BY NEXT *August*

THE AUGUST SERIES

ASHLEY PIERCE

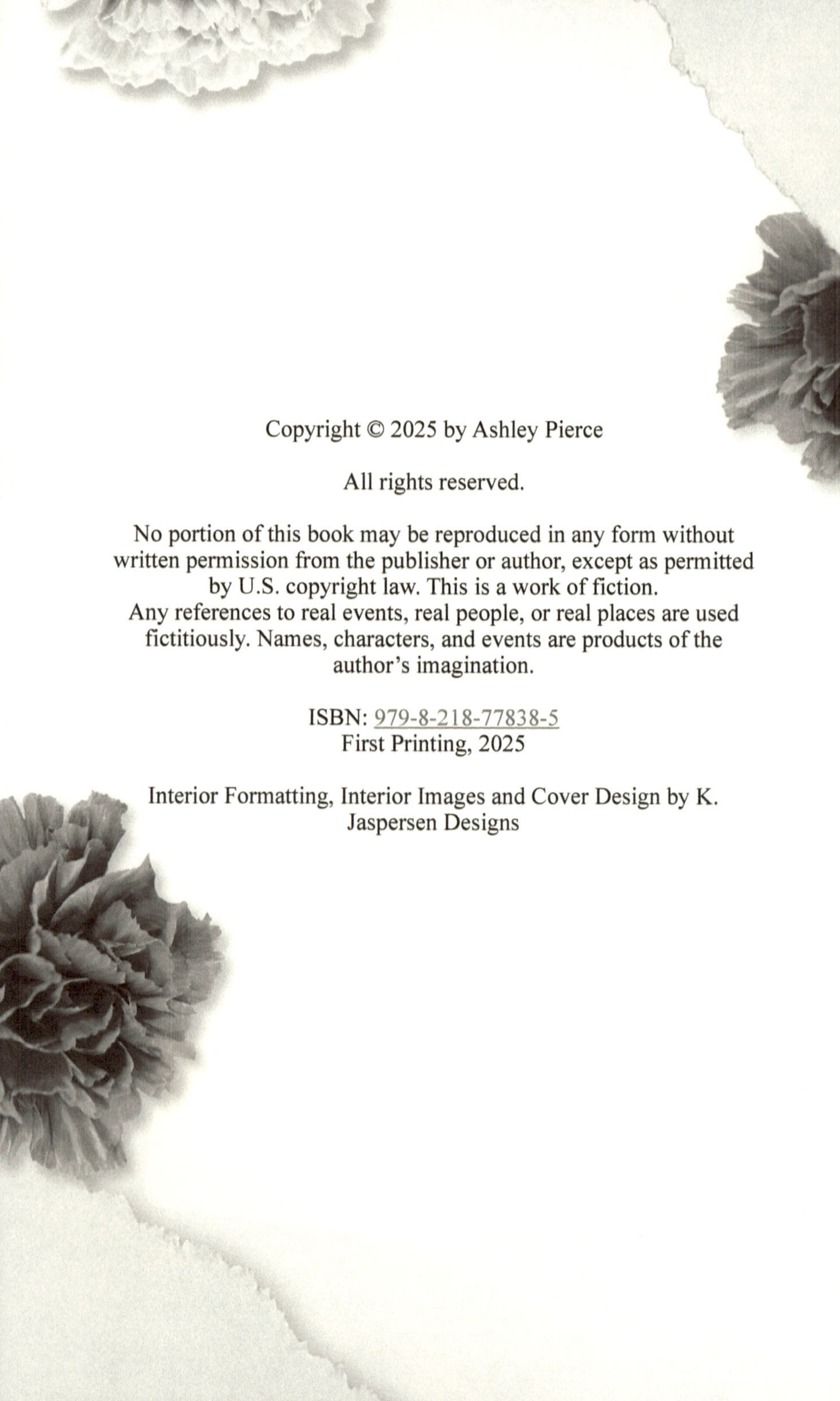

ISBN: 979-8-218-77838-5
First Printing, 2025

Interior Formatting, Interior Images and Cover Design by K. Jaspersen Designs

For the ones who are stubborn, who love fiercely, fight harder, and somehow always finally learn the hard way—this one's for you.

PROLOGUE

November 24th 2019

The music is too loud, the drinks are too weak, and my girlfriend is too busy whispering about the same thing everyone else is. Jimmy's here with Autumn—who is not Becca, his wife. She is also here with someone else. But everyone is eating it up like they're so surprised. I don't know why—I'm not. And anyone who's been paying attention as closely as Izzy has definitely shouldn't be.

I didn't even want to come. This isn't my reunion—it's hers—but she insisted it would be fun. I didn't expect it to be, though, and turns out I was right. I look over at her, and she's leaned in close to her friend, whispering about the love triangle in the room. For someone who insisted on my coming, she hasn't looked at me once since we sat down.

I clear my throat. *Nothing.*

I tap her leg. "You good?"

She waves me off. "Just a sec. I can't believe this."

Yeah. Me either.

I knew this night would be potentially messy thanks to Jimmy, but I just didn't expect to feel this… detached from my own relationship. Izzy and I have been circling the drain for months—maybe close to a year—and tonight confirms it. She's more interested in drama than me. More invested in other people's chaos than our own quiet unraveling.

I lean back, letting the noise wash over me. Looking around the red, black, and white cloaked gym, I see someone else. Someone that other people aren't watching, like a side show.

She's standing near the table Jimmy and Autumn are sitting at, smiling at something one of them said—Autumn, I presume. Her dress is black, fitted, and stops at a length that makes my throat tighten. I almost didn't recognize her—her normally bouncing curls slicked back and tamed at the back of her neck in a bun. But she's still stunning. *Always has been.*

Her smile is effortless. Her laugh is real. She has an aura about her that is impossible not to be sucked into. So does her best friend Autumn, and when they're together it's like a force field exudes around them, and it's impossible not to get engulfed in their world if you get too close. It's no wonder Jimmy fell into what he's in now.

She's magnetic.

She used to sit in the row next to me in AP Lit, always with a book tucked under her arm that wasn't a class requirement. I'd watch her twirl her mechanical pencil between her fingers while she read, her curls bouncing every time she laughed at something no one else knew about. I hid a grin behind my fingers once when she got scolded for not paying attention—her response being *'I could be skipping behind the gym and doing drugs. God forbid a girl just like to read something that's not boring,'* before being sent to the office.

Another day, she dropped her notebook onto the floor on her way out of the classroom—not realizing she lost it. It was lying there open, the pages were full of scribbled thoughts— quotes, ideas, little poems. I didn't read much, just enough to know she saw the world differently.

I wanted to talk to her so many times. I almost did that day. But she was dating some guy from the football team, which I was reminded of when I shut the notebook and saw *'I <3 Logan,'* and hearts with the number fourteen doodled all over the cover.

I look over at Izzy, who has left the table without saying anything. And I didn't notice. So, I think tonight has really just confirmed what I already knew.

Suddenly, I'm the side of the magnet that Izzy's force is repelling, while Kory's is dragging me in. I decide to talk to Jimmy—at the table she's sitting at.

I make my way over, nodding at a few classmates I barely remember.

"Yo," I say, clapping Jimmy on the shoulder like I'm actually over here for him.

He turns, eyebrows raised. "What's up, man! You good?"

"Yeah. Just needed a break from the gossip mill." I glance over my shoulder, where Izzy is still glued to anyone else but me.

Jimmy chuckles. "It's a circus, man. Sorry about that."

"You're not kidding," I say as I catch him smirking over at Autumn.

But I'm not really listening, just like I don't really think Jimmy is listening to me.

He's watching Autumn, and I'm watching her best friend.

Kory's sitting at the table just behind Jimmy, sipping something brown from a glass, her lips pursed in thought. She's not watching the drama. She's not trying to be seen. She's just… *here.* Her eyes scan the room, and for a second—just a second—they land on me.

Deja vu settles in, and my chest tightens.

I turn back to Jimmy, trying to play it cool. "You seen Brett?"

"He's probably outside hitting on someone's wife."

I laugh, but it's hollow. I'm not over here looking for Brett.

She's joined Autumn, sitting down at the table. Jimmy keeps talking, but his words are not registering as I listen to those two talking joyfully and taking selfies on Autumn's phone.

Kory Brooks.

We've never been single at the same time. Not once.

But one of these days, the stars will align.

And when they do, I'll be ready.

I glance back again. She's laughing now, head tilted, eyes bright.

I swear, she glows.

"You sure you're good?" Jimmy asks again.

I nod, eyes still on her.

"Yeah," I say. "I'm great."

CHAPTER ONE

Kory - July 2023

People always leave.

Fictional Peyton Sawyer from the fictional city of Tree Hill said that once, but turns out it's not so fictional after all. People do, always leave.

Nathan, ironically enough, wanders quietly around my apartment gathering his things. He didn't live here long, probably just long enough that I'm sure I'll still find a few random things even months from today. We had a good year and a half. At least I thought we did. It was good for me.

We met on a dating app and talked for six months before even going on a date. He lives in the next town over, but we talked all the time. After we finally met up for our first date, we found every excuse to be with each other.

Until he decided he was taking a job in Phoenix.

To be honest, as blindsided as I was, I didn't even argue or ask why. Phoenix is obviously just an excuse. No one takes a job in another state without mentioning it to their significant other if they actually care about them and want to be with them. He took this job as an excuse to leave and to feel like not *that much* of an asshole.

But he is an asshole. For almost two years, I thought he could be my future. Yet instead, now he's just another name on the list of people who left me back here in Michigan.

My parents- Florida

My brother- Tennessee

My best friend- New Jersey

My now ex-boyfriend- Phoenix

I'm not mad at any of them, well, maybe Nathan at the moment, but it all still sucks.

My parents weren't all that present growing up anyway. My dad traveled regularly for work, and my mom just did whatever while he was gone. What she did, I don't know, but she was also gone a lot. My brother, Elliot, is three years older than me, and once he was eleven or twelve, he basically became my legal guardian.

I know my brother loves me and always has, but he got away from our parents as soon as he could, as far as he could, leaving me to fend for myself. I was so mad at him for a while; we didn't speak. At first, I thought a few years in the woods would do him some good. He'd go to college there, have his fun laid back mountain man life, then he'd come home.

I was only half right. The mountains did him so much good that he never came home. Rarely even to visit.

Our relationship has gotten better over the years, but unfortunately, we still don't talk all that often. I wish we did more.

Even though he was running from them, my parents acted just as anxious to take off for good, too. Once I graduated high school, that meant their job was done, apparently. Not two weeks later, they left for Florida, also never to move back.

Believe it or not, a few weeks later, my best friend Autumn also informed me that she was leaving, to go to college in Wisconsin. I knew why she was leaving, but just like my brother, it didn't make it suck any less. It took ten years, but eventually she did come back. Just to leave again two years later. This time for New Jersey, and this time I think it's for good, too.

So at this point, I'm not the slightest bit surprised that another state is ripping apart my relationship.

"Are you sure my other headset isn't here?" Nathan crashes my pity party.

His gaming headset, of course. That's what he's concerned about. I don't think he can breathe without that stupid gaming system. I know, I know, we're fresh in our thirties and playing video games should have been a red flag, but I didn't mind it. I love to read, and he loves to game. It worked for us. We could both participate in our beloved hobbies while also quietly enjoying each other's company.

Now that I think of it, maybe if we spent more time doing things together, rather than existing parallel to each other, he wouldn't have just ended things with an emotionless three sentences. He actually didn't even say *'it's over.'* But, *'So I took a new job. It's in Phoenix. I'm sorry.'* Followed by gathering his stuff. That said, the words his mouth didn't.

"No, it's not," I tell him and pick up my book.

If he wants to be emotionless, I can be emotionless. Never in this lifetime or the next will you see me begging someone to love me.

He runs his hand through his black hair and looks around again. "Alright. I think that's everything then."

I slide my finger against the bookmark and begin to open it when I look back up at him, and he's staring at me. I watch his face, and he looks sorry. Not really sorry we're breaking up, but sorry that he's doing it this way because now that we're awkwardly staring at each other, he knows he's still a *huge* asshole.

His shoulders shrug and his lips tighten. *Really? The smile you give to strangers on the street?*

"I really am sorry."

There it is. "Me too," I say quietly and open my book. "Drive safe."

Is he driving all the way there? I don't even know. But it comes out before I stop it.

"I will. Bye, Kory." He says before leaving the apartment.

I sit in silence for a minute, staring at the words on the pages, but not actually reading. I sit and wait for something. *For anger? For sadness? Even relief, maybe?*

But nothing comes. I don't feel anything in this moment.

I'm sure at some point it will hit, but right now, all I feel is the all too familiar reminder that people always leave.

CHAPTER TWO

Dom

The steak sizzles to perfection on the cast-iron pan in front of me.

I take in a strong whiff, usually able to tell when it's done by the smell. It helps that it only needs a quick seven minutes on each side—leaving it perfectly pink in the middle. It's the only way to eat a steak. If you like it still bleeding, you're a psycho, and if you like it well done, then you're a criminal.

Once it's ready, I flip it onto my plate along with some broccoli and a sweet potato. It's one of my favorite meals, and actually my exact order from the local steakhouse—the only steakhouse around here. It's not a bad place to eat, but I prefer to cook at home. Plus, the girl at the to-go window has asked for my number multiple times—despite me politely declining every time—and that's put me off from going there regularly.

I do really enjoy cooking, though, which may be a product of my being on my own for quite some time.

After my family left for New York, I spent the first few months exclusively eating take-out, but that got old fast, and cooking became something I actually enjoyed. Izzy—my ex-girlfriend—was around for a few years, but we never lived together. She came over a lot but always insisted on the take-out option. It never compared to what I could make myself, so in the years since we've been broken up, I think I've ordered out maybe four times.

Sometimes it's weird, though, to cook one portion size of everything. Not so much this meal, but just about any pasta dish, leaves way too much left over. *Why don't they sell individual serving sizes of pasta for habitual bachelors like me?*

One of these days I'll have someone to cook for, but I'm not in a rush. After wasting a few years with the wrong one, there's no reason to play the field until the right one finally enters the game.

What is nice about being on my own—there's no one to complain about what I put on the TV or the fact that I sit here with a tray in my living room instead of at the dining room table.

There is a small dining room right off the kitchen, but sitting in there by myself just feels—*lonely.* The dining room can wait until there's someone to join me in it.

I haven't always been one to enjoy silence. As a teen, you'd rarely find me at home. I was always out and about, enjoying things and living life like they say you're supposed to. But in my early adult years, my family's leaving changed everything. It didn't just leave me alone; it left me with a silence that used to feel like punishment. Now, I've made peace with it. I've built a life around it.

My townhouse isn't large by any means, but it's bigger than my last apartment and, most importantly, has a small garage for my bike. All shiny black, my GSX-R1000 looks slick like a rocket ready to launch. Polished fairings, shiny black accents, and a growl that sounds like pure attitude—its speed wrapped in midnight paint. When I ride, it feels like the rules of gravity don't apply. It's the best escape.

I'm no longer the guy who needs a crowd. I'm not the guy who needs attention. I'm the guy who shows up, does his job, goes home, rides his bike or goes to the gym, then does it all again. I manage one of the two *Home Team* stores nearby, and while it's nothing fancy, I take pride in it.

After we broke up, Izzy insisted that I was just emotionally unavailable. Maybe she was right. But I think it's more than that—I just don't waste energy on things that don't feel real. I've seen what real love looks like—my parents had it. And I've seen what it looks like when it's gone.

After I finish my dinner and a war movie in peace, I see my phone light up. Two texts. One from Jimmy.

One from Blake.

These two texts about sum up the existence of my social life at the moment. Jimmy—whom I've known since high school—would be who I consider my best friend, though we don't see each other much. We regularly go to the gym, but not all that often outside of those walls. He lives the complete opposite life from me—living in a big house on a nice street in town with his wife and daughter.

I met Blake at work. He, too, lives a different life than I do—leaning more in the *'ready to mingle'* part of being single. He's a good guy, though, and it makes most work days more entertaining than boring. I reply yes to both of them as I normally do. While I love going to the gym and going even if Jimmy can't make it, I really only go out to the bars when Blake invites me. I enjoy my solitude, but I can't deny that leaving the house and acting social every so often feels like a nice change of pace.

Blake is insistent that one of these days he'll convince me to take some girl home and *'learn the fun parts of being a single guy in a small town.'* But that doesn't sound appealing to me in the slightest. We do live in a small town, which means on any normal day, we know pretty much any girl in that bar already. It is tourist season, near Lake Michigan, which means the chances of meeting a stranger are higher, but most people who vacation here are families, so the chances are still very slim.

It doesn't matter how hard he tries to convince me to change my mind; I won't. There's only one person in this town that I am interested in, and she is not a stranger—*technically.*

CHAPTER THREE

Kory

Olivia throws a dress at me, and it wraps around my face as it makes contact.

"Put it on. Let's go." She demands.

I remove the stretchy fabric from my mouth and laugh. This is normally my job—refusing to let my friends mope around. Not that I'm moping, but my redhead friend is using my breakup as an excuse to go out. Just like I would.

She stands in front of the mirror, smoothing out the blue body-con dress swaddled around her thick, curvy body. I've always been envious of her curves, the kind of envious where friends appreciate attributes of their friends, not the kind where I hate her for being curvier than me. I'm on the taller side, which, to me, makes my curves look stretched out sometimes, especially standing next to Olivia.

Her hair, long and burnt orange, hangs down her back. I've always loved her hair color, unique in its own right. It's definitely in the *'red'* category, but not bright orange like most. It's like a brown orange, more than strawberry blond, but still not just brown. It's definitely not a color you can get from a bottle. She gathers it up in her hands, debating wearing it in a ponytail before dropping it back down.

"We're both going to be seriously overdressed. Nowhere around here requires this amount of skin to show." I say as I slide it over my head anyway.

"I know that did not just come out of your mouth."

We switch places so I can look at myself, and I laugh because she's right. But I'll embrace the roles we're in tonight. Me going through a break-up, and her being my over-the-top, but sweetly supportive friend. This tight red dress shows each of my curves just right. The ruching at the waist accentuates all the right places. I don't look stretched out today. The bright crimson, although not my usual color, always looks good with my olive skin and dark chocolate brown hair that is just as curvy as Olivia's hips.

I hold it all together, having the same debate Olivia just did, then also decide to leave it down, letting the curls bounce back onto my shoulders.

"Overdressed usually means attention, which usually means free drinks, right?" She winks as she mocks something I've said plenty of times, and I shake my head as we wait for the Uber.

Olivia's been one of my best friends since middle school, almost as long as me and Autumn. We were all tight back then, and even though I've always been closest to Autumn, Olivia is the one person who's physically always been there for me. I consider them both my best friends. Autumn and I have a bond that can't be broken, but with her living states away for the majority of the last twelve years, life would be really lonely without a best friend who is actually here.

And I don't want to jinx myself, but Olivia is the last person I see moving out of this state, like everyone else. Unlike mine, her parents are very involved and very financially supportive. They work in real estate, specializing in lakefront properties, i.e., money. If you have ever looked into the prices of Lake Michigan properties, you would understand. Olivia's also mentioned they know a lot about investing in stocks. Whatever it all is, it's working.

Olivia still lives with them, technically, in their *'in-law'* suite. Basically, her own house—it has its own driveway and yard for God's sake. Early in my adult years, I thought that was so odd, but now at thirty-two, I realize it's kind of a dream, and I don't blame her one bit. She doesn't work either. She's had a few random part-time jobs, but that was just to keep her from being bored. Most of the time, she just finds new hobbies to hyper-fixate on. Her latest one? A podcast. Does she make money off any of her hobbies? No, she doesn't need to. She just does it for fun until the fun's not there anymore.

Like I said, a dream.

Once the Uber drops us off, we make our way into the dim bar. As expected, we stick out like two sore thumbs dressed for a party in a downtown club, not a hole-in-the-wall bar in a town most people have never or will ever hear about. There are only three bars anywhere near us, and I work at one of them most evenings. Everyone stares as we find two seats at the main high-top counter.

Living quite the opposite life from Olivia, I have two jobs. During the day, I work at *Home Team*, a sports apparel store. It's a small brand started by someone who's from here, which is why it's in a random small town like Scotville. It's a relatively new brand, with only two stores, one here and one about thirty minutes away. It's not a bad job, but the sales associate's pay isn't quite enough. Maybe had I stayed in college, I'd have a better job, but it wasn't for me. Olivia and I both got bored freshman year and dropped out, and while that wasn't really a life-altering decision for her, it probably was for me.

But I like *Home Team*, the people are mostly cool, and you get different crowds during different sports seasons throughout the year.

"Two Washington Apples." Olivia requests putting her card on the bar.

"Seriously? Starting with shots?"

"Yup. You're finally single again, and even if you aren't depressed, we are going to pretend you are and drown your imaginary sorrows."

"Can I get a Crown and Coke too, please?" I ask the fast-moving guy behind the bar.

"That's the spirit." She squeals. The bartender returns with our shots. "Just add hers to my tab. Thanks so much, handsome." She winks flirtatiously as she takes the shots from him and hands one to me. Expectantly, she lifts hers in the air. "Cheers to Nathan leaving you in July, giving us just enough time to enjoy the rest of the summer with that newly single, shimmery glow. He was boring anyway."

I lift mine to clink it to hers and laugh. Again, she's right. "Cheers to a single, shimmery summer." I echo.

Three shots and two drinks later, we both feel great. She took over the touch tunes an hour ago, and it's been our own millennial throwback karaoke session since.

"Oh my God, Kooorrryyy," she says, touching my arm and leaning into me so heavily I think we might fall. "You know what sounds SO good right now? Double-fried pickles from JAX!"

I groan. "Seriously?" Why do you always do this? I hate going there on my day off, it's weird."

"Pleeeaaaassseee," She whines. "They're my favorite. And it's not weird, it's like tradition or something. I NEED those pickles."

I roll my eyes and pull out my phone to call another Uber. She watches what I'm doing and shrieks happily, asking the 'handsome' guy behind the bar to close her tab. A few minutes later, we leave the patrons of that bar to return to their regularly scheduled music and head to my work, which unfortunately *does* seem to be tradition when she drinks.

"I'm going to get two orders." She says with her eyes closed and head back against the seat.

Walking into JAX, I see exactly who I expected to see on a Friday night. Lisa is behind the bar with Boy Corey. Our coworkers affectionately nick-named us *'Boy Corey'* and *'Girl Kory'* to keep us apart when being spoken about. Grace and Leah work the floor. Lisa waves, and we plop down at a table this time.

"Hey, stranger," Grace says as she comes to the table.

"Two orders of double-fried pickles, please." Olivia requests before I even take a breath. "Oh! And a Crown Apple and Sprite! Or Ginger Ale. Surprise me!"

"I'll take a burger. And a water." *One of us has to make sure we make it home.*

Grace scribbles then disappears, not engaging in small talk, and I'm not offended. Even for a small town, Friday nights are busy, and even though I like the people I work with, I wouldn't consider any of them friends outside of this place.

JAX is the liveliest of the three bar options we have nearby, which is why I chose to work here. If there was a place considered to be a party scene, that's where the money would be. Most young people around here come here for their twenty-first birthdays and then continue to party for a few years after that. The younger ones almost always spend the most money. They drink now, and think later. And that works for me.

"I'm going to the bathroom," I yell over the music. Olivia is not paying attention, obviously more intoxicated than I am.

Making my way to the back of the bar, I hear my name. I turn to see Matt, the owner, waving. I throw my hand up to return the gesture, but in just that short second of distraction, I walk right into a wall.

Except it's not a wall, as the warm hands on my elbows would suggest.

"Sorry." I spit out as I look up and see a pair of green eyes.

They are the greenest eyes I've ever seen, like emeralds, and vaguely familiar. His hair, dark like mine, is slicked back, and his face has just a dusting of matching facial hair along his carved jaw. His skin is fair, which is illuminated by these bright neon lights. The combination or contrast of the light skin, dark hair, and bright eyes is jarring.

"You're okay." He says, a smile creeping across his lips. "Well, I guess I should ask. Are you okay?"

"I'm fine," I say, suddenly more embarrassed than I've ever been. I'm not quite sure why, though. I've done way worse. "Sorry again," I say as I run away from the stare that I can feel burning right through me.

But the face sticks with me, because he does look familiar. I picture him in my mind as I wash my hands, but I can't figure out from where. I'd know that face. I'd remember that look.

As I walk back towards Olivia at our table, I see where he is sitting on the other side of the room. He looks up and sees me too, smiling again. I ignore the fact that his eyes move up and down my body as I get closer. I pretend it's not that action that's making my heartbeat faster.

"Dom, you're next!" someone calls from the pool table. He nods and waves without looking away from me and… *shit*. I wish I hadn't just heard that.

Because now I know exactly why he looks familiar.

CHAPTER FOUR

Dom

The hard billiard balls clack loudly together, knocking the 8-ball into the hole and leaving the purple one he was aiming at, bouncing off the edge and rolling casually to the other side.

"Damn it." Nick groans as he taps his stick on the floor.

"You really suck at this." I tease.

Poor guy can't play without beating himself. Blake grabs the stick out of my hand, and I go back to the table to grab a new bottle of beer out of the ice bucket.

I can see her across the room, sitting with her friend, her back to me. I've seen her a hundred times, but I'm not sure we've ever had a conversation. Part of that is due to me being in a relationship for a few years, but that's been over for a while, and I haven't run into her since I've been single.

The smell of her shampoo lingers in my nostrils. The smell is citrusy and sweet, and intoxicating.

"I'm going to put a song on." I lie to the guys before walking towards their table.

Her back is still to me, but her friend sees me coming and very obviously reacts. It makes me laugh as I pull my shoes across these sticky floors. If she realizes I saw her eyes grow, her slap Kory's hand, lean and whisper something, she doesn't appear to care.

Just as I make it to the table, Kory turns toward me. "Hey again," I say with my best smile.

"Hi." She responds quickly before turning back to her friend.

"I was just thinking that I didn't introduce myself." I extend my hand, making my introduction formal. She grabs it and shakes it one quick time, but doesn't smile back.

"I know who you are. Jimmy's best friend, right?"

I laugh. "Unfortunately, I think I am."

She doesn't seem to appreciate my joke, but her friend does and bellows a laugh.

"Oh my God, Kory, you're being so rude." The redhead looks at me. "Her name is Kory and she's newly single."

"LIV." She says with a tilted head and wide eyes.

"Newly single, huh?"

"Yes, but not looking." She says quickly.

"Yes, you are." Her friend interjects.

"No, I'm not." She grits back.

The whole exchange between the two makes me laugh some more. I watch her hazel eyes dart back and forth, trying not to look at me. She sips on some water, and even though she appears not interested in this conversation, I couldn't be *more* interested. The way she's looking at me right now is *not* the way she looked at me twenty minutes ago. The way she looked at me twenty minutes ago didn't happen for no reason, and I know that's exactly why she has gone cold.

"Well then, I'll let you ladies be," I say, pretending to take the hint.

Kory nods, then her friend speaks up again. "Sorry about my rude friend. It's been a while since she's been single. She works here, though. Come see her one night."

She slurs it out so fast that Kory couldn't have stopped her if she tried. Her eyes were pleading it across the table, but the words were already spoken before any telepathic message could be received.

"I might do that. Have a good night." Another chuckle escapes as I walk back over to my friends.

I sit back down at the table, but my mind's not on the game anymore. Blake's already halfway through another beer, probably scanning the room for someone to flirt with. He's got that easy charm that works on most girls—even though anyone here should know better by now—but it's all about sex for him. He doesn't get it—doesn't get why I'm not interested in just anyone.

Olivia's loud laugh cuts through the music from across the room. She's got a palpable energy that makes people feel like they're part of something. Makes them *want* to be a part of something, whatever it is. Kory's different. She's quieter, and from what I remember, she used to be the one bringing life to a room.

I watch and wonder what she's thinking right now. I wonder if she still reads. I wonder if she'd ever let me in.

I take another sip of my beer and lean back in my chair, eyes drifting toward her again.

"My turn," Blake says in my ear, causing me to jump.

I don't get a chance to ask what he's talking about before I see him sauntering over to their table. My teeth clench with an unexpected jealousy. As I stand to go stop him from even trying with Kory, my body rigid, he leans on the table—rudely —in front of her, his attention clearly on Olivia. My jaw and muscles relax as I watch her pull herself from their conversation, leaning back in her seat and looking at her phone.

Jimmy's best friend. She's clearly decided that I'm guilty by association. I get it. Best friends are like that. What Jimmy did to Autumn wasn't cool and ultimately ended mine and Izzy's relationship, too. But little does she know, I'm nothing like Jimmy.

Well, maybe kind of similar. Similar in the sense that I've wanted Kory way longer than I've ever admitted to anybody. I've noticed her repeatedly since we were teens. The problem has always been that we have never been single at the same time, but now we are. I introduced myself to her as a way to start a conversation, but I knew who she was.

But unlike Jimmy, I know exactly what I want, and I go for it.

CHAPTER FIVE

Kory

Cutting myself off when we got to JAX was the best choice I made last night. Had I not, I would likely be graveling in front of the toilet right now, next to Olivia.

"Okay, I admit it. I'm too old for this." She whines, laying her head on her arm.

I hand her some water and sit on the edge of the tub for moral support.

"Yes. We are. But thank you. I had fun."

She starts to throw up again, so I decide she needs space more than moral support. I did have fun, except I wish I hadn't run into Dom. *Literally.* Once we started talking, I remembered him more clearly, but I didn't remember him looking like that. *I wish he didn't.*

He's not Autumn's ex, but he's her ex's best friend, which is too close for me. To be involved with him means being associated with Jimmy, and I will not. I plan to hold a grudge forever because if it weren't for him, my best friend wouldn't have run away. *Twice.* If it weren't for his inability to admit he was always in love with her, I wouldn't have had to hold her while she cried so many times. If it weren't for his deciding to admit his love for her while being married to someone else, his wife wouldn't have made a scene, screaming at me in a Starbucks, assigning me as guilty by association. The same wife he decided to stay with after all.

I know I shouldn't have supported Autumn when I found out about their affair, but everyone knew they loved each other, and I thought maybe, since she was back, she could finally have her happy ever after. But they didn't. He disappointed everyone, so yeah, I have some feelings about him and don't plan to let them go.

And those feelings are what make Dom off-limits. If I were guilty by association, so is he.

But I keep picturing him. His hair is so dark, it's almost black. His criminally green eyes and the neatest facial hair I've ever seen. He must have just seen a barber, like that day. His shoulders are so broad and his body so firm, I really thought I had hit a wall. It's starting to get under my skin how much I can't stop thinking about it.

But it doesn't matter.

Olivia comes out of the bathroom, and my hand covers my mouth, containing my laughter. Her poor face is pale, and her hair is thrown up in a pile, one that tilts slightly to the right. She has no pants on, just an oversized T-shirt of mine that I let her borrow last night. One that I'm pretty sure now might have puke on it. She is straight out of a PSA that shots are only acceptable in your early twenties.

"Can I just stay here all day?" she asks as she plops down, stretching across my couch. "I can't imagine driving anytime soon."

"I don't care." I laugh. "But I have to work, so I can't stay here and babysit you all day."

She turns herself onto her side while I fill my coffee cup. Normally, I'd offer her some, but I know that's the last thing she wants right now. Just as I'm comfortably reclined in my chair, coffee in one hand, and a book in the other, she starts talking again.

"Did we meet a guy last night? I feel like I remember a guy."

"Yeah, we ran into one at JAX, and you told him I worked there and to come see me. Oh, and that I'm single. Thanks for that."

Her face tightens in a squint. "Sorry. Was he hot at least?"

"Doesn't matter if he's hot."

"Why not?"

"Because it was Dom Rissi."

Her eyes widen, then shrink in judgment. "Dom, who dated Izzy? Seriously? He is hot. Why wouldn't…"

I cut her off. "Just not going to happen."

Her still-judgy eyes linger just briefly before succumbing to her hangover headache. That's the end of the Dom conversation for today. Olivia's always been good at reading my mood, and while I'm sure it will come up again eventually, she'll let it go for now.

But then again, maybe it won't, because *why would it need to?* Maybe he was just as drunk as she was and doesn't even remember following me to my table, or that I'm single, or that I work there.

"You met a guy, too."

Her head lifts just slightly. "I did?"

"Oh, yeah. Lover boy was trying WAY too hard, and you were eating it up." I laugh thinking of the incessant flirting that was happening between them. "It was quite obnoxious if you ask me."

"Who was it? Did I like him?"

"Liv, you like everyone when you're that drunk." I sip my coffee. "But it was Blake, I think. Blond hair, blue eyes. Definitely your type, but he seems like he's everyone's type."

"Nope. Don't remember that at all. Too bad."

I shake my head. "That's probably for the best. I've seen him in there before. Doing the same thing."

"You wouldn't have let me leave with him anyway." She rolls over and covers her head.

"You're absolutely right about that. Especially not as drunk as you were."

Especially because that would mean I was left there alone, susceptible to Dom and his green eyes, rock-hard muscles, and tattoos again. I can only keep hoping he doesn't remember anything she blabbed because I do. I remember the look on his face when we bumped into each other. The smile that crept across his lips when she said I was single. The way that smile made my gut twist. But I want to forget, so I move on to reading where I left off last–willing myself to forget.

However, the way the cowboy in this book looks at his PR representative is not helping.

CHAPTER SIX

Dom

Football season is almost here, which means a store makeover. This and baseball season are the two busiest seasons, and unlucky for us, they overlap, and if either of the teams does good that year, it gets even crazier.

For us, football season used to be slow. College football fans kept us afloat. The Michigan/Michigan State rivalry was way more interesting than the Detroit Lions for a long time. But last season seemed to be a turnaround year for our beloved/stressful NFL team. So, we're riding that wave and expecting this season to be even better.

"We need to start rotating," I explain to the four staff here with me. "Tigers' stuff will move over to section C, while the Lions' stuff will move up front to A. Section B will be College, Michigan, on the right side, State on the left. Same with the Jerseys. Baseball to the back, football to the front."

We all look up, mutually dreading the task at hand. Both sides of the walls, from the entrance to the back, are lined with hundreds of jerseys. They're high above the tallest of us, meaning whoever starts work on the jersey sections will be climbing up and down a ladder all day. By whoever, I mean me, because I'm a great manager and love leg day, so I don't mind the steps. I'll take the job no one else wants to do, because sometimes, that's the boss's job.

"Jasmine and Blake take baseball, Devin and Kyle take football. I'll do the jerseys."

They all collectively sigh in relief, then scatter to start their tasks. I head back to my little office, where the owner, John, is waiting for me. We're a small company, so his presence is not as unusual for us as it may be for others, but I didn't know he was coming until six this morning, so the reason for his visit has been on my mind all morning.

"Sorry about that," I say as I round the desk and take a seat in my chair.

"Not a worry." He says, adjusting himself in his seat. "You run a great store here. I'm sure you were up to something good." He laughs, and I join him, relieved that his visit seems positive.

You'd never know he's the owner because he doesn't dress like one. He sits in front of me in a black hoodie with the *Home Team* logo stamped in the center. One thing about John —he's proud as hell of what he's built. He almost always has *Home Team* gear on. Jeans complete the casual outfit, down to his sneakers. The only thing that might give him away as the owner is his age. I'm guessing he's in his fifties, with a clean bald head and mostly grey goatee covering his chin.

"Thank you, and yes, seasonal rotations are starting today."

He nods. "Ah, yes, of course. Well, that's why I'm here, actually."

I feel the wrinkles appear in my skin as my eyes squint. "For seasonal rotation?"

A chuckle slips out with the shake of his head. "Not exactly. But the way you run this store. This is our top-performing and highest-rated store, and that hasn't gone unnoticed."

"Thank you again," I say and slide him a water bottle. I take the compliment and ignore the fact that there are only two stores.

"*Home Team* is growing. We have four more stores we plan to open in the next few months. We'd like to enlist you to travel and help set these new stores up for success by training the managers to be."

My eyes blink a few times before my mouth registers movement. "Wow. I'd love to. But what about here?"

"Happy to hear that. As for here, I was hoping you had a reliable employee here who could cover for you in the interim. They'd be compensated, obviously."

Blake for sure. "I do, yes. So what does this look like?"

"Well, we want you as a manager. We are going to choose an employee from the other store to help the sales associates. We don't want to leave one store too understaffed. Starting next month, you'll travel to each location and spend a week there. We want you to give an overall training, help with store set up, then we'd like you to work one-on-one with the manager for a day or two."

I take a sip from my water bottle, thinking about everything he just said. Nothing about this sounds bad so far. He continues talking as if he can read my mind.

"On top of your regular daily pay, you'll be paid a per diem rate of $100 for each day you are gone, including travel days. You'll have a company credit card for gas."

"So if the drive there is only four hours, it will be a full day's pay and $100?" It sounds too good to be true.

"Exactly." He smiles, then takes a sip of his water, knowing this is an offer not many would pass up. "And we'll take care of the rooms, but you'll have that card with you just in case there are any complications. Speaking of which, don't you know someone who has hotel connections?"

"Yes, my friend Jimmy is a regional manager."

"Perfect. Get me his contact information. Nothing wrong with saving a little when we can, huh?"

"No, not at all," I reply.

"So what do you think?"

My head nods, giving him an answer before my mouth does. "I'm in."

"Cheers," Blake says as he taps his mug of beer to mine. "To both of us and our promotions."

"Cheers." I laugh back and take a drink.

"When do you leave?"

"I'm not sure yet. He said sometime next month. I'll hear more once they figure out who else is going."

"Well, hurry up. I'm ready for my raise."

The amused shake of my head relieves a little crack in my neck that I got from looking above my head the rest of the day. I stretch it from one side to the other when I see *her* walk in the door.

Her dark head of hair is thrown up on her head. Even though it's secured, the curls bounce as she walks. She disappears into the back for a second, then reemerges, tying the short black apron around her waist. The waitress had warned us it was about to be a shift change, and I was just hoping my lucky day would continue. And so it has.

It takes a few minutes for her to approach our table. She sees me before she reaches us, and I watch her eyes roll. It does not escape me that she forced the faint smirk away first. It's adorable.

"My name's Kory and I'll be taking over for Leah. Do you need anything right now?" She asks flatly, obviously directing the question toward Blake, not me, but I speak first.

"Another round, please."

My smile alerts Blake that something is up. She continues to ignore me as she asks him what our drinks were.

"Who is that?" he asks once she's left the table.

"No one." I drink down the rest of my beer. "Yet."

A few moments later, she returns with two frosty glasses. As she sets them on the table, her hair falls forward, wafting the scent in my direction. She smells as good as she looks. It perks me up more than the sight of her.

"Thank you, ma'am."

She shoots me a look. Little hazel daggers for eyes. She didn't like *'ma'am,'* though I didn't really expect her to.

"Kory's fine."

"Yeah, sorry. So Kory, what's the best thing to eat here?"

"I like the burgers. But the twice-fried pickles and Cajun onion rings are pretty popular. Haven't you eaten here recently?" She shoots the sarcastic question out, but doesn't look at me. She pulls her notebook out of her pocket and opens it, preparing to write.

I laugh. "I've been here a few times. Usually just for a drink or two, though. Thought it might be worth seeing what else this place has to offer."

I wink because she finally looks at me, and well, I can't help it.

"Drinks and food. That's what we offer." She says quickly, then looks back at Blake. "Anything for you?"

He shifts in his seat, trying to hide his amusement. "I'll take one of the burgers."

"I'll take one too," I add. "And an order of both popular things."

She scribbles in her notebook, then scurries away from the table again.

"So she's why you wanted to come back here?" Blake's face and voice are both full of amused accusation. I just nod and take another drink. "Does she know that?" he asks.

I look up and catch her staring from behind the bar. The light catches the glass liquor bottles on the wall, adding a shine behind her. She quickly looks away, trying to pretend like she wasn't.

"I think she does now."

CHAPTER SEVEN

Kory

Unfortunately for me, Dom was *not* as drunk as Olivia when she blabbed that I work here.

Whatever else this place has to offer. Yeah, Okay. Not going to happen. But this is my job, so serving them I will do because, well, I like this job. I don't *love* it, but having a second one and using the tips purely for spending money helps me keep up with Olivia's carefree, budget-less lifestyle. My phone buzzes with a text from Autumn.

I type back.

I slide the phone back in my pocket and survey my tables. Everyone's drinks are still full, so I check in on the kitchen. "Five more minutes on the pickles!" Jay calls out.

I turn to go back out by the bar when my phone buzzes again. I expect to find a reply from Autumn, but don't. It's Nathan.

> Hey, I've been thinking about how I ended things. I'm sorry again. I'd love to talk if you'll call me. Miss you.

Really?
That text had more words than he spoke to me in my apartment that day. *Is he serious right now?* My cheeks are hot with irritation, and the tightness in my chest surprises me. *What is the point of us talking? To add another long-distance relationship to my life?* No thanks.

I'm frozen in a daze, deciding whether to write back or not, when a voice startles me back to life.

"You okay?"

I look up and am met with those stupid green eyes. My stomach betrays me briefly, and I fumble to put my phone back in my pocket.

"I'm fine."

I have no choice but to look right up at him as I'm standing against the wall. I wish I weren't, though, because with him in front of me like this, I'm back in another daze. His tattoos, which I tried not to pay attention to before, stretch the length of both arms. Black ink in various shapes rides the hills of his muscles. I hate that for a split second, I'm curious about the ones I can't see.

"You are. But I asked if you were okay." His right eyebrow arches slightly, and he smirks. Suddenly, my daze is over.

"Did you come here just to bother me?" I cross my arms in front of my chest, but immediately unfold them when I watch his eyes drop to the cleavage it causes.

"Bother you? No. Talk to you? Yes, I hoped so."

His honesty surprises me, but I shut it down. "Well, I can't talk. I'm working. Speaking of which, your food is probably done."

I brush against him to walk past, and I can't help but notice how warm and solid his body feels again, so it wasn't just my imagination.

As expected, their food is sitting under the lamp, so I grab it and take it to the table while he's not there. But unfortunately for me, he's on his way back from the bathroom once I deliver it and turn around.

"What about your number then? So we can talk when you're not working?"

A huff escapes my lungs with a chuckle I can't hold back. "No, thank you," I say without stopping, then effectively avoid the table for the rest of my shift.

The worst part about working two jobs is definitely when the schedules fall back-to-back. I slowly work the diffuser in my hair, getting ready for work again. I was at the bar until two, then got a solid five hours of sleep before waking up for my ten-to-six shift at the store. At least with this job, I don't have to worry about Dom showing up and being… Dom.

He didn't bother me anymore after rejecting his shot at my phone number, but he was still there for a bit. Still smiling at me with those obnoxious white teeth any time I looked his way, so I simply stopped looking at him. *Well, I tried.*

The drive to *Home Team* is a good twenty-five minutes, but I don't mind. Driving, staying busy with both jobs has done a great job at occupying me without all of the people I'd rather be doing things with. Maybe that's why my relationship wasn't as strong as I thought it was. Not everyone else is accustomed to being close with people they don't see all the time, as I am.

Speaking of Nathan, I never did text him back. I didn't see the point. I still don't, nor do I have anything to say. I'm not interested in staying friends with exes. All that does is cause trouble. He also hasn't tried again since, so he can't possibly miss me that much.

Once at work, I stop at the computer to clock in, then put my purse in my locker. Before I can head out to the floor, my manager, Derric, calls my name.

"Can you come see me first?"

Great. This is never good. "Yeah, no problem."

I sit in the plastic chair that is across from his metal desk as he sits in his. "How ya doing today?" he asks as his chair swivels.

He's never called me in here before, so I can't gauge if this is normal for him, or pleasantries before bad news. We usually don't hear much from him at all. He's a very black and white manager. He comes in, tells us what to do, does what he needs to do, then leaves. He's nice, but not very personable.

"I'm doing good. You?"

He nods. "Good. Good. So we've had this opportunity come up. Something I thought you would be great for." He stops like I should say something, but in my relief that I'm not getting fired, I just look at him. "*Home Team* is expanding. They want to open a few more stores over the next few months. They asked for a Sales Associate to be a part of the team to travel and help prep the new stores for opening." He pauses again to sip his coffee. "You are one of, if not our best, Sales Associate. I want to offer your name for this position."

"Wow," I say, surprised. While I've never been called in here for anything bad, I've never been recognized as the best employee either.

"Before you decide," he continues. "For this project, you'll become salaried. Paid a flat rate for each day worked, including travel days. You'll also receive a stipend for meals each week. Part of this job would be to help train their sales team, so the salaried rate would be at the manager's pay."

"I'd love to," I say immediately.

He laughs. "Well, good. I know you've mentioned another job before, so I wasn't sure if you'd be able to."

I shake my head. "No, well, I do, but I'm not worried about that."

"Sounds like a plan then. I'll get you more details today or tomorrow, and we'll go from there."

"That's great," I say as I stand up. "Thank you."

"Not a problem. Now, please do me a favor and make sure Neil is not scaring people away again."

"Sure." I exit his office with a laugh.

A smile remains fixed on my face as I join the team on the sales floor. This is perfect timing. I'm sure the bar will have me back when I'm done, but if they don't, oh well. I'll find another one.

One that hopefully isn't frequented by tall, dark-haired, green-eyed, tattooed men who smell like heaven on earth.

CHAPTER EIGHT

Dom - August

My only stipulation for this trip was that we drive something I can pull my bike in or on.

The last two months that I'm guaranteed riding time, cannot be spent with no access to the bike. October in Michigan sometimes still has a good chance, but come November, it's typically over until next April, March if we're really lucky.

John and I talked it over and decided on a small U-Haul. It may cost more in gas, but what we save in rental car fees should still come out cheaper. Plus, it gives the bike protection from the weather. We start next week, hitting Traverse City first. We'll spend a week there, then head to Grand Rapids. After that, we'll come home for two weeks, then leave again for Kalamazoo and Lansing, two more weeks at home, then the last stops in Ann Arbor and Detroit.

I still don't know who I'm working with, and I know that will make or break this trip. All I hope for is someone with a halfway decent sense of humor. And I hope it's someone who actually wants to be doing this. Traveling for days on end with someone miserable will not work for me.

I'll know soon, though, because we have a dinner meeting with John in thirty minutes.

I rub the towel over my freshly showered head. A few passes with the towel, then the tiniest amount of styling gel usually does the trick. All I need is a good five minutes, and I can be ready to go. With the towel now around my waist, I walk to my closet and grab my clothes, just a casual black T-shirt and jeans. We're only going to that one local steakhouse, so I don't see the need to dress up any more than this. Outside, the weather is a perfect eighty-two degrees and sunny, which leaves no question that I'll be taking the bike there.

Upon pulling up to the restaurant, John's car is parked right outside, the *Home Team* logo not so inconspicuously slapped on the door. I take my helmet off, hang it on the handlebars, then go inside.

I see him at the table alone just as I walk in. He smiles when he sees me and waves me over.

"How's the week treated you?" John asks as I sit down.

"Pretty good actually."

"Good. We're just waiting on the sales rep. She's a few minutes behind."

My eyebrow arches as I take a sip of the water that was waiting for me. "She?"

He nods. "Yes. She. That's part of why we're meeting tonight, to make sure we have an agreement on acceptable behavior."

I laugh, "You mean to make sure that I, the man, understand to keep my hands to myself."

"Pretty much." He smiles behind the glass lifted to his lips.

"I can assure you that you won't have any problems from me. I'm already interested in someone."

"Good." He nods. "But I'm sure it will be comforting to her that we have this conversation before she hits the road with you."

My head mirrors his nod as the waitress approaches to ask if we're ready to order. John orders calamari and spinach dip for appetizers. She smiles and retreats, then John perks up.

"There she is."

I turn in the direction of the door, and our eyes meet straight away. Her steps pause briefly, and her head rolls back with her eyes. I turn back around and lift my finger to my mouth, trying to hide my smile.

"Kory!" John exclaims as he stands to greet her. "So happy you could join us."

"Me too." She says, but with sarcasm dripping off her words.

He holds his hand out towards me. "This is Dominic, he'll be the manager traveling with you."

She holds her hand out to shake mine, acting like we've never met before. "It's nice to meet you, Dominic." Her words are still layered in sarcasm, but I see the faintest smirk in the corner of her thick lips. I ignore how it makes me feel, especially coupled with my full name rolling off them with teasing emphasis.

"This is Ms. Brooks." He says as I extend my arm and take her hand, immediately hexed by the way it fits in mine, and how soft her skin feels.

"Dom is fine. Nice to meet you, Ms. Brooks."

Her cheeks brighten, and she quickly pulls her hand away, fidgeting with the curls that hang closest to her face.

"Kory's fine."

"Should we eat first, then business?" John interrupts, oblivious to the tension that has now settled at the table with us. "I don't know about you two, but I am starving."

Kory nods, and I follow suit. Then, as if on cue, the waitress appears to take our orders.

The only conversation that happens while we eat is between John and me, Kory only adding an occasional one or two-word response, while actively avoiding my eye contact. I wonder if he can feel it yet, the tension, or if we are pulling off appearing as two strangers who are awkward because we just met.

I can't help but look over at her during the times of silence—eating bites of ravioli after she swirls them around in the sauce. She's got an orange shirt on that's sleeveless and bold compared to the monochrome attire both John and I are wearing. This color also makes her olive skin look even more tan than it usually does.

Once our plates are almost empty, she finally looks up. She doesn't shy away this time, though. Her eyes lock on mine, and she stares right at me as if this is a challenge. I stare back, raising my eyebrows just a tad. After a few seconds, I smile and to my surprise she does too, just briefly, then looks at John.

"So let's talk about this trip."

He starts rambling on about all the stuff he and I have already talked about. The cities, the schedule, *bla, bla, bla.* I zone out watching her listen. She twirls her hair while her eyes remain on John attentively. It's not until he assures her that I'll be a total gentleman that she looks back at me.

"Right, Dominic?" John stresses.

"Yes. Right. I promise to be on my best behavior." I say while holding her gaze.

Once again, she doesn't waver. Neither of us does, and in that stare, I realize she may actually be challenging me. Challenging me to the promise I just made to remain on my best behavior.

CHAPTER NINE

Kory

Go fucking figure.

Of all the people in the world. Of all the people in the state of Michigan. Of all the people who work for *Home Team*, Dom is the one I'm traveling with.

The last person I would want, besides maybe Nate. No, you know what? I think I'd rather be stuck with Nate because he doesn't look like *that*.

His elbows are on the table, allowing his chin to rest on his hands, his fingers lazily hiding the smirk on his face. Sitting this close and under these fluorescent lights, the emeralds he has for eyes sparkle unfairly, putting mine to shame. I get distracted by his tattoos again, feeling my eyes follow along each black trail, as if my brain isn't even connected to the action.

The slight tilt of his head and the arch in his brows promptly stop me from thinking any further, once again, about the tattoos I can't see. *Damn it.* He is loving this. The smile that plasters his face leaves little to the imagination. But I am not giving this opportunity up, so I decide to smile right back. He may think this has worked out for him, but two can play that game.

We make it through dinner, John seemingly oblivious to Dom's inability to find anything else to look at. I ignore him and pretend I don't notice. We agree on all the necessary details and that Dom will pick me up in ten days. John gives me his phone number in case of emergencies, or if Dom gets inappropriate. I caught the insinuation from the scheduling of this meeting. While I appreciate it, it's also a little insulting. I'm perfectly capable of taking care of myself.

Despite the fact that it's 2023, John obviously doesn't know me at all. I'm probably one of the last women who would find themselves as a damsel in distress. Being practically on my own my whole life has forced me to be tough enough to be able to handle myself, or to handle one horny dude at least.

John pays the bill, then we all get up to leave the restaurant. Once outside, we say our goodbyes, and John goes to the right of the building. Naturally, Dom follows me to the left side.

"I know you promised to be a gentleman and whatever, but I don't need you to walk me to my car."

"I hate to break it to you, sweetheart, but this isn't chivalry. This is just me walking to my own vehicle."

His voice saying sweetheart heats my stomach, and I roll my eyes to fight the response. He doesn't need to know I'm rolling them at myself and not him. We walk a few more feet until he veers towards the street. He approaches a black motorcycle with a helmet hanging off the handlebars.

"That's you?"

"Nope. But it looks fun, doesn't it?"

He sticks a key in the ignition, then grabs the helmet. *Of course, it's him.* Not only was that a dumb question, but look at him. The muscles, the tattoos, the slicked back hair, the attitude, of course, he has a motorcycle. All he's missing is a leather jacket.

He laughs, reading my annoyance. "Want to go for a ride?"

Before I can speak, I laugh too. "Definitely not. No thanks." I can't pull my eyes away while he throws one leg over to straddle the bike. He pauses, staring at me, that stupid smirk sitting way too comfortably on his lips.

"I don't know why you have to make this so difficult, Brooks."

Ew. Calling me by my last name. He cannot start this trip by giving me a pet name.

"And what's that?"

"Falling in love with me."

A combination of a laugh and a snort floats out of me, my head tilting back as it does. "Yeah. Right. You're insane."

"I might be, but I'm also right. By this time next year, you'll be so in love with me you can't stand it."

"Yeah. This time next year, while we're sitting on the beach during a snowstorm, maybe then."

"A snowstorm in August? Be careful what you ask for, baby. Don't forget we live in Michigan."

He laughs and slides the helmet over his head. The baby comment goes in one ear and right out the other because all I can see while he adjusts the straps is his eyes, piercing me through the open visor, illuminated under these streetlights.

"Fight it all you want, Brooks, but you'll see."

"My name is Kory." I petulantly reply.

"See you next week, Kory Brooks. Bright and early." Then he winks, turns the key in front of him, and roars the bike to life, making me jump.

I turn to walk away without saying anything else. Behind me, I can hear the bike's engine rev a few more times. I refuse to look backwards, but as soon as I reach my jeep, it sounds like he finally takes off. I get inside and take a deep breath, cursing at myself for feeling the way I do around him. The sound of the bike gets louder just briefly as it passes by me, then almost instantly fades away again.

I lean my head against the seat for a minute before pushing the button to start. I close my eyes and tell myself the money is going to be worth it. It has to be worth it because every *second* that I'm around him, he somehow gets deeper under my skin.

CHAPTER TEN

Dom

I should be packing.

The duffel bag is still half-empty on my bed, a few shirts tossed in like I started and got bored halfway through. I've got a checklist somewhere—probably under the pile of clean laundry I haven't folded. But instead of checking it off, I'm in the garage, elbow-deep in grease, fiddling with my bike like it's going to tell me what to do.

It's not about my bike, really. It's about the distraction. About keeping my hands busy so my mind doesn't spiral into the same loop it's been stuck in since she walked into that restaurant, and I realized it was her I'd be with for the next couple of months.

I've liked her for years—quietly and from a distance. From across the hall, across the store, across the damn town. Always just far enough away to admire, never close enough to reach. Timing was never on our side. She was with someone. I was with someone. But now we're both single, and will basically be together for a few months, and the weight of the situation has caused my mask of confidence to crack.

Talking to her is easy, but getting past that tough exterior is going to be the challenge. I don't even know how to start trying to convince her that I don't just want to sleep with her, because I'm sure that's her assumption.

The honest truth is that I'm a mess at the thought of messing this up. She's not the kind of girl you flirt with and forget. She's the kind that sticks with you. That much I know already.

I tighten a bolt that doesn't need tightening and wipe my hands on a rag. The bike's fine. It's been fine. But I keep checking it like it's going to fall apart the second I climb on it again. Maybe I'm the one who's not ready.

I walk over to the workbench and sit with a huff. She has changed, though I guess we all do. But this seems different. She's guarded. She's sharp. Which means she's been hurt—and obviously isn't going to let me in easily, even if I wasn't Jimmy's best friend.

Blake would say I'm overthinking it. He'd tell me to just make a move, crack a joke, buy her a drink. But Blake's never had to earn someone's trust. He's good at surface-level. I'm not interested in surface-level. The thing with him, he's what people nowadays refer to as a *'fuck boy.'* While I like him, he's made it perfectly clear that he's not interested in anyone enough to be tied down for more than a night, maybe two.

It fits him, though, with his pale blond hair and baby blue eyes. If you googled the term *'fuck boy,'* his picture may actually pop up. I imagine if I knew him in high school, he would've annoyed me. But as adults, his conquests don't affect me, so his love life can remain his own problem. I definitely won't be taking any advice from him, though.

Thinking of high school, I remember one of the first times I saw Kory, laughing with Autumn at a football game. The bleachers were packed, the air thick with the scent of concession stand hot dogs and the chill of an early fall evening. The stadium lights buzzed overhead, casting long shadows across the field. The crowd roared after a touchdown, but all of that faded into the background when I saw her.

Kory and Autumn were both wrapped in school colors with paint on their faces. They flew up onto their feet, cheering and clapping with the rest of the crowd. As they stopped to sit back down, they were both laughing with excitement. Her laughter—it was light, effortless, but her smile hit me like a punch to the chest. I knew then that she was something special. Maybe it was the way her eyes sparkled under the lights, or how she leaned into Autumn's shoulder, gleefully and radiant.

As Jimmy and I were climbing the steps, on our way to join them, I thought I caught her glance. For a second, I thought she might have been looking at me. My heart picked up speed, and I rehearsed a line in my head like a middle schooler—something casual, maybe funny. Just enough to start a conversation. But before I could say a word, a guy jumped up the steps past us, sliding into the spot beside her. He leaned in and kissed her on the cheek, and she smiled, turning toward him with the same warmth that had just lit up my world.

And just like that, the moment passed. Jimmy sat down by Autumn, and I sat by him—the complete opposite end of Kory and her boyfriend.

I still remember that feeling—the sharp twist in my chest, the way my words dried up before they ever reached my lips. It wasn't heartbreak, not exactly. But it was something close. I've gotten better with my words with age—but spending this much time with her is going to change everything.

It happened again, right after Izzy and I had become official. I saw her out to eat with the same friend she was with at the bar. I wanted to let myself be sucked in, to approach the table like I did the other night, but I had just committed to someone else, so I wouldn't let myself. There was a similar twist in my chest that night, one that I couldn't really describe. I still can't. I really liked Izzy at the time; I wouldn't have made her my girlfriend if I didn't, and I really wanted to be with her. And I didn't have the thought to leave Izzy and be with Kory; it was never like that. But it was for sure that there was a part inside of me that knew I needed to know that girl.

I return to the bike to make sure I haven't left any loose tools on the ground. I run my hand along the seat, imagining Kory behind me, arms wrapped around my waist, head tucked into my shoulder. I wonder if she'd trust me enough to lean in. *To hold on.*

I wonder if she's thinking about me right now. If she's packing for the trip. If she's nervous. If she's hoping I'll make a move—or hoping I won't.

Again, I should be packing. I should be checking my gear, printing the plan, and texting John to confirm the hotel. But instead, I'm stuck here. Wandering around my garage like I'm lost. And in a sense, I guess I am lost—in my thoughts.

Because this trip isn't just about work, it's about her. It's about finally maybe getting close enough to reach her.

Eventually, I toss the rag onto the bench and kill the garage light. The sun's dipping low, casting jagged shadows across the driveway. I take one last look at the bike, then head inside.

In a few days, we hit the road. And maybe, just maybe, I'll figure out how to convince her to give me a chance.

CHAPTER ELEVEN

Kory

As soon as she walks in the door, my world feels normal again. Of all the people in my life whose absence lingers, Autumn's is the worst. I forcefully grab her by the shoulders and pull her in tight.

"God, I missed you!"

"Me too." She replies.

I step back, leaving my hands on her shoulders, taking in the new person in front of me. "You look amazing." I gush.

She really does. One thing about my best friend is that she's always been as predictable as they come. From the moment I met her at ten years old, she's always had long blond hair with bangs across her forehead. That never changed for almost twenty years.

But now I'm looking at a whole new woman. She no longer has the bangs, and instead of her hair hanging down her back, it sits just slightly past her shoulders: split down the middle and curled slightly into golden waves. It honestly suits her more than the bangs ever did.

"Thanks." She smiles as we plop down on my couch like we haven't missed a beat.

"So, what's new? How's Jersey? How's the guy? Tyler?"

Another thing about Autumn, she falls hard. *And fast.* I knew she was smitten with this new guy just from talking on

FaceTime, but now I know for sure without her even responding. I can see it in the sparkle of her blue eyes.

"Yes, Tyler. He's good. He's here, actually."

"Here?! Like sitting in the parking lot?"

She laughs. "No. Just in Michigan, dork. With me. He dropped me off."

"Why didn't he come in? I have to meet him."

"Because I've barely seen you in two years. He can wait."

That right there. That's why her being missing from my life hurts the worst. I throw my arms around her again.

"Ugh, I love you." I spit out. "But I can't wait. So spill. Everything."

She spends the next twenty minutes gushing about him. She tells me the story of how they met (again), about how they spend five nights a week together, and how she can't sleep the two nights that they're apart.

"He wants me to move in."

It feels too soon to me, but I know they've been together for over a year. That together has just been in New Jersey, not around me.

"What do you think?" I watch her face, because again, I'll know the answer before she says it. A smirk slowly creeps across her lips. She wants to.

"I'm nervous. I've never lived with anyone. But I think I want to." Her voice grows sheepish.

I squeal and pull her back into another obnoxious hug. If she's happy, then I'm happy, and thank God she's in a better place than the last time she was here. She pulls back.

"What about you? I'm sorry about Nathan. You doing okay?"

She also didn't personally know Nate because of our distance. We met shortly after she left again. It is funny, though. Despite the physical space between us, we're still so close that we both know just about everything there is to know about two guys we've never met.

"I'm fine," I say with a shrug. "I wasn't that hurt, so it obviously wasn't meant to be. I was more pissed off than anything."

"Still sucks." She gets off the couch, making herself at home in my kitchen. She gathers some snacks and rejoins me in the living room. While munching on some chips and water, we continue talking for two hours. She asks if I have any shifts at the bar while she's in town, and I realize I didn't catch her up on my job situation. *And Dom.*

"Oh, shit. I forgot to tell you. I quit."

"Quit? Why?"

"Well, Kind of quit like a temporary thing. Next week I'm leaving for a road trip for *Home Team*. They're opening some more stores, and I was hand-picked to travel and train new associates." I flutter my eyelashes dramatically.

"That's awesome!" she exclaims. "Better pay?"

"Way better."

"So you get to drive around by yourself? Or with a team?"

I pop a chip in my mouth and chew before answering. She notices my delay and narrows her eyes at me. "Yeah, that's the only problem. It's me and one other person."

"And?"

"It's Dom."

She laughs. "Like Izzy's ex, slash Jimmy's best friend, Dom? The one with all the tattoos?"

"Yeah. Him."

"Interesting. I didn't know you two worked together."

"I didn't either. He's the manager at the only other store that exists. For now."

Autumn cocks her head to the side, narrowing her eyes once again. "So why is this a problem?"

"Because he's Dom."

"And?"

I widen my eyes at her like she should already know. She should, and she does. She laughs again, louder this time, with her head thrown back.

"Okay, so is this a problem because of me? Or because you think he's hot?" She takes a sip of water, those annoying narrowed eyes returning for a third time. If I didn't know her, I'd think she was judging me at this point, but I do know her, and these looks are because she knows me, too.

"You, obviously." She stares silently, waiting for a different response. I hang my head against the couch and groan. "Fine. Both, I guess. Yeah, he's hot, but because of you, that's why I need to pretend he isn't."

"Seriously, Kay? I don't care about that." I don't say anything back right away, so she continues. "You're just using me as an excuse."

"He's Jimmy's best friend."

"And? Everyone in this town is linked to someone somehow. That's why I left, remember? Have some fun. Road tripping alone with a tattooed hottie? Sounds like the perfect ingredients for one of your romcoms."

"Maybe."

"Does he still ride a bike?"

I roll my eyes. "Yes."

She laughs. "Oh my God, even better. If you don't take advantage of this, you are crazy."

She may not think she cares, *but how could it ever actually be anything?* I wouldn't ever put Autumn in the position to deal with Jimmy. That's why I don't blame her for getting the hell out of here, as much as it sucks for me. She's right. Everyone in this town is or ends up connected one way or another. Running away is the only way to avoid it. So there couldn't be a future between me and Dom, but maybe she's right about fun. Maybe there *could* be some fun.

There's a knock at the door, and she jumps up. "That's Tyler. Be nice."

I put both hands up in the air, declaring my innocence as she turns to the door. He walks in after kissing her, and she introduces us as we sit at the table. He tells me about himself and his version of their beginning. I'm sure Autumn probably expected me to hold more of an interrogation, but I'm only half in the conversation.

The rest of my brain has veered off, focused on the idea of having *fun* with Dom.

CHAPTER TWELVE

Dom

The last day at *Home Team* before we hit the road feels like I'm quitting—or got fired.

I trust Blake, but I remove my things I have from this office, allowing him to fully take over until I'm back. Shuffling through the drawers to make sure there's nothing *too* personal in there, he comes in and plops himself down in the guest chair.

"So, you come up with a master plan already?" He plasters on the smile he wears when talking about conquests at the bar, so I know exactly what he is insinuating.

"There is no master plan," I say flatly.

"Oh, come on." He laughs. "You drag me back to that bar just to see her, and now you'll be traveling *alone* with her, and I'm supposed to believe you don't have a plan?" He stares at me incredulously, waiting for an answer.

I stare back, wondering if we would have ever become friends had we not met here—*probably not.* Our friendship officially started with a drink after work, right after Izzy and I broke up. She showed up at the store one day, trying to convince me to change my mind. She didn't cause a scene, but was obviously emotional as hell, which bothered me. I didn't end it to hurt her; we were just so wrong for each other, I couldn't let it go another day longer.

Blake witnessed the fiasco and could tell it threw me off, so he invited me out for a drink to get my mind off of it. Turns out we clicked, and he's one of the few people I enjoy hanging out with. Going out that one day after work turned into a once-a-week thing—sometimes more if there's a game he wants to watch.

But we have become pretty close, and the look he's giving me now is because he knows I'm actually full of shit.

"Yeah, I am aware that we will be traveling alone, but that doesn't mean that there is a *'plan,'*" I emphasize the word plan with finger quotes.

"Whatever you say. But you can't tell me you haven't thought about it. You're infatuated with that broad. I can't say I blame you…"

"Don't call her that." I cut him off before he says anything worse. The word *'broad'* already causes a tightness in my chest.

He laughs. "See. I didn't even know that was a bad word."

"Don't you have work to be doing?" I ask him.

He chuckles as he stands, and my annoyance with him grows. "K. Fine. Clearly, I struck a nerve. I won't talk about her anymore." He pauses in the doorway. "We're still on for drinks tonight? Before you leave?"

"Yeah, we'll see. I have a lot to do."

"Exactly why you need to come out."

"I said we'll see."

He shakes his head with the same grin he wore on his way in here before leaving.

Of course, I've thought about what this trip could mean for us—Kory and I—that's all I've been thinking about. But the only plan I've come up with is to play it cool. I've already made my interest clear. I've waited too long for this to mess it up by appearing *too* cocky—like Blake. That's the last impression I want her to have of me. I'm sure she may already think that, but right now it's just an assumption. The confidence I try to carry has often been mistaken for the cockiness of a playboy, but that's not me. And she's the first person I actually care about understanding that. But finding the balance between playing it cool and *'not interested'* will be the problem.

I grab the rest of my things and then head for the car. Speaking of playing it cool, we exchanged numbers but haven't used them yet. We haven't really needed to, but that could be my way to still play it cool and also keep myself on her radar.

After getting home, showering, and popping leftover spaghetti in the microwave, I decide to rip off the Band-Aid.

> Hey. It's Dom.

Playing it cool.
The microwave beeps, and I pull the steaming bowl out. My phone buzzes as I'm sprinkling Parmesan cheese on top.

> Hey. It's Kory.

I'm not the slightest bit surprised that's all she says. Copying me word for word. Snarky—just the way I like her.

> Just wanted to make sure you had my number.

> Bold of you to assume I need it.

I laugh through my too-hot bite of pasta.

> You may not now, but you will.

> I do get bored and need someone to bother from time to time.

She writes back instantly. My smile persists through the chewing of my food. This is how I know she doesn't actually hate me. She could just ignore me, but she doesn't.

> Bold of you to assume you'd bother me.

I ricochet her snark right back to her.

I'm sure I could, but I'm in Jersey right now, so don't expect me to be bored the next couple of days.

The response surprises me just a bit because I wasn't expecting much back and forth, but this feels like an opening, so I keep it going.

Jersey? What's in Jersey?

Autumn. Helping her move into her boyfriend's place.

That makes sense, but it adds to my surprise because I know Autumn is a big part of why she wants to avoid me. But that's also why I'll keep fighting to keep myself on her radar. I go for broke.

Ah fun. Don't work too hard. I need you in excellent physical shape when you get back.

Part of me regrets it, but then her response calms my nerves.

I'll do my best.

CHAPTER THIRTEEN

Kory

This has got to be another joke.

That's all I can think of as I watch the U-Haul truck park against the curb in front of my apartment building. When the window rolls down, it gets even worse. Dom's in the driver's seat, wearing a backwards baseball cap, sunglasses, and a shit eating grin.

"Morning, Brooks." He says as I approach the window.

"Dominic." I greet formally, curtly nodding my head and avoiding eye contact.

"Oh, full first name again. I like it."

The weight of my annoyance causes my eyes to roll before I even look into the cab and take in the lack of space for my three bags. He notices my observation and jumps out, rounding the back of the truck and throwing the back open. As it slides up into the top, the need for the U-Haul becomes visible and is strapped down tightly. He reads my mind and comments before I even say anything.

"Can't go the rest of the summer without it." Then he winks.

Remember when we were kids and your parents would tell you to stop making that face, *or it would be stuck like that forever?* I fear by the end of this project, mine will be stuck rolled into the back of my head. It's the only reaction I can seem to muster up when I'm around him.

We silently get situated, and he pulls onto the road. The big truck bounces at each bump, and it actually might be the perfect thing to lull me to sleep. But Dom turns the knob for the volume on the radio, and country music fills the small cab. I open my book to where I left off last, perfectly content paying attention to the tattooed main character on the pages, versus the one sitting next to me.

But with the more words that leave this page and enter my brain, I realize that I picked the wrong book for this trip. Stella, the female main character, describes the man who just walked into her coffee shop—tall with muscles covered in tattoos on display due to the tank top he is wearing. The baseball cap he wears is backwards, which has the same effect on her as it does on me.

I strain my eyes to the side, so as not to be noticed, and it's possible he is the main character in this book. The only difference is that Dom is in a white T, not a tank top. But the tattoos are still just as prevalent, showing beneath the taut fabric, then fully exposed all the way down to his hands. I strain a little harder, trying to take in the full picture, his one arm on the steering wheel, flexed so that a vein is also visible. His head faces forward, but the hat is still tortuously backwards. His lips turn up in a smirk, like he can feel me watching him.

"Can I help you with something?"

I guess he could. "Just wondering if you forgot how to talk."

He laughs. "Nope, you just didn't seem like you were in the talkative mood."

"I'm talkative with people I like."

He switches which arm is on the steering wheel as he laughs again. "So you admit you like me? If you want me to be talkative?"

Shit. Insert foot in mouth.

"I didn't say that. But we're stuck together, so it's going to be more agonizing than it already is if we spend this whole time in silence."

"I agree." His ever-present smug little smirk is still comfortable as ever on his face.

"Good," I say.

"Good." He copies.

An ironic, awkward silence returns as we both stare at the road ahead. *What do we even talk about?* I have no idea, but I know we're off to a horrible start.

"I didn't take you as a country music fan?" he finally says.

"Huh?" I turn my head back toward him.

"You're humming. You must know the song."

I didn't realize I was. "Oh yeah, it's fine. I like a little bit of everything."

"So I'm not stuck on a road trip with a crazy Swiftie?"

I laugh. "Not quite. I like a lot of her songs, but I'm not a superfan. That's more Autumn's forte." He laughs, but something tells me he wouldn't have cared if I were. "What about you?"

"Me? A Swiftie?" He turns his head towards me just briefly. "I'd never tell you if I was."

"No," the word comes out mixed with another laugh. "I meant what kind of music do you like?"

"Same as you—a little bit of everything. I get bored after a while and have to change it up. Chances are I'm good with what's on the radio, though."

For the next hour, we intermittently ride in silence and ask questions. It's been a game of "Twenty Questions" about all the basics.

Favorite music: Both Everything.
Favorite colors: His black. Mine purple.
Favorite seasons: Both Summer.
Favorite type of food: Both Steak.
Favorite Holiday: His Fourth of July. Mine Christmas.
Favorite time of day: Both evenings.
Favorite Snacks: His Salt and vinegar chips. Mine chocolate-covered pretzels.
Favorite drinks: His Light blue Gatorade. Mine Vanilla Coke.
Favorite alcoholic drink: His Vodka Cranberry. Mine Crown and Coke.
Least favorite chore: His laundry. Mine dishes.
Least favorite food: Both hot dogs.

It was all seemingly surface-level, unimportant things, but it made things in this truck so much more comfortable already.

We stop for gas and food, just sitting down in the fast-food place connected to the gas station. I carry our tray of cheeseburgers to the table he's sitting at after filling up the truck and taking a bathroom break.

"I'll be right back," I tell him, needing to do the same.

After washing my hands, I look at myself in the mirror, trying to smooth the frizz of my hair. My natural curls are my favorite thing about me, and beautiful when I treat them right, but I rushed out the door this morning with my products already packed. As I'm about to give up finger smoothening and just tie it all back, I realize I am being stupid. *Why do I care?* It's Dom. I don't care what he thinks I look like. *I really don't.*

Back at the table, most of his fries are gone already.

"Hungry?"

"Honestly, I was starving. I almost started on yours, too."

I laugh, then pop a fry in my mouth before he can steal them all. "So," I start, now comfortable with the cadence of firing off questions. "Tell me about your family."

I add a second fry to my mouth and wait for his response, but there isn't one. Not right away. For a second, he tenses, and I see his jaw clench. He stares down at his burger as if he's lighting it on fire. It's the briefest of moments, but I catch it.

"What about them?" he asks, still not looking at me.

"I don't know anything. Siblings? Just getting to know you, I guess."

"We went to school together. You should know this."

After swallowing the bite I'm chewing, I scoff. "I barely remember anything from school. Honestly, I don't really remember you that much. Anyway, I have one brother, Elliot. We were super close growing up, but he moved away after he graduated. My parents, too, although they were gone most of my teen years, doing God knows what anyway. That's why we were so close, we practically raised ourselves."

I take another bite, and he does the same, nodding in response, but not yet adding anything. After another bite and obviously some quiet deliberation, he finally speaks.

"I have a twin sister. Kami. We were also really close. Until she and my parents left for New York."

"Wow, both our parents and siblings left us in the dust for another state. What a crazy coincidence." I chuckle and bite down on another fry.

"Yeah. Crazy." He says flatly.

I watch his Adam's apple bob and understand that this question has changed his mood. I take it as the end of our "Twenty Questions" game, and we finish our meal in silence. We get back in the truck and finish the short drive just as quietly. I go back to reading, and he concentrates solely on the road.

I can't help but continue to peek at him out of the corner of my eye. Not just because of the way he looks, but with a newfound curiosity. There's something he's not telling me. Something he doesn't want me to know, and that's probably because it's none of my business.

But now that we're stuck together, it's definitely something I am going to try and figure out.

CHAPTER FOURTEEN

Dom

No surprise I'd be the one to mess it up.

Kory was finally opening up to me, well, at least not actively pretending to hate me—and I shut the whole thing down, not with words, but with my attitude.

I don't know why I didn't expect her to ask a question like that—we'd been interrogating each other for almost an hour. But it surprised me nonetheless, and I wasn't prepared with an answer. I hoped giving her something would come off less defensive than *'I don't want to talk about them,'* but it didn't.

We didn't speak for the rest of the drive. Even once we got to our hotel, we both quietly checked in and went to our rooms. They were directly across the hall from each other, so even the walk down the hall felt ominous. A total shift from just shortly before. I thought about saying something before we split up for the night, but she had already adjusted to the mood and clicked her door shut without a word.

Once my clothes are pulled out of my suitcase, I sit on the edge of the bed deciding what to do next. I'm hungry again. And we should talk about tomorrow. I need to fix it so she doesn't go back to fake-hating me. I decide to send her a text.

Thankfully, three little dots pop up as she starts typing.

> I was actually planning on staying in. I've already changed. Driving makes me tired.

I try to hit her with the humor I normally would, to let her know that I'm good now.

> Driving? When did you drive anywhere?

> Haha. RIDING makes me tired.

I begin typing *'is that so?'* but before I can hit send, another from her comes through.

> Don't even think about it. Ignore that whole text.

I laugh, relieved that it seems like things may be able to return to normal after all.

> I don't know what you're talking about. Want to order in? We really should plan for the week before we get there.

> That's fine. From the restaurant downstairs?

> Sounds good. Your place or mine?

> Mine. I'm too tired to walk that far.

I laugh out loud.

I guess I'm ordering too. But this is good. I didn't screw this up after all. Today has actually been the most she's ever given me, which means we're moving in the right direction. I spent the fifteen minutes waiting for the food straightening up. Not the room, but myself. I know I turn into a whole different person when people bring up my family, but I need to get that under control. The weirder I get, the more questions there will be.

It's been years since they left, and Kory isn't the first person to bring them up, but she is the first person I can't just walk away from.

She was right, though—it is crazy that we both have one sibling and parents who moved away. I shouldn't be surprised with everything else we have in common, but it also has me more on edge. If she knows it's something she can identify with, she may be more likely to want to talk about it again.

So I need to get my shit together.

Only a few seconds after I knock, she answers the door, and I lose my breath. Her mahogany curls are piled high on her head, and black square-framed glasses sit on her nose. The pajamas she referred to—a light blue silk tank top with matching shorts. Something about that color makes her skin look as silky as the fabric. I've never seen her like this. I didn't even know she wore glasses, but I know that she's never looked better.

She motions to the desk, and I get the food boxes out of the bag. We grab our respective meals, then I sit in the desk chair while she sits in the accent chair by the bed. She grabs the remote and flips through the channels, stopping on Impractical Jokers.

"I love this show," I tell her through a mouthful of asada nachos.

"Me too. I think I've seen every episode and still laugh every time."

"Same," I say with a smile, which she mirrors.

I watch as she adjusts herself to be sitting with both legs on the chair, crisscrossed underneath her. I can't help but notice how this new position makes the shorts slide up her thighs. She doesn't say anything, but when I look up at her face, her eyebrow is raised inquisitively, *or maybe invitingly?* Either way, she definitely sees me staring.

"I didn't know you wore glasses." I take another bite.

"I usually don't. Only at night."

"I like them."

"I hate them."

With a small laugh from both of us, we finish our meals. She gets up to clean the to-go containers, and each time she walks past me, I get a whiff of her scent. It's so unique to her. If only she'd let me get close enough to engulf myself in it. But she won't yet, so for now, I'll appreciate what I can get. Once the garbage is all cleaned, she moves to the bed and plops down on the edge of it, which makes the silk around her chest bounce.

"Well?" she asks.

I blink. "Well, what?" My eyes grow wide, confused.

"You said we have to make a plan?"

"Oh, haha." I nod. "Yeah, we do."

I lean down to grab the training manuals from the bag on the floor. Silently cursing myself for letting the anxious boy side of me creep out for a second. Of course, she isn't inviting me onto the bed.

I hand hers to her, and as she reaches for it, her tank strap falls to the side, revealing a sliver of the strapless bra underneath. Her eyes linger on mine for just a moment before moving the packet in her hands.

I sit back in my chair and flip through mine, but I'm not reading it. My eyes are looking up at her while my brain is working overtime. I know I won't make it through this project without falling for her.

But there's nothing that matters to me more right now than making sure she falls right along with me.

CHAPTER FIFTEEN

Kory

The first week went off without a hitch. Dom was surprisingly easy to work alongside, and I could see why they liked him as a manager.

Training the floor staff was also surprisingly fun. It was mostly younger kids- seventeen to twenty-one-ish, but they were excited and eager for the job, or maybe just the 45% off staff discount.

This location is a big store, which made setting up the layout easy. The store I work at is small, so there is half the staff and half the space to make all the displays John wants out. We spent the first few days walking them through everything, then the last two working alongside them and observing.

"We should go out to celebrate," Dom says as we walk to the truck.

"Celebrate what exactly?"

"That the first job is done?"

"Sure, you're not just trying to get me drunk, Dominic?"

The hardest part about this week? The way he looks at me. I always catch him staring, and the look in his eyes belongs in one of my books, not on the workplace floor. It makes ignoring my attraction to him almost impossible. And the thoughts of *'fun'* are a forever-spinning pinwheel.

"I didn't say anything about getting drunk. You did." He smiles as we both hop in and buckle.

"Fine, but let's shower and change first."

"I thought you'd never ask." He responds effortlessly.

I shake my head. "Just drive."

Back at the hotel and out of the shower, I look through my limited options to wear. I did bring a few different things just in case, but nothing that really screams *bar*. Surprisingly, though, I do really want to go. I miss being myself. I was always the fun one. I was the one who would drag all my friends to places they didn't want to go, but with Autumn leaving again, then Nathan doing the same, I just stopped caring about fun.

But there is something about being around Dom that seems to be having a positive effect on me. *Unfortunately.*

Did I put that set of pajamas on purpose before he came to my room? No. *Was I wearing them because that's all I brought on this trip?* Yes. I didn't expect him to end up in my room, though. I said I wouldn't let him in. But on the very first night, there he was.

My phone begins vibrating, and I see it's a FaceTime from Olivia. I prop the phone up on the mirror and answer.

"Hey, girl," I say while blending my foundation into my skin.

"Sup, babes." She says, then instantly gasps. "Why are you putting makeup on on a Friday night? Are you going out on a date with a sexy stranger from out of town? That's hot. I love that for you."

I laugh and shake my head, moving the beauty blender to the other cheek. "No. I'm just going to get a few drinks with Dominic."

"Oh. My. God." She says slowly, enunciating each word as her face fills with excitement. I cut her off before she can go any further.

"No. Don't do that. It's nothing."

She laughs and rolls over on her bed. "It is most definitely *not* nothing. It's too insanely hot, people—*no*—coworkers, who are going to a hotel bar together while away on a work trip. I LOVE it."

My eyes roll as I grab my mascara. "Exactly. Just co-workers. On a work trip. People do that all the time."

"You know what else people do all the time? Get drunk and have an affair with the coworker they secretly have the hots for."

"Not going to happen," I argue.

"Then why are you grabbing lipstick right now?"

I pause and stare at her with the tube in my hand. "Because I'm going to a bar, Olivia."

"Mmmhmm." She hums sarcastically. "Don't think I didn't catch the fact that you called him Dominic."

"That's his name."

"Said no one ever. Who actually calls him that?"

"I do, I guess." I pause to paint the red across my stretched open lips. "Anyways, did you call for anything other than harassment?"

"Nope." She says happily. "Just bored and you've been all mopey lately, so I figured you'd be in bed already. But clearly you have much better things to do, so I'll leave you to it. Don't forget a condom."

"GOODBYE," I say firmly before ending the call.

Just as I get up to put on the casual black T-shirt dress I decided on, my phone beeps again.

> I'm going to head down. Be there or be square.

Before I can text him back, another message comes through, from Olivia.

> Nice to see the old you coming back.

I pause for a minute, looking at the text and deciding how to respond. Instead, I leave that message and open Dom's and let my old self type back.

> Nothing square about me.

I purposely waited a few more minutes so I knew for sure he'd already be sitting somewhere once I got there. I found him easily at the bar with two drinks in front of him. He has on a white T-shirt again, this time with black jeans. A modest silver chain hung around his neck with a #1 symbol on it. His hair was still damp from his shower, the little bit of length hanging in a loose strand down the middle of his forehead. He almost looked like he was covered in sweat, and as soon as it happened, I wished I hadn't thought that.

"Crown and Coke." He says and slides me one of the glasses. My face must appear surprised because he follows it up with, "Twenty Questions, remember?"

"Right," I say and take a drink, silently appreciating that he remembered.

"Cheers." He says, raising his glass. "To a kick ass first week."

I laugh. "Are we teenagers?"

"Excuse me." He says, faking offense with a smile and a hand to his chest. "You don't have to be a teenager to appreciate a good toast. It's an American tradition."

"I wouldn't go that far. But fine, cheers."

This drink is made so perfectly that the taste and smoothness cause just the tiniest moan to escape my throat. I take another big swig, then look back at him, and both his eyebrows are raised at me.

"Tell me more." He says before downing the rest of his.

I follow suit and finish mine too, just as the bartender approaches asking if we want another round. He says yes without taking his eyes off me. Goosebumps cover my skin, and a fire ignites somewhere deep inside me.

Our second drinks come quickly, and I lift it to my lips, only sure of one thing—if they keep going back this smoothly, I am in trouble.

CHAPTER SIXTEEN

Dom

I learned a lot about Kory this week. Tonight, I learned that she *really* likes those drinks, but she can't handle them.

Much to my amusement, it was pretty obvious that the alcohol had taken over. It was adorable, though, watching her unwind at a level I've imagined, but never witnessed. Noticing what was happening, I switched myself to water five of her drinks ago. One of us has to get us to the room safely.

"I looooooooove this song!" she exclaims as a new pop one comes on.

She begins to sing into her cup as a microphone while I sip from mine, enjoying the show. She sways her head from side to side, passionately belting the lyrics. Her hair bounces with her movements, and the cut of her dress shifts with her weight.

I don't even try to remove the smile from my face. Not one single thing about her has been a turn-off, including being sloppy drunk. Before the chorus plays for a second time, her eyes suddenly grow wide, and she hits her hand on my forearm.

"We should go swimming."

"Swimming. Right now?"

"Yes. Right now. Come on." She grabs my hand and jumps off the stool, but I grab her in return to stop her.

"Hang on, let me pay the bill."

"Fine." She slurs and leans against the bar.

Swimming in the state she's in is definitely not safe, so she's not going alone. She is not going anywhere alone like this.

Once I get it paid, we go to our rooms to change. I almost didn't bring a swimsuit, but now I'm glad I did. After I'm dressed, I knock on her door.

Once again, the door opens, and she takes my breath away. I wonder if that will ever stop. I prepared myself for the possibility of a bikini, but it wasn't enough. It's a typical bikini, hot pink, and it fits her perfectly. I can finally see the curves I've been imagining, and I'm the farthest thing from disappointed.

"Are you going to stare all night, or are we going to go?" she demands.

"After you," I say and motion for her to walk in front of me with a laugh.

She takes the lead, not a care in the world that she only has this bathing suit on, while she struts through the hotel.

The ties of her bottoms sit perfectly on her hips—resting effortlessly in the curve that bridges them to her waist. From behind, just enough of her cheeks are exposed to confirm her ass is as round as it looks in jeans.

In the pool room, she makes no time jumping in. I follow, but use the steps like a sober adult. But once again, I watch her in amusement. And awe maybe. There's that aura about her. A happiness that exudes from her, and I can't get enough. I've wanted to be a part of that happiness for so long. And now it's here in front of me, even if it's alcohol induced.

"Quit being boring and come swim with me." She taunts.

"I am swimming."

"Sitting on the stairs is not swimming, Dominic." She emphasizes my name, like I'm a child being chastised.

"Fine." I push off with my feet and float towards her. As I reach her, I stand so we're face to face. "Better?"

"Yes." She says with glistening eyes, not from tears, not from the pool water, but from happiness. *It's in her eyes, too.*

She stares at me for a minute, and I'm not sure how to take the look. Before I can sort it out, she closes the gap between us, her fingers trailing my chest. I shiver then suck in a breath. I was not expecting her to touch me, and now I'm frozen. After a second, I realize she's tracing over my tattoos.

"I've never seen these."

"That's because you've never seen me with my shirt off."

"Why's that?"

With that question, both her hands are on my chest now, not her fingertips. Her palms glide up my pecks to my shoulders, and I think she's short-circuiting my heart.

"Because you haven't asked." My words are barely a whisper.

She looks up at me through her wet lashes as her hands trail circles on my shoulder, then onto my neck, then the back of my head. Her lips part as she grips my hair, and I don't know who closes the gap, but it's gone.

Her lips are on mine, and her legs wrap around my waist. I hold her in the water with my hands, finally cupping the ass I've been dreaming about. Her tongue skates across my teeth and finds mine, while her hands move feverishly through my hair. I move mine along her back, and this is everything I could've hoped it would be. I can feel almost every inch of her skin against mine, including the warmth between her legs, as she tightens her legs around me.

"Take me upstairs." She moans.

I want to. *So badly.* But not tonight. Not when she's this drunk. A kiss is one thing, but I won't sleep with her right now.

"Not tonight." I croak, wishing more than anything we could.

She freezes for a moment, then jumps off of me and heads right for the stairs.

"Kory, wait," I call to her, stumbling up the wet concrete.

"I'm going to bed." She says as she fumbles to get the door open.

"Let me walk with you," I say while I grab a towel and try to hand it to her.

"Do whatever you want. That's all that matters anyway."

"Kory, come on, I'm sorry. You know I want to, but…"

She cuts me off. "But what?"

Before I can answer, the puke flying out of her mouth interrupts, landing all over my feet.

"I'm so sorry." She spits out before her body flies forward, jerking with more heaves.

I move behind her this time, grabbing her hair, waiting to see if there's more to come. Thankfully, after a few extra fruitless heaves, it appears that I got the brunt of it. I help her into a chair while I rinse my feet off at the pool shower.

When I get back to her, she is snoring. I shake my head with a laugh. This girl just tried to jump my bones, puked all over me, and is now snoring. Yet somehow, I'm still not turned off. I sweep her up in my arms and head out of the pool room. She's as limp as a wet noodle strewn across my arms. I can't help but smile as I look down at her, eyes closed, mouth parted just slightly. This should also be a turn-off, but it's not. I push the glass door open with my hip and head to get her to safety before she gets sick again.

"She puked in there, sorry, dude," I say as we pass the front desk, not stopping long enough to see their annoyance.

In front of her room, I realize I don't have her key. She left the room in nothing but this bikini. She doesn't have her key either.

I turn around and go to my door instead, somehow managing to get my key out of my pocket without dropping her. In the room, I lay her down on the second bed and laugh because she is still out cold. She hasn't moved an inch, just sprawled out flat exactly where I laid her down, tan skin and bright pink bikini against the white sheet. I could stand here and marvel over the sight, but considering she's passed out drunk, that feels just as creepy as physically taking advantage of her.

I leave her to sleep it off in peace while I go take a very, very cold shower.

CHAPTER SEVENTEEN

Kory

I know before my eyes are even open that I've made a terrible mistake.

My head and stomach both ache in the telltale way of too much whiskey. Such a tricky, asshole of a liquid. It tastes so good that you forget this is the way you feel the next day. I roll over and let out an exaggerated groan. I blink hard, trying to force my eyes to adjust to having slept in my contacts all night. They protest the unfamiliar feeling, and I have to rub them into submission.

I know better than this. *What was I thinking?* I don't even remember getting back to my room. I don't even remember leaving the bar. I watched Olivia make a mess of herself just a couple of weeks ago, proud of myself for knowing better— then Dom came into the picture and I forgot it all. I lift my hands to my forehead.

"Stupid!" I say to myself.

"Speak for yourself," Dom responds.

I jump up, clutching the blanket. *What the hell? Oh No.* "Why are you in my room?"

He laughs. "Your room?"

My eyes follow his, scanning my surroundings, and I realize this is, in fact, not my room. It's his. I got drunk and woke up in his bed. *Damn it. Damn it. Damn it, Kory.* It's only then that I feel the shirt I'm wearing. It's not mine, and my bathing suit is untied underneath. My bottoms are still on, thankfully. *But my bathing suit? What in the world?*

"Relax," he says as he sits on the chair, taking a sip of the coffee provided in the room. "I slept in the other bed."

"Why am I in my bathing suit, though?"

He laughs. "Well, after six or so drinks, you insisted we go swimming." I don't remember a second of that. He watches my eyebrows crease, then continues. "Then you puked on me and passed out in a pool chair. So I carried you safely to a bed."

Good God. That might actually be worse than what I initially thought.

"I am so sorry."

"Don't be. It was quite amusing. I had a great time."

I shoot him a look of disgust. "At least nothing happened."

"I didn't say that. I said I slept in the other bed." He says, then sips another drink through his smirk.

Well, that's lovely. So everything that possibly could have gone wrong went wrong last night. I am never, ever drinking again. Not one drink. I wait for him to say more, but he doesn't.

"So, we had sex, then you just went to the other bed? How very gentlemanly of you."

He laughs. "I didn't say that either."

I can't stand him or this game he is playing. I'm too hungover for this. I tilt my head back and suck in a breath. "Can you just tell me what the hell happened? It's bad enough that I don't remember. I deserve to know."

He smiles. "We didn't have sex, Brooks. Of *any* kind. You did try to jump my bones in the pool, though. We kissed for a bit, you begged me to bring you upstairs, then got mad at me because I said no, because you were too drunk. You tried to storm away, but when I caught up to you, you threw up on me instead. I carried you to the room like a sack of potatoes and set you right in that bed. You haven't moved since. Happy?"

I rest my forehead in my hand. Of course, I did all of that. *But he said no because I was drunk?* That replaces some of the agitation I felt with gratitude.

"When we got back to the room, I took a shower, and you were still passed out. I put the shirt on you and untied the straps. My sister used to complain about how tight they were after a while, so I figured sleeping in one wasn't a great idea. Then I went to sleep."

And he didn't even undress me. *Who is he?* "Thank you, I say meekly. "And I'm sorry."

"It's fine. Technically, it was my fault anyway."

"I'll go to my own room now. We leave today, right?"

"Yeah. About that..." he tosses me some sweatpants. "You left the room in just your suit last night. No key."

I groan as loudly as I did when I first woke up. "So I have to do the walk of shame to the desk like this?"

He laughs. "I'll come with you with my company card, so hopefully they don't give you too much of a hard time not having your ID."

"Yeah, because that will only make this walk of shame look worse," I complain as I slide his pants on.

But I know he's right. If everything is in my room, there's no way to prove that the room belongs to me, so he's my only hope. I follow him out the door, staying behind his tall frame, avoiding eye contact with anyone who may see us in the hallway. It's obvious I'm in his clothes. Both the shirt and pants are three sizes too big for me. I look like an eight-year-old playing dress up in her parents' clothes. I don't even brave a mirror to know what my hair looks like.

Thankfully, the front desk doesn't give us a hard time. The girl behind the computer looked between us a few times, smirking, but she gave me a new key without issue. Both Dom and I are quiet the whole way back to the rooms.

"Thanks again. Seriously," I say, hesitating by my door, looking up at him, suddenly coy.

"You're welcome. But you should probably go brush your teeth."

Coyness gone. I smack his chest, then escape into the lovely solitude of my own room. I fall onto the bed, allowing myself to finally feel the magnitude of mortification.

I got wasted. Blackout wasted. I made out with him. *For a bit? What does that even mean?* Got mad at him for turning me down, then puked on him. I still can't believe it. Olivia is going to love this.

Olivia. *My phone!*

I jump up from the bed, frantically searching for it, praying it's somewhere in this mess and not left at the bar.

Thankfully, it starts to ring and I hear it on the floor near my suitcase. It's Autumn.

"Hey," I say breathlessly, and I fall back on the bed.

"Whoa. You look like shit, Kay."

"Ha. Thanks. It's been a morning."

"Drunk sex with Dom?" I gasp, and she laughs. "Olivia texted me that you stopped responding last night."

"Of course she did. Drunk, yes. Sex, no."

"Really?"

I shrug. "That's what he says. I don't remember."

"Well, shit."

"He said we kissed, though."

She smiles widely. "There it is."

"Then I puked on him."

Autumn belts out a laugh so loud, I think Dom might hear it across the hall. "Oh my God. This almost couldn't get better."

"Yeah, yeah. Go ahead and laugh, but I need to start getting my shit together. We have to check out soon."

"Okay," she says, "Love you. Behave, or don't. Who cares?"

I roll my eyes and share an *'I love you too'* before hanging up.

In my messages, I see that Olivia texted me six times before giving up. She called three. I send her a message to let her know I'm alive, even though I'm sure she and Autumn are already talking about it.

> Hey. I'm alive. No freaky business. Talk later.

I linger in the shower longer than it takes to repack my things. I just stand here, letting the hot water cover my body, reveling in the embarrassment before I leave my room. Once I step into the hallway, I will be cool, calm, and collected, like sober me knows I need to be. But hidden in the shower, I can revel in how stupid I feel.

Every little thing about last night went wrong. Except for maybe him saying no—or maybe actually that too.

I didn't take him as the chivalrous type, but part of me thinks if he had just let it happen, maybe it would be less awkward now, stuck back in this truck together. This small cab feels stifling and reeks of oil. The air conditioning hums but feels like it's barely blowing. And we've hardly spoken.

The mood in here is no longer light and playful like it was a week ago. It's not full of questions and laughter anymore, but it's also not anger or hostility that I feel. It's frustration and tension. Tension so thick that I feel like it may be affecting our gas mileage. At least this drive is only an hour.

I feel like I should apologize, but I've already done that— *a few times*. I want to go back to acting like I'm not attracted to him, but my drunk alter ego already outed me. I guess I could still try—tell him I was just drunk and he was just there —but I think that might hurt his feelings, and I've realized I don't want to hurt his feelings.

Crap.

CHAPTER EIGHTEEN

Dom

The drive to the next hotel felt like forever.

I don't bother her once we settle in, though. I can tell she's still uncomfortable, but with what part, I'm not sure. *Embarrassed for being so drunk? Freaked because we kissed and she doesn't remember? Or because she woke up in my shirt?* Probably a little bit of all of it. But I'd like to note that she didn't offer to return that shirt or my pants yet.

I hope she believes that we didn't sleep together. But her silence has me convinced that maybe she doesn't, and that's why she seems so uncomfortable. I can understand her not knowing me enough to feel like she can trust me. That's what I'll have to work on at this point. I place an order for dinner to my room and send her a text.

You okay?

Short and sweet, but hopefully coming off as genuine.

Yeah. About to go to sleep.
Thanks again.

I reply.

The second week at the newest *Home Team* goes by as easily as the first one did. I'm wrapping things up in the office when Kory knocks on the door. I look up and find her smiling, which eases me. I've tiptoed around her all week, which, quite honestly, has sucked. She's done a good job mostly avoiding me, though, except for the rides to and from work every day.

"Another good week, huh?" she says as she comes the rest of the way in.

"It was. I think we're a pretty good team."

"Yeah." She says, twirling a curl of her hair around her finger, as she sits down in one of the chairs. "What are you doing tonight?"

My eyebrows pull together in surprise, but I try to fix them before she notices. The pull of the corners of her lips tells me my reflexes are too slow.

"I was planning on going for a ride on my bike. Maybe eat eventually, we'll see."

She laughs lightly but just says, "Oh."

"What are *you* doing tonight?" I ask as I stick some papers into the drawer of the desk.

"I was going to see if you wanted to go to dinner." She pauses, then clarifies, "No drinks."

It makes me laugh as I organize the last of what's on this desk, clearing it for its rightful owner to take over. "There's no restaurant at this hotel. You want to go out somewhere?"

She tucks a piece of hair behind her ear. "I've been in that hotel room all week. Somewhere sounds great."

"Somewhere it is then."

We smile at each other before she taps both hands on her thighs, pushing herself up to stand. "I'll see you in the truck." She says, then disappears.

My cheeks adjust to the smile stuck to my face, stretching from ear to ear. With a little space, maybe we're back to getting somewhere. And as I've been contemplating all week, I think I may have come up with an idea to gain her trust.

A couple of hours after getting back to our rooms, we're both showered, changed, and back in the lobby.

She's gorgeous as always, with half her hair pulled back, revealing silver hoops hanging from her ears. She has on a tight, low-cut white shirt with a cropped black jacket over top. Her jeans are painfully tight—*painful for me, not her*—with slivers in the material that show off peeks of her skin underneath. The short little boots at her ankles bring her up an inch or two closer to my eye level.

We greet each other with silent smiles, then head to the truck. As she reaches for the door handle, she notices me walk past it to the next parking space.

"What are you doing?" She asks, rounding the truck and seeing me putting the key in my bike.

"Riding my bike. I told you that's what I was doing tonight."

She squints her eyes at me. "And I'm just supposed to meet you there in the truck?"

"No. You're supposed to ride with me."

She snickers and tosses her head back. "Yeah, right. That thing is not made for two people."

"Sure it is. People do it all the time."

Her arms are folded in front of her, and her foot taps anxiously as she tries to come up with an excuse. "What about my purse?"

"It's technically a little backpack, right? That's perfect." I watch as the word *'shit'* runs through her mind. "You'll be fine. Just lean into me and hang on."

"You'd like that, wouldn't you?" she sparks, and a chuckle escapes me.

I would like that, but that's not what this is about. Her petulant resistance makes me wonder if she notices the change in her attitude when she is trying to act like she isn't interested in something. *In me.* The sweet Kory who asked me to go to dinner earlier is all of a sudden back in fight mode, all at the thought of getting on this bike with me. But I think she knows as well as I do that her fighting her attraction to me is like a child fighting their sleep. It can only last so long. I grab the helmet, and she throws out another excuse.

"See, I don't even have a helmet."

"You'll wear mine."

She stares at me, blinking a few times before finally saying something. I pull my baseball cap securely on my head in the helmet's place.

"I've never been on a bike before."

"That's fine. You can trust me," I say as I hand her the helmet.

Another couple of stubborn seconds pass before she lifts the second strap of her purse onto her other shoulder and takes the helmet. She slides it onto her head, and her eyes appear in the open visor space.

Assuming she doesn't know how to do the strap, I get closer to her and reach out for it. Neither of us says anything, but she stares up at me—the brown that circles the green in her eyes, glowing in the golden hour sun. As my fingers brush against her throat, I want to yank on this strap and crash my lips to hers again. But I won't. *Not yet.* But as I feel her throat swallow against my knuckle and we continue to stare at each other just inches apart, I wonder if she would stop me.

"All set," I say, then quickly turn back to the bike. Stealthily adjusting myself in my jeans once my back is to her. I throw my left leg over one side of the bike, then firmly plant both feet on the ground. "Have you ever ridden a horse?" I ask, as she takes a couple of apprehensive steps toward me.

"Yes."

"Good. Get on kind of like that. Grab my hand like you would the saddle, then step here with that foot, as you swing the other around."

My hand reaches out, and after the same brief hesitation as with the helmet, she grabs it. I do my best to ignore the memories that her skin on mine brings. Worse than that, what I imagine they could bring if she'd let it happen.

She jumps up like a pro and wraps her hand around my waist. "Damn, Brooks. You sure you've never done this before?"

"Not that I remember."

"That doesn't mean anything."

Her hand swats my stomach, and I feel her body bounce against mine with a laugh. I'm glad she catches the jab and takes it as the joke it is. Once again, I'm hopeful that we're back in business.

"Ready?" I call back to her.

"As I'll ever be." She says, tightening her grip.

"Good. Now hold on tight, spider monkey."

"A Twilight fan too, huh?"

"Add that to the list of things I'll never admit."

I feel another chuckle on my back, then roar the bike to life. The whole machine vibrates underneath us, and the throttle growls louder each time I warm it up. She tightens her grip some more.

I'm glad she can't see the smile on my face right now as I feel the chin of the helmet on my shoulder and her arms under mine. I imagined this moment more times than I'd like to admit, and here we are. It's better than I thought it would be; she feels better than I could've ever imagined she would.

But more important than how any of this makes me feel physically is how it makes me feel emotionally. If she didn't trust me before, she definitely does now.

CHAPTER NINETEEN

Kory

I can feel the firmness of his abs through this thin T-shirt.
What am I even thinking right now? This is the most insane thing I have ever done. The jolt in movement as the bike begins moving through the parking lot causes me to grab his shirt with my fingertips. I have nothing else to grab, considering both his abs and chest are solid as a rock. I hope with everything that is in me that this thin shirt will stay intact if I start to fall off this thing, because I am not letting go. This helmet is heavy, and I feel like a bobblehead. That alone has me worried I may topple right off if I don't give all my attention to balance.

We pause at the exit, and just as a car passes, he taps my leg. I don't know what that means, but my gut says to hold on even tighter, so I do—with both my hands and my thighs, tightening them against his. A second later, we take off onto the street. I can feel us moving, but my eyes are closed. I can feel the wind going into my jacket, causing it to flail and the faux buckle straps to tap my legs. After those first few terrifying seconds, I open my eyes. Buildings zip by as strobes of bright colors. The sound of the bike echoes in my ears louder than any other sound, screaming just a bit more each time we accelerate.

I watch the world fly by us and feel a smile start to grow. *This isn't so bad.* That realization turns into acceptance, which turns into embracing. I tighten my arms around him just a bit tighter and lean my heavy head on his back. Then I have another realization—this is much more intimate than I thought.

But the part that surprises me the most—my disappointment when we pull into a new parking lot and come to a stop.

He reaches his hand out and I grab it again, swinging myself in the opposite direction than I did last time. As I lift the helmet off my head, he's standing in front of me, which, for some reason, catches my breath. He puts his hand out, and I hand him the helmet.

"Thanks," I say as it switches from my hand to his.

"You're welcome." He hangs it by the straps on the handlebars. "What did you think?"

"Not as bad as I thought." I play it cool as he pushes the restaurant door open for me. I may as well be transparent, though, because I can tell by his smirk that he sees right through me.

Once seated, we order right away, both clearly famished. Afraid we're going to fall back into the awkwardness of the week, so I decide to jump into another round of Twenty Questions.

"So, what do you do for fun?"

"For fun?" his eyebrow arches. "You just did it."

"That's it? You don't do anything else?"

"Not really. Go to the gym, work, and ride my bike. That's about it for me."

"And watch Twilight and listen to Taylor Swift." I joke. He smiles and takes a drink while we stare at each other, but he doesn't deny it.

"The bike was my dad's," he adds unexpectedly.

It surprises me, both because the last time his family was brought up, he shut down, and his bike isn't the kind I imagine a middle-aged man owning.

"Your dad had a crotch-rocket?"

"Yup. One he had no business with. My mom hated it. Called it his 'Mid-Life Crisis Machine.'" He laughs at his own comment.

Our food comes quickly, which gives me a few seconds to decide what to say next. I want to keep him talking, but don't want him to shut down like before.

"All my parents gave me were abandonment issues." I shrug, making light of my situation, then take a bite of food. He mirrors the action.

"I know the feeling."

Although he responds, I still see a change in his disposition. I can tell it's time to change the subject. But just the tiniest bit of insight has done something to me. Not many people I know know what it's like to be left behind by the two people who are supposed to be there for you forever. But he does.

"What about you?" He asks, right on cue, for a subject change. "What do you do for *fun*?"

"Read, obviously. And I love the beach. Reading on the beach is top tier! But honestly, that's pretty much it for me, too. I was working this job and at the bar, so that left me pretty busy."

He nods, and we each take a couple of bites of our food before I decide to let him into my world a little, hoping that it will ricochet.

"I used to love hanging out with my brother, Elliot. We were really close."

"My sister was my best friend." He says, staring at his plate.

"My brother, too. Then Autumn. Sucks trying to stay close to people who are physically far away."

"Yeah." He says, stirring his fork around the almost empty plate.

Damn it. I did it again.

We finish what is left of our meals with much lighter conversation, mostly around work this week, and what we're going to do with the two weeks off. I hadn't thought about being back home, and I suddenly feel weird about not seeing him every day.

Back at the bike, he straps the helmet for me again. I could've figured it out both times, but I'm ashamed to admit how much I enjoy watching him and his backward baseball cap while he does it instead. *Or maybe I'm not.*

The ride home is the same as the way there. Well, actually it's not. It's definitely colder, but I'm also more comfortable, so I don't care.

We walk down the hall to our rooms, now next to each other, mine being first, and I pause at the door.

I don't know what it is about this moment, but my breathing quickens. I look over at him near his door and watch his chest expand with his own deep breath.

"Thanks for tonight," I tell him.

"Thanks for not puking on me." He says, taking a few steps toward me.

His hand rests in his pocket, not searching for a key. His eyes, though, his eyes are definitely searching. Searching for something that can't be put into words. My cheeks heat through my smile and realization that my back is now against my door and he's still getting closer to me.

"Must have been the kiss," I quip, voice barely audible.

My eyes are on his as he's just about closed the space between us. I try to focus on the feeling of the hard wall against my back and not on everything that I'm feeling inside. He's right in front of me now, and maybe I read too many romance novels, but I find myself silently pleading, *Please God, don't let him do what I think he's about to do.*

My eyes flick to his lips, then back to his eyes, just as it happens. He leans forward just enough to raise his arm above my head, resting his hand on the wall. He hovers over me, and my insides are a hot, mushy mess. I inhale deeply to catch the breath I lost, but that makes it worse because his smell is all around me. All of that physical reaction happens in just a second, and I know I've failed at playing it cool before he even hits back at the kiss comment.

"Want to test that theory?" his voice is low and gravely.

His usually bright green eyes are dark now. So dark it should be scary, but it's not. Quite the opposite of scary, actually. No sooner do I nod my head does he grabs my face and pushes my body into the door with such force that I lose my footing. He catches me before I fall and, in one fluid motion, picks me up without our lips ever coming apart.

My hands knock his hat off and tangle into his hair, reciprocating the aggression. Our tongues battle just as fiercely, and until I feel him slide his finger into my pocket, then hear the beep of the key unlocking my door, I forget we are in the hallway.

As soon as we cross the threshold of the room, I fight to get my jacket off like it's the worst thing to ever be put on my skin. He sets me down on the desk, where we finally tear apart. His eyes are still dark, maybe darker now, and his mouth is stuck open. His chest moves in and out, and his shoulder moves up and down. His lips are wet and smeared with the color I had on mine.

We stare for a moment, silently questioning what is about to happen next. Him gauging what *I'm* going to let happen next. I reach out and grab the hem of his T-shirt. He stays silent, lifting his arms so I can slide it off. Revealed underneath are the tattoos and abs I feel like I've only imagined, because I don't remember seeing them in the pool. I run my hands across his pecs, then down across each divot of his abdomen. He remains still watching me for a moment, and for some reason, that spikes my body temperature even higher.

I raise my hands, and he follows suit with my shirt, leaving me in the purple lace bra. One with about as much coverage as that bikini top I had on, and his reaction is immediate. And physical. His lips meet the top of my chest, then pecks, licks, and sucks up my neck. My head tilts back, and through a ragged breath, I say, "I haven't puked yet."

Moving up from my neck, he makes it to my earlobe and makes me whimper with a nibble.

"I think we need more tests." He whispers, then slams his mouth back to mine.

I respond by sliding my hand up the back of his neck and returning some bite with my nails. His groan rumbles right into my mouth, and I pull away to reach behind myself and unstrap my bra. It comes undone, and I let it fall. His eyes scan all over me again now that my torso is completely bare. He has sweat glistening on his head, and already the few strands of longer hair on top hang down his forehead. He closes the gap once more, this time with one hand cupping my chest and the other wrapped around my back.

He pulls me in so close that I can feel every inch of his exposed skin against mine. The weight of his body has me leaning back with one hand on the desk to brace myself from falling backwards. He goes back to kissing my neck, my bare chest, then back up my neck like he can't get enough. He tries to sink his hands into the back of my jeans, but they're too tight.

"The bed," I whisper, and he immediately scoops me up with one arm and turns around to lay me on the bed.

I push up on my hands, maneuvering the buttons, but with two fingers, he pushes my shoulder, causing me to fall back on the bed. Lying there on my back, I watch him undo the buttons on his jeans first. Our eyes never leave each other, and I know I've never in my life experienced something hotter than this moment. I hear his pants hit the ground, but I can't look away. There's something about the way he is looking at me that has me entranced. He bends again, presumably lowering his briefs this time, but our eyes still stay locked. Neither of us wavers even as he unbuttons my jeans the tosses them to the side.

Our eyes remain locked as he crawls up my body and lowers himself on top of me, then one strong motion finally breaks that, causing them to roll into the back of my head.

CHAPTER TWENTY

Dom

The now familiar citrusy aroma wakes me up with a smile.

As my eyes open, I can see Kory's hair pooled on the pillow in front of my face. We're both facing the window, and the sun is beaming in just enough to alert my eyes. She doesn't seem bothered, though. Her breaths are steady and calm, unlike last night.

I welcome the smile that comes from the memories. After the first week we had, I never expected that this would be how our second week would end, but it was the best surprise. Careful not to wake her, I slide out of the bed. It's 7:24 a.m., which is right on schedule for me. I've never been able to sleep in much—if I make it to 9:00 a.m., that's a shock. After I get dressed, I see a notebook on the desk with a pen stuck in the wire binding. The desk makes me smile, too.

I open it up and leave her a note before leaving the room.

Going to my room to shower. You were sound asleep, so I didn't want to disturb you. See you at checkout. ☺

The smiley face seems lame, but a heart would probably be worse. I want it to appear as though I'm not just skipping out on her like some douchey frat boy—like Blake would—

but also not like I'm in love with her after one hook-up. Even if the latter might be true.

I should shower before heading to the workout room, but I don't. Instead, I relish in the remnants of her sweat on my skin. There's not much in this *'gym,'* but it will do to pass the time. After running on the treadmill for twenty minutes to warm up, my arm curls a worn dumbbell as I watch my reflection in the mirror. Watching myself, hoping maybe the reflection version of me might have the answer to the questions that jumble around in my mind. *Where do we go from here? Where do we stand? What was this to her?*

If it were ten years ago, I'd call Kami. That was the best part of having a female twin- more importantly, one who was my best friend. I told her everything, and she would tell me exactly what to do. The confidence I had with girls in High School? It was really Kami in my ear, and she never steered me wrong.

But now she's not here, and even if I called, she wouldn't answer. That's probably why I stayed with Izzy longer than I should have. I knew it was over long before I left, but I just couldn't find the words to end it. Kami would have though.

I push away the yearning to call my sister with the shake of my head. It's been a while since that's ached me the way it is. I used to a lot—wish I had my best friend back—but after a while, I got over it.

There was nothing I could do to change her move to New York or the fact that my parents decided to go with her. I wanted her to be happy, I really did. But I didn't expect everything that came after the move, and how that would ultimately end our relationship completely. So in the end, I traded sadness for anger, and I try to just live life like they never existed.

Until Kory—who gets me to talk about them and has me wanting to call my twin for the first time in years. I rest my head in my hands, my body useless, and decide it's just time to go shower.

She's sitting on a bench waiting for me outside the doors by the time I make it to the lobby. Playing on her phone, she doesn't notice me right away, and I brace myself for what her reaction to me will be today. To my relief, a big smile graces her face when the doors slide open and she sees it's me walking through them.

"Sleep good?" I ask as she stands and grabs her bags.

"Great." Her smile grows just a tad.

"Good," I say, and then we head to the truck.

The first half hour of the drive passes quietly. But it doesn't feel like it's from the awkwardness from before. I steal a glance over at her. Her bare feet are up on the dashboard, exposing her long tan legs. Her book is open, resting against her thighs, and remembering what they felt like in my hands last night causes my Adam's apple to bob in my throat with a tight swallow.

Looking up over her sunglasses, she catches me, raising them to push her hair back. "Can I help you?"

I shake my head with a laugh. "Tell me about that book you're reading."

"My book?" She looks confused, but then laughs to herself. "You'll never believe me."

"Try me."

She shuts the book closed. "It's about this girl who meets this guy she shouldn't be with. He's got tattoos and rides a bike, and well, eventually it gets a little spicy."

"Wow. You're right. I'm not sure I believe you."

"Told you. He's got a real motorcycle, though." She says before opening it back up and returning to reading.

That causes me to laugh loudly, and I reel my head back, feigning offense. "Excuse me, I'm pretty sure it has two wheels and moves, which makes it a *real* motorcycle." She giggles quietly, not looking up from her book. "Sounds like they had fun though," I say and look back at her, hoping that she catches what I am insinuating.

"They definitely did." Her tone alludes to the fact that she got it, but after a quiet moment, she speaks again, quieter this time. "But Dom," Her words are now short, and her tone is low. *And she called me Dom.*

"Yeah?"

"I don't think they can do it again."

And just like that, the mood in the truck shifts once again.

CHAPTER TWENTY-ONE

Kory - September

"You're stupid." Olivia so eloquently says to me from across the room—judging me for not allowing anything else to happen with Dom.

"No, I'm not," I argue. "There is no future, so there is no point in *now*."

"Why isn't there a future? Because he's friends with Jimmy?" She scoffs. "Again, that's the dumbest thing I've ever heard. Who cares?"

"I care, Liv. What would that future look like, huh? 'Here, Autumn, be my maid of honor. Have fun walking down the aisle with the one who ripped your heart out and threw it in the trash.' I don't think her, Jimmy, or Becca, for that matter, would enjoy that."

"Easy. Just have me be your maid of honor then." She winks, but then laughs off her comment, knowing the bond Autumn and I have always had and that no one else could ever be my maid of honor. "I still think you care more about this than either of them does, but so what? Fine. There's no future. That doesn't mean you can't be friends," she pauses to wiggle her eyebrows, "with benefits."

I take a drink of my Coke, unable to come up with an excuse she won't slice right through. We could do that. I've replayed the night we had in my mind over and over. I'd lie if I said my body hasn't hoped I'd change my mind every day since we got home, but the thought of this becoming an ongoing thing scares me.

"See, exactly." She continues. "You've already done it once and said it was the best sex of your life, right?" She pauses for my response, but I don't give her one. I take another drink instead. "Right. Exactly. So again, why not? You guys are stuck together for two more trips, right?"

"Yes."

"It's a no-brainer to me. Friends with benefits. Sex no strings. What could go wrong?" she laughs as she gets up to fill her glass.

'What could go wrong?' Everything. He could fall for me. Or worse. I could fall for him. I don't like the way I feel when I'm around him. It's equal parts comfortable and uncomfortable—*but in a good way, or a bad way?* I don't know, and that's a huge part of the problem. The fluttering in my stomach that I've ignored gets stronger and stronger every time I'm near him. It's like the butterflies multiply with each minute we spend together.

It's also the feelings that creep up when I'm not with him. Somehow, I've turned into the person who hopes a text is from a certain someone. I've looked at the calendar a couple of times to see how many days are left until we leave again. I've thought about going to hang out at JAX, hoping maybe he'd be there too. And that's why I'm scared.

But what if we could just have sex? If we both agree that this is what it is and don't do couples shit, maybe it'll be fine. We just need boundaries. Rules. *Yes. We need rules.*

"When do you leave again?" Olivia asks as she sits back down.

"Early in the morning. We have a farther drive this time."

"Yuck." She says and starts flipping through the channels on the TV, comfortable as ever in my apartment. Her house sitting for me while I'm gone has only added to her comfort.

I pull out my phone, suddenly energized to text him. We haven't spoken much in the time we've been home. I didn't want to make it worse. I don't know what we are, so I didn't really know how to handle the conversation. It bordered on flirty when we first started sharing texts, but considering I had no intentions of crossing that line again, flirty texts felt wrong. So I left the phone dry. But if I can set some boundaries and he can agree to them, then I can work with that.

Hey, what's up?

I send.

Not much, just repacking. You?

Same. Well, actually, I'm done. I wanted to see if you wanted to get food.

A few seconds pass before he responds.

Sure. I haven't eaten yet. Anywhere in mind?

It hasn't missed me that his texts are also very business-like—no traces of the flirtatious guy from before. I respond just as neutral until we agree to our terms.

The diner on Main. 1 hour?

See you there.

In my bedroom, I throw on some leggings and a T-shirt since I thought I was in for the night, I was already in my pajamas. I also already have my glasses on, but I don't go through the process of putting my contacts back in.

"Change your mind that quick, huh?" Olivia laughs as I walk back into the living room. She smiles sarcastically before popping a pizza roll in her mouth. I shake my head, not able to deny her snarky comment, then throw my purse over my shoulder.

"I'll be back in a bit," I say, quickly passing her.

"Have fuuuuunnnnnn!" She exaggerates loudly as I shut the door.

Just as I jump out of the jeep in the familiar diner parking lot and shut the door behind me, I hear Dom's bike approaching. I hate that I know the sound of it already—and that it makes my heart beat faster. He pulls up into the spot right next to me, and I am both fascinated and frustrated by how ridiculously hot he looks, even though he hasn't even taken the helmet off yet. *I hate that too.*

Once he does get it off, it doesn't help. The whole sequence of actions actually makes it worse. Lifting the helmet above his head-running his fingers through his hair, hanging the helmet on the handlebars, effortlessly lifting his leg over the bike, then topping it off with a perfect smile. I turn around to roll my eyes at myself. *GET IT TOGETHER.*

"I was wondering how long it'd take you to miss me." He says, then I roll my eyes at him. Flirty Dom is back.

Ignoring the comment, I go inside and sit in my favorite spot by the window. It's still warm and sunny outside, and these giant glass panes magnify it. It won't be long before the sun is replaced with depressing grey clouds for six or seven months.

Once our drinks are ordered, he starts right back up. "So if you're not going to admit you missed me, to what do I owe the pleasure of this date?"

"It's not a date." My eyes meet his. "But it is kind of what I want to talk to you about."

"You want to ask me out on a date? Brooks, I'm flattered. Who knew you were so non-traditional?"

I take a deep breath and glare at him through my eyelashes, ready to get straight to the point. "No, Dominic. I don't want to go on a date with you, but I do want to keep having sex with you."

His eyes grow wide with surprise. He obviously didn't expect that blunt a response. Neither did I, honestly.

"So you brought me to a public place to do it? Kinky." He takes a drink of his water just as the waitress puts food on the table.

"Can you be serious for two seconds, please?"

"I'm always serious with you." He says before tossing a fry in his mouth and smiling in a very non-serious way.

I take a bite of my own, then begin the spiel that I had planned. "No attachment. Just sex. Friends with benefits. No feelings. We can enjoy each other's company while we are on these projects, then go our separate ways."

He eats in silence, staring at me while he does. Obviously —*hopefully*—contemplating what I just said. I expect any guy to immediately love the idea, but he doesn't look convinced. He hasn't said a word.

"But we need to both be clear," I tell him. "To have boundaries—so I wrote these." I slide the piece of paper that I wrote on in my jeep across the table.

He takes it and I watch his eyes scan the words, but he still says nothing.

CHAPTER TWENTY-TWO

Dom

Rules
1. No kissing unless sex is involved.
2. No meeting the family- especially kids.
3. No sitting close enough that our thighs rest against each other.
4. No lingering stares from across the room.
5. No sleeping in the same bed, even if there's only one.
6. No nicknames.
7. No romantic walks on the beach.
8. No tucking strands of hair behind my ear.

"Rules?" I ask.
"Yes. So no feelings get involved. No blurred lines."
I laugh. "These are oddly specific, and kind of random."
"Not for a romance reader, they're not."
"Do those things even translate into real life?"
"Not sure, but I don't want to find out."
I stare at her, unable to figure her out. *Why won't she let me in? Why would she want this? Do I want this?* No. Not like this. *But am I willing to say no and have none of her at all?* No.

But I want her to trust me, so I followed her lead, and it got us here, so I'll keep doing it. This may not be what I want, but it's what she wants, so I'll do it. Impatient for my response, she speaks again.

"So what will it be, Dominic? Do you want to keep having sex with me?"

I laugh before I can talk because while I've never known her to be shy, I didn't expect to hear any of these things come out of her pretty mouth. Not to mention, for such a suggestive topic, she's treated this whole conversation like a business meeting. *Maybe to her it is.*

"Yes, boss. I will keep having sex with you." I hold my hand out to shake on our deal. With that, a sly smirk appears on her lips. Clearly satisfied with my response, she meets my hand with hers.

"Good." She says as she shakes.

When we get to our vehicles, she pauses, looking at my bike. "I noticed *'no bike rides'* wasn't one of your rules."

She laughs. "That one's still up for debate."

"Want to go for a ride then? We're pretty good at testing theories."

She doesn't fight the smile that comes from that comment, her eyes gliding from me to the bike, then back to me again.

"For research?" She asks. The business look in her eyes has softened, and I know if she gets on this bike, we'll be riding right to my house.

"Research purposes only." I throw my hands up, showing my fake innocence.

"Okay."

Before I know it, my hips are sandwiched between her thighs, her arms are wrapped around my waist, and my helmet is on her head. I fly through familiar streets this time, traveling the routes I like to take when I'm riding alone. I get on the freeway for a mile or two, just to see how she reacts. She doesn't, so I know she enjoys this much more than she's led on.

Not long after we get off the freeway, we pull into a beach entrance. It's getting late, and the sun is starting to set. People are gathered—there are always people watching a Lake Michigan sunset.

"No romantic walks on the beach, remember?" She says as soon as we're off the bike.

"We're not walking on the beach," I say and point to a lookout with wooden benches.

She smirks but doesn't argue, and we get comfortable looking at the colors of the sky. "So." I start talking. "What do you think?"

"That I should have added no romantic sunsets on the list."

I laugh. "Noted. But I meant about the bike."

"Oh." She pauses. "It falls under the kissing rule."

"The kissing rule?"

"Yeah." She smirks. "No bike rides unless sex is involved."

The spit in my mouth gets caught on the way down, causing me to have to clear my throat. "Well, I don't live far."

"No." She clips, then stands and grabs my hand.

I follow her shamelessly, letting her pull me wherever she wants. She leads us to the building that holds the bathrooms and showers. By divine intervention, I chose the beach that has private family showers, and that's exactly where we end up. The lock on the door makes a loud *thwack*, then she turns to me.

In a hot, rushed second, her hands are pulling my shirt off, and her tongue is dancing with mine. Only a few seconds after that, our pants are also off, and she's turned with her hands against the wall, giving me the most glorious view of her from behind.

I can't figure her out; besides that, she always does what I least expect her to. I never know what is going to happen next, but the one thing I do know is that I plan on breaking all of those stupid fucking rules.

All of them except for one.

CHAPTER TWENTY-THREE

Kory

Things that need to be added to the list of rules.

No remembering my favorite snack or getting it for me without me asking.

No, buying me lunch because you remembered my order from last time.

No, wearing a fucking backwards baseball cap.

Who am I kidding? Everything he does is a problem. Those rules are for me because I can't let myself fall for him.

With our clear understanding and boundaries in place, our longer drive was a piece of cake. There was no awkwardness from what happened in the bathroom the night before because it was all part of the deal. We don't have to tiptoe around it this time or wonder how the other person feels. We both want this. And we both agreed to it.

These past two weeks have proven that it's a good deal. A worthwhile deal. We've eaten dinner together every night—whether out or in one of our rooms. Dinner was always followed by dessert. A dessert I don't think I could ever get sick of.

Two straight weeks of this have been a breath of fresh air to my mood—I even catch myself humming while re-folding T-shirts that customers carelessly dropped back on the shelf. It normally irks me, but here I am—*not mad*—and humming.

The wordless tune of a Lizzo song leaves my throat as Dom comes up behind me, scaring me and causing me to drop the shirt in my hands.

"Damn it." I curse and smack his chest.

"What are you doing later?" he asks, low and breathy against my ear.

My body shakes away the chill that comes from the sudden warmth on my skin. "Stop it, Dominic. We're at work." He looks over both shoulders, not so subtly pointing out that there is no one around us. "A ride sounds fun though," I whisper back before he can respond.

"What kind of ride?" His eyebrows wiggle obnoxiously, and I'm embarrassed by the giggle that comes out of me.

"Let's see how the bike ride goes first, tough guy."

"Rules are rules, right?" he challenges.

I turn around to leave the area when his hand connects with my ass with a quiet smack. I jump and swing back around to face him. "Don't do that," I say through gritted teeth.

He pulls my move and rolls his eyes, so I follow with his move and smirk. "See you later," I add a wink before walking away.

We've started a dangerous ride, but it's too late now.

Each bike ride we've taken has gotten longer, and I've enjoyed it a little more. I get it now—why people do this. The feeling of floating or even flying is a hard one to replicate any other way. When we enter a freeway or a long back road absent of stop signs or streetlights, I close my eyes, lean into that feeling—and the feeling of my arms around him—reveling in both.

Tonight, we stop at an ice cream place that all of the locals told us we had to try before we left. After placing our orders for the *best frozen custard on the planet,* we take a seat at a sticky green patio table.

"What's your favorite part of riding?" I ask, then take a bit of my cannoli sundae—impeccable as promised.

He takes a bite of his banana pudding sundae, and the roll of his eyes leads me to believe he agrees with the locals, too.

"It works no matter what." He takes another bite. "If I'm happy, I want to ride. If I've had a shit day, I want to ride. If I need to think, I need to ride."

I nod, completely understanding now. I'm not sure how to describe exactly what it feels like, so I imagine he can't either.

"It's hard to imagine what I did with my time before riding." He continues. "I never had any interest in riding until my dad left it here. I had a bad day one day, and it was like sitting in the garage calling to me. I said fuck it and grabbed the keys." The corner of his lip picks up before he continues. "The first turn I tried to make, I went down. Scratched the shit out of the right side of the bike and myself. Rookie mistake. I'm still not sure how I didn't break anything." The green in his eyes sparkles while a chuckle escapes his lips. This is somehow a pleasant memory for him.

"And after that first impression, you became obsessed?"

"Oh yeah. That tends to happen to me." His pause, then subsequent smirk, causes the ice cream in my stomach to roll. "That short cruise before the turn was enough to make me want more. I just had to be smarter and learn how to ride first."

"What about riding with someone?"

"What about it?"

"Was it harder to learn?"

"Not really. It actually went much smoother than I thought. It helped that you seem to be a natural."

My spoon briefly floats in the air as I realize what he just said. "Are you telling me that you never took anyone for a ride before me?"

"Nope." He pops a bite in his mouth with a proud smile. I reach out and smack his arm.

"Dominic! How dare you! What if we crashed?"

His smile turns into a laugh. "I'm confident enough in my riding now that I wasn't worried about it. But I've still been careful. The more comfortable I've gotten, the faster we've gone."

"So that wasn't for my comfort and security?"

"Me not telling you that you were my first passenger was for your comfort and security." His smile elicits an eye roll out of me as usual.

He has a point, but I won't tell him that. He still shouldn't have tricked me, even if that tricking was just omitting important details. *But why, though?* I find it hard to believe that no other girl has ever wanted to climb up there with him. But that gives me an opening to ask about Izzy—the only ex of his I'm aware of. I know they broke up a while ago, but I haven't really had a reason to ask about her. Now I can be nosey.

"What about Izzy? Weren't you guys together for a while?"

"A little over three years. But she never wanted to. She hated the bike."

"Is that why you broke up?"

It sounded dumb as soon as it slipped past my lips. Of course, they didn't break up because she didn't want to ride the bike. I could've worded that question differently, but my curiosity beat my brain to it.

He chuckles. "Not quite. But it did boil down to differences. I grew apart from her while waiting for her to grow up. The gossiping got old." He pauses, contemplating his next statement. His eyes flicker, avoiding mine briefly, before settling back. "What happened with Jimmy and Autumn was the final straw."

Right. Izzy was the one who called Becca to tell her she saw them together.

"So would you have rather him kept cheating?" My voice is surprisingly tinged with annoyance at the mention of his name.

"Calm down, killer. That's not what I said. It just wasn't her place to pull some vigilante shit. What he was doing was wrong, but I watched my best friend's life get turned upside down…"

"Yeah, me too." I interrupt.

"Knowing she was the one who brought it out made me resentful towards her. I tried to stay, but after the reunion, I was done."

My body still tingling with annoyance, I can't glance over the fact that he looks at Jimmy's mess as Izzy's fault. "That's a crazy thing to say, though. Jimmy's life turned upside down because of his own choices, not because of Izzy."

"Hey," he says calmly—clearly trying to take this conversation another direction. "I get it. But at the end of the day, it wasn't her business, and Jimmy's my best friend. Just like Autumn is yours, you know, his mistress?"

I don't particularly care for his tone, but again, he's got a point. She is my best friend, and I supported her, despite her being with a married man.

"She really loved him," I say quietly, scraping my spoon around the melted cream in the bottom of my cup.

"I know. He really loved her, too."

We fall into an awkward silence, our custards both long gone. I get it, too, and I can appreciate that about him—his loyalty to his best friend. But I'm just as loyal to mine, and this whole conversation was just a painful reminder of why there has never been the possibility of a future for me and Dom.

CHAPTER TWENTY-FOUR

Dom

I don't usually scroll Facebook, but I'm killing time waiting for Kory to finish talking to one of the store employees when I see it: **Fall Book Fest in Downtown Grand Rapids.** Local authors, cider, live readings, and a pop-up poetry wall. What we're doing tonight is not even a question.

I look up at her, dodging this kid's compliments like a pro. Maybe I should feel jealous, but I watch in amusement as she effortlessly avoids each time he says something that might give him a segue into asking her out tonight.

She steals a glance my way, and I raise my eyes at her, silently asking her if she's interested in him tonight. She knows exactly what my look meant and laughs with a shake of her head and an eye roll. She's been quieter today. Not cold, just… distant. But I know that look. It's the one she wears when she's thinking about something she won't say out loud—thinking about the fact that last night didn't end the way either of us wanted it to. But she hasn't iced me out completely, so it's my mission to make sure today doesn't end the same.

"Hey," I say as we finally jump into the truck. "You trust me?"

She squints at me. "That's a loaded question."

"Just say yes. I know you do."

She rolls her eyes but climbs in anyway. "Fine, but if I end up in a corn maze with a chainsaw guy, I'm haunting you forever."

I laugh as we pull out of the parking lot. We're not even going back to the hotel first. I don't want to risk her changing her mind and staying in, not for this one. She obviously does trust me because she doesn't even pay attention to where we're driving. Her nose is stuck adorably in her book like it always is. Fifteen minutes later, we're pulling into a blocked-off street lined with tents, string lights, and the smell of cinnamon and paper. Her eyes widen as she reads the banner.

"Dominic," she says slowly. "Is this a book festival?"

I nod, trying not to look too proud of myself. "Saw it online. Figured you'd like it."

She doesn't say anything for a second. Just stares at the crowd, the tents full of tables and books, the cider stand. Then she turns to me, and her face softens in a way I haven't seen before.

"Why are you like this?"

"Like what?" I ask with a laugh.

"Kind of amazing when you want to be," she says.

I shrug. "Only for you."

She ignores my comment but squeals with excitement as she throws the door open. Rounding the truck to her side, she's already feet in front of me. I laugh as I pick up my stride to catch up to her, and by the time I do, she's already got a book in her hands.

We walk through the booths, her fingers trailing across covers, her body halting to read blurbs. We don't talk much. I don't think I've said a word at all, just following behind her and watching her light this place up. She has a bag full of books, bookmarks, stickers, pens, notebooks, you name it. The last booth we stop at is full of old books with old, worn leather covers. She spends the most time there, pulling books off shelves, carefully inspecting the pages, and even smelling a few.

The worn brown cover she holds now hides her face. All I can see is the open book and her curls of hair surrounding it. If there was a picture for the quintessential 'book worm', I'm pretty sure this would be it. When she lowers the book, she must notice the crease between my eyes, because she defends herself.

"There's nothing better than the smell of a book. Especially old ones. Here." She holds it up to my face.

Her tone isn't defensive, it's confident, like she knows she's absolutely right about this and I should already know it. I take a deep breath in—smells like paper and leather—a little musty if I'm being honest. But her eyes glow as she waits for me to reciprocate her love for this smell, so I nod in agreement.

"New books don't smell the same anymore." She smiles, then takes another whiff before putting it back on the shelf.

Before we leave that booth, she buys a small poetry book that she says is way too much money, but a classic. She lets me buy her a hot cider, and I pretend not to notice how she keeps brushing her arm against mine as we continue walking. The rules say our thighs can't touch, but apparently that doesn't count for our shoulders.

At the pop-up poetry wall, she grabs a marker and writes:

People always leave, forever leaving scars. Silent wishes of return lost to life on Mars.

I read it, and something tightens in my chest.

I approach it after her and grab a marker of my own. Right under hers, I write:

Some people never left. They were just waiting to be seen.

So much less poetic, but the point is clear. She reads it, then looks at me. Her eyes are glossy, but she doesn't blink them away.

We somberly walk to the curb and sit with our cider—now cool enough to drink—watching the sun dip behind the buildings.

"So," I say, nudging her shoulder. "What kind of books do you actually read? Besides the ones about tattooed bike riding men."

She laughs. "Mostly romance, the spicier the better." Her eyes twinkle briefly. "But when I'm in the mood, a good psychological thriller always hits the spot too."

"Spicy romance and murder mysteries. That tracks."

She grins. "I like to listen to poetry. It's calming. Especially old poetry. Listening to the smooth cadences of words just feels good."

"I never thought about that."

"Try it sometime," she says, nudging my shoulder this time.

"I used to write poetry, too. Back in high school. But I stopped."

I nod. "I remember."

Her head tilts. "You do?"

"You dropped your notebook once in class. I picked it up. Saw a few lines. Something about stars and silence."

Her mouth falls open slightly. "You remember that?"

"I remember a lot of things about you."

She doesn't speak. Just stares at me like I've said something that cracked open a door she didn't know was still locked.

"I still think about that notebook," I say. "I knew then that you saw the world differently. I liked that."

"How come we never talked?"

"In high school?"

"Yeah," she says, looking up at me. The urge to kiss her bites at me.

"I wanted to. A few times. But you always had a boyfriend."

Unexpectedly, she laughs. "I did not *always* have a boyfriend. I actually only had a couple during high school."

"Well, yeah, but sometimes I had girlfriends. And it seemed like every time I didn't, you did."

"We still could've been friends."

I shake my head. "I've never wanted to just be friends with you, Brooks."

Her eyes glow at me like they did at the poetry wall, but she doesn't say anything else. She leans her head on my shoulder, and I let her. I don't move. I don't speak.

I don't know if we're going to end up in one of our rooms tonight, but I don't care. Because this—*this quiet, this closeness*—is everything I've been waiting for.

CHAPTER TWENTY-FIVE

Kory

Now all that's left, both near and far, are silent nights and distant stars.

That's all I can remember from that poem Dom brought up. Besides that, I wrote it during my senior year, missing my brother.

My hotel room is obnoxiously quiet tonight, except for the hum of the mini fridge and the occasional creak of the heater. Dom's next door, probably asleep or scrolling through his phone like he does when he's pretending not to be tired. I'm alone, finally, and I can't stop thinking about today.

The book fest was… unexpected. *Thoughtful.* Sweet in a way that made my chest ache.

He didn't pull over for cider and books. He pulled over for me. For the girl who used to scribble poems in the margins of her notebooks and pretend she didn't care if anyone saw them. For the girl who stopped writing because all she could ever write was depressing, she started reading happy endings instead.

But Dom remembered. He remembered something I didn't even know he knew. He remembered I dropped a freaking notebook. I didn't even know he saw it. I didn't know anyone did. I try to think back to those days, but I cannot remember his face at all, which makes me feel like a real jerk. *How can he remember so much about me, and I can't even remember being in the same room as him?* Maybe he looked different then, like so different that you couldn't believe he was the same boy before and after puberty. That has to be it. Because there is no way I wouldn't have noticed him if he looked the way he does now.

Then there was the poetry wall.

I grab one of the notebooks I got and rewrite our words from earlier:

Mine:

People always leave, forever leaving scars,
Silent wishes of return lost to life on Mars.

His:

Some people never left. They were just waiting to be seen.

Then I add:

Sometimes, if you'd look beyond where you've always been,

You'd find far more than just silent nights and distant stars.

I stare at the words, heart thudding. It's not perfect. It's not polished. But it's mine—*ours*. His words with my words, both new and old. I don't remember what the full poem in my high school notebook said, but I know I like this one better.

Like a true sap, I lie back on the bed, hugging the notebook to my chest. Dom saw me today. Not just the version I show people—the sarcastic, guarded, *'I'm fine and fun'* version. He saw the part of me I buried. The part that even I almost forgot about.

And yet I'm lying here alone. *Why did I let him walk me to my room but not invite him in?* He didn't have to do any of what he did today. An event like that should've been against the rules because now I'm in my bed wishing he were here under the sheets with me. But I panicked. His surprising me with that had the feelings inside of me so jumbled that when we got back to the hotel, I got nervous, stumbled over my words, and ran into my room to hide like an embarrassed teenager.

I picture him earlier—the look on his face when I made him sniff a book—has my cheeks tight from a smile. I try to wipe it away, but can't. Instead, I lay the notebook on my face to hide it from no one but myself.

This is not what we agreed to. FRIENDS with benefits. No feelings. My stomach shouldn't feel like this if I have no feelings.

I picture him again, sitting on the curb—the way his biceps flexed just from him lifting his cider cup to his lip. How I watched his lips surround the hole in the plastic lid, regretting going to my own room last night just because the conversation left me annoyed. Not so much at his comment about Jimmy, because he was right. Both Jimmy and Autumn were wrong, but as their best friends, we stand by them. Annoyed wasn't even the right word for how I felt last night— disappointed is more like it. Disappointed that Dom could be so perfect, with no chance of a future. Only fun *for now*.

Yet again, I'm in here alone. It takes one more vision of him to change that. Him watching me earlier at work— breaking the rules—watching while I tried to concentrate on organizing the clothes and explaining to Tanner how they should be, without him asking me another question about myself. Something about the way we silently shared a thought, and how even that sends tingles down my spine, has me jumping out of my bed and heading to his room.

I ignore the alarm bells going off in my head—that I shouldn't do this tonight—not after that trip to the book fest. That I shouldn't jump into bed with him while these feelings also swirl inside of me. But I ignore them because this *is* what we agreed to. Sex while we're on the road. There's nothing else that I want to be doing right now.

But then, as my knuckles tingle from the knock, and just as quick as I convinced myself to come to his room, the agreement suddenly feels like a lie.

Because it's not just about the sexual chemistry that we stopped ignoring. It's about the way my heart stumbles when I hear movement in the room. The way I take a deep, nerve-calming breath before he answers the door.

You like him, my brain whispers. *You know you do.*

I shake the inner voice away. I can do this. I can keep it casual. While my heart is starting to be a little louder than my brain, I can tuck it away for a little longer and just enjoy the moments we have. That's the truth. It has to be.

But then the door swings open, and he instantly pulls me into him. The lips I stared at earlier are now on mine as if he'd been sitting at the door waiting for me to realize I didn't want to be in here alone again. No words are needed as he moves me toward the edge of the bed. I sit here as he pulls my shirt above my head, then I watch him remove his. All the inner dialogue I struggled with earlier is obsolete.

I love watching him. Watching him drink cider, watching him get on his bike, watching him hang jerseys on the wall—honestly, I think I would watch him do anything. But this, watching his eyes darken as he prepares to take over me for as long as I'll let him, is definitely my favorite thing to watch.

CHAPTER TWENTY-SIX

Dom - October

It feels good to be back in my own gym at home. Hotel gyms are fine for basic cardio and light weights, but it's not what I'm used to, or want right now.

I drop the bar off my shoulders and move out of the way for Jimmy. "So how's the work thing going?" He asks as he positions himself in place.

"Good. Almost done. I'm going to miss two weeks on, two weeks off. It's nice."

"And Kory?" he asks through a strained grunt.

"What about her?"

"Come on, dude." He holds his squat for a second, then pushes back up. "I'm not dumb. You like her."

I shrug, playing it cool—*again*. "We're stuck together. I have to like her or this would suck."

He repeats the rep once more, then we start to walk to the locker rooms. "So what it sounds like is that you like her, but she doesn't like you back?"

"What is this? Fifth grade?" I snap.

"I'm just saying. You talk about her a lot. You think I missed that you took her on your bike?"

I sigh, defeated and busted. "Fine. Yes, I like her. I *know* she likes me back, but says she doesn't want anything but friends with benefits."

Jimmy's eyes grow. "Wait, so, you slept with her?"

"Yeah," If I'm confessing, I might as well tell him everything. I can't help but smile thinking about it. *About her.*

"Yep, I knew it. You're a goner."

I open my locker, shaking my head. "I am not a *'goner'* and even if I was, it doesn't matter."

"Why not?" he asks as we both shut the locker doors. I sling my bag over my shoulder, preferring the shower in my own home.

"Because of you." I spit out. "You and Autumn."

"Oh," he says, with no need to elaborate.

"Yeah. I didn't think it was that big of a deal, but one of the last nights we were in Grand Rapids, we went for a ride, got ice cream, but then she went to her own room for the night. That wasn't the routine we had going, so I know it had to do with you two coming up in conversation. It changed her mood for sure. But then the next day we went to a book festival and I know she loved that. We went back to the hotel and she went to her room, but less than an hour later she was knocking on my door and all of a sudden it was like the night before didn't happen."

"Have you talked to her since?" He pushes the gym door open so we can step out.

"I mean, we rode home together the next day—small-talked during the ride—but hardly at all since we've been home. It always gets weird once we're back in this town."

"So you have sex every day for two weeks, then don't for two weeks? No wonder you're a grouch."

He's not wrong. I am craving her body with mine, but also so much more than that. The scent of her hair that I'm obsessed with. Her laugh. Her voice. Her eye roll.

"Just text her, dude." He opens up the trunk and throws his bag inside. I toss mine into the back seat of my car, parked next to his. "Get your girl, get laid, loosen up a little. This isn't like you."

He may be my best friend and know 99% there is to know about me, but this is the 1%. This is actually like me when it comes to Kory; I just never told him. I understand her apprehension about Jimmy because Autumn is exactly why I never brought her up to him. I almost did, not long after high school, almost asked him to help through Autumn, but instead, he spent that day distraught over the fact that she was going away to college. He moped around about it forever. After she left, Autumn became a subject no one could talk about around Jimmy. It would always go one of two ways—he would with clam up and shut down, or he wouldn't shut up about it.

His calling her *'my girl'* flared heat in my chest, *and fuck*, he's right. I am a goner, and I just miss her. She's a tough cookie to crack, but I've made a dent, so I can't stop now. "Yeah, I'll try. Talk to you later," I say and sink into my seat.

Once I get the car started and the AC pumping for this still annoyingly warm weather, I pull out my phone to text her. At the same moment, a message comes through from John to both me and Kory in a group chat.

> Hey, dream team! Great work out there. We have been invited to a Lions game. We'll have a booth to share some gear as a brand partnership. Since you two will already be in Detroit, it makes the most sense for you to do it. A couple of extra days on the last stop sounds okay?

Another one pings.

> Oh, and you'll be working (and paid), but rest assured, you'll be set up where you can still watch the game.

Kory replies.

> Sounds good. I've never been to a Lions game!

I send.

> I'm good with that, too, as long as Kory can handle dealing with me for a few extra days.

I've handled myself this long just fine, haven't I?

It's hard to know if she's smiling at her phone, but I am—missing our back and forth. Also smiling because John has no idea that she's full of shit. The way *she's* handled herself—or me—is just about everything he lectured *me* not to do.

Good to see you guys are getting along. I'll email more details and game info.

Kory responds with a thumbs up, so I do the same before switching to a chat with just her name.

I'm not sure John would consider our arrangement 'handling yourself.'

Good thing he's not a part of the deal then.

Ahh, there it is. My smile grows.

What are you doing right now?

Waiting for you to invite me over.

And it's back—the confidence I had before. But then a twang of annoyance with myself. She's been waiting for me to make the first move. I'm going to get her to crack. It's going to happen. My response is short and to the point.

765 Arden. Give me twenty minutes.

Nineteen minutes later, I step out of the shower to a knock on the door. When I open it, there she stands as glorious as ever. Her dark brown curls fall along her shoulder just above the chest that's begging to make its way out of that shirt. I watch her eyes survey me, moving up from the towel wrapped around my waist, slowly to my face.

"Hey." She says quietly with a small smile, almost like she's shy all of a sudden.

"Hey." I copy as she passes me, and I shut the door behind her.

She continues the rest of the way through the entryway, looking around, taking in her surroundings.

"Nice place." She says—making obligatory small talk because there really isn't much *'nice'* about it. Just an average townhome. "Nice towel too." She adds, and I watch her eyes sparkle as she takes her jacket off.

The words *'I've missed you'* fight so hard to roll off my tongue, but I don't want to ruin this moment. So I say, "Thanks."

She comes closer with a devilish grin on her face. I stand still, waiting to welcome whatever she is about to do. Heat bubbles up inside of me as she reaches for the towel, and I ache to kiss her. As I lean in to do so, she rips the towel off and takes off down the hallway.

Stunned and suddenly naked, it takes me a second to realize what she's just done. I hear her giggles and follow the sound.

"Where do you think you're going to hide? You've never been here before." I call out.

Another giggle. There are only three doors she can go through—two bedrooms and the bathroom. I get closer when I hear movement to my right, but then a second later, she zooms across the hallway from one bedroom to the other like she's a ghost in a scary movie.

Once I'm also in the spare room—hyper aware that I'm still naked—I know there's only one place she can go—the closet.

I swing open the door, but she's not here. I turn around and see the faintest hint of movement between the open bedroom door and the wall. I tiptoe in that direction and, as I approach, I use the length of my arms to slam the door shut, leaving her exposed and up against the wall. Her smile is huge, laced with amusement. *God, I really fucking missed her.*

My hand starts at the neckline of her shirt and slides up her throat, agonizingly slow, on purpose. I feel her swallow hard, and it sends a jolt of electricity right to my core. My hand stops right at the base of her neck with a little squeeze. "You want to play games today, huh?"

"Maybe." She whispers, and I watch with familiarity as her breathing changes and her eyelids briefly flutter.

"Too bad, because I don't."

Gripping under her jaw, I pull myself into her, using my lips against hers to push her into the wall. Her fingers get tangled in my hair, and as if she can read my mind, she lifts her shirt over her head. She returns the assertiveness I just showed by pushing me away from her until I reach the bed and fall backwards on it. I watch as she continues to peel her clothes away, enjoying every second. Once she climbs on top of me on the bed, I get reunited with and lost in the taste of her skin and the feel of vibration from the moan on her throat against my lips.

"I missed this." I groan against her skin—unable to hold it back any longer.

"Me too." She whispers between breaths.

But as I bring my lips back to hers, I can't help but wonder if she actually misses the same things I do.

CHAPTER TWENTY-SEVEN

Kory

My finger follows the black trail on his arm.

Solid black lines span from his wrist, going different routes across his forearm, along the curves of his biceps, then over his shoulders to connect across the front of his chest. I trail my finger tips from one end to the other like completing a maze in a children's activity coloring book.

We're lying in his bed, neither of us having attempted to put our clothes back on. The room is softly lit by only the light of a couple of lamps, looking as sensual as it feels.

"What do these mean?" I ask, still gliding my fingers across the ink.

"Nothing really. They were popular back when I started getting tattoos, so here I am."

I lean onto him, resting my elbow on his chest and my face in my hand. I can feel the still sensitive skin of my chest resting against his side. He looks at me a smiles for a moment.

"I just like them. Sorry to disappoint you with a boring story."

"Liking them is reason enough."

I lay my head down, and we stay there for a few more minutes. This feels good. Lying here with his skin against mine, and I don't feel awkward. Not at all. Just comfortable. I feel his heartbeat against my ear and his fingers now moving along my shoulder blades. The comfort I feel has me closing my eyes, but then the realization of our situation has them opening back up just as fast.

"You ready for this last trip?" I say as I sit up and begin looking for my clothes. It takes him a second to respond, and when he does, he doesn't answer my question.

"You don't have to do this, you know?"

I freeze after clipping my bra together. "Do what?"

"Get up and run away, like I don't want you to stay. Or that you don't want to stay."

If he only knew. I do actually have to do this because if I stay here—cuddled up on his chest for much longer—I'll end up with my heart broken at the end of all this.

"Come on, Dominic, don't be such a softie. I like this. I really do. Let's just keep having fun, okay?"

An obvious flicker of disappointment crosses his eyes. He doesn't try to hide it. God, I am such an asshole. *Why is the one man in the world who wouldn't take this opportunity someone I can't have?* But maybe if he *were* eager about our situationship, I wouldn't wish things could be different.

"Plus, I have a trip to go get ready for. I'm excited for this one."

His lips pick up into a small smile. "Me too."

Once fully dressed, I realize he hasn't moved—or covered up—from the bed. He's just been sitting here, obviously watching me, hoping I'll change my mind, and suddenly I feel awkward again. Walking across a hallway to my own room was one thing, but leaving him here to drive to my own home after just feels… cheap. I ignore the voice in my head also telling me it doesn't have to be this way, and that I felt comfortable when I was in the bed, but not since I've been out of it.

"See you Saturday?"

He nods. "7 a.m. sharp."

I catch myself still lingering, realizing it also feels weird not to at least give him a quick kiss goodbye. *Something.* We stare at each other awkwardly—both feeling it—but I can't break my own rules.

"See you then," I say, before turning and running to my car like a coward.

I may have felt awkward in the moment, but it couldn't be that bad that I left him at his apartment. Once he picked me up for our trip to Ypsilanti, we went right back to normal and spent the whole week there like the previous trip. Dinner and alternating trysts in his room or mine.

Getting ready to leave his room for the night, I see a text from Autumn.

We need to talk. NOW.

My stomach falls to my feet because it's not often she sends messages like this, and when she does, she's serious.

You okay?

Yeah. Just call me.

Shit. Okay.

"What's wrong?" Dom asks, clearly sensing my distress.

"Nothing. I just need to make a call. See you in the morning."

I leave and walk down the hallway, my room farther away than across the hall. I already have her phone ringing before I make it inside my room.

"Hello." She answers.

"Hey! What's up? What's wrong?" I ask, out of breath.

"Where are you right now?"

"In my room?" I answer questionably.

"Where were you like thirty minutes ago?"

I blink, unable to hide my apprehensive reaction. She stares back, waiting for me to answer. "I uh…" I stumble over my words, trying to think of something, but fail because she cuts me off.

"Actually, I already know what you were doing because you butt dialed me and left me a disgusting voicemail, you nasty bitch." Her face lightens with the last comment, and she lets out a laugh, allowing me to breathe a sigh of relief. She's not upset—just giving me shit.

I cover my forehead with my hand. "I am *so* sorry." I laugh back with her. "Did it at least… sound good?" I raise my eyebrow, and she laughs some more. This is normal conversation for us.

"Why do you think I called you a nasty bitch? Jealous."

We both laugh some more. "Please don't do that to me again, Autumn. I thought you were mad at me."

"Well, I was. Why didn't you tell me?"

"Because it's not even like a *thing*. We're not together."

"And since when has that ever stopped you from oversharing with me specifically, before?"

She has a point. "I didn't tell you because it's him," I admit.

"And?"

"Jimmy's best friend?"

I watch her head roll back with frustration. "Kay, I already told you I don't care about that. Maybe I'd care a little if it were Jimmy you were sleeping with, but you're not." I'm quiet for a moment, thankful she's not upset and glad Olivia isn't here to tell me she told me so. "No more secrets. We've never had them before, let's not start now."

"Technically, we did. How did I find out about you and Jimmy?" I correct her.

"Touché." She says with a laugh. "So we're even. No more. Starting now."

"Even. But I am tired. I'm going to shower and go to bed."

"I bet you are, nasty."

"Love you bye," I say and hang up with a laugh.

After my shower, I see unread messages on my phone. The first one is from Autumn.

> Stop worrying about me. I'm happy. You should be, too.

The next one is from Dom.

> Ride tomorrow? Weather looks good.

I respond to Autumn.

> Love you.

Then to Dom.

Sounds great.

I crawl into my bed and lie still, staring at the ceiling. His text makes me smile more than I should. As I realize my sheets still smell like him from last night, I realize there's another rule I should've added to our list.

No smiling at your phone like a giddy teenager.

CHAPTER TWENTY-EIGHT

Dom

Once we've made it to Detroit and settled into our rooms, we decide to go for a walk by the river.

We stand for a moment, soaking in the scene. Downtown Detroit is incredible and nothing like I've imagined. Our little *'downtown'* is a half-mile strip of road lined with quaint little brick buildings that have been there for years. It's nothing like the massive metal buildings and abundance of both people and traffic here.

And there's the river. The Detroit River spans as far as you can see, with a colorful view of Canada's shoreline just on the other side. It's so close, you can actually see the details of the buildings.

"It's beautiful." She says, obviously thinking the same as me.

But it isn't nearly as beautiful as the sight next to me. She has her hair bundled up on top of her head, some waves falling loose, refusing to be restricted. Her aviator sunglasses are still on her nose, even though the sun is starting to set.

When she looks back at me, I see a faint peek of her eyes above the frames and something about the look in them lights a fire in me that I have to contain—until we get to the room at least.

"It's even beautiful this way." I turn around, pointing towards our hotel. It's a tall tower that appears to keep going into the clouds. We don't have buildings even half this size back home.

"Crazy to think we're on the 36th floor, huh?"

"And that's still only halfway up."

John set us up in a hotel right in the heart of downtown since we're going to be participating in Sunday night football at the end of the week. It helped that we had been working with Jimmy all this time, getting a significantly discounted rate on our rooms. That gave them some wiggle room in the budget to let us splurge a little on this last trip.

Last trip. That sucks to say because I don't want to stop doing this. I look over at Kory as she tightens her cardigan across her chest. It's not really cold yet, but standing near a body of water in mid-October easily makes it feel ten degrees cooler than it is. I want to wrap my arms around her—keep her warm—but I'm too afraid she'll pull away.

When she offered this friends with benefits deal, she said *'while we're traveling,'* and that's been on my mind heavy this past week. What does that mean after we're done here? *Do we just stop talking? Act like we're strangers?* We're definitely not, and I don't think I can go back to not talking to her.

She turns towards me with a shy smile, having caught me staring. "Want to do the river walk?"

I nod. Of course I do. I want to soak up every single second with her until this is over. We turn to the left and go a couple of steps down to walk along the brick path. The sky has started to turn shades of indigo, pink, and purple, like the clouds are tie-dyed.

As much as I wanted to wrap her in a warm hug, I want to grab her hand right now and lace my fingers with hers, but that would probably make this walk *'romantic.'*

"Hey." I interrupt the silence. "Isn't a romantic walk on the beach against your rules?"

"Technically—we are not on a beach—so I'll allow it."

Neither of us says another word as we move in unison. We stay quiet until we get to the end, and the path directs us to turn around. We begin back the way we came when the silence becomes too much for me.

"So," I start, "if you could go anywhere, where would it be?"

She slides her glasses up into her hair. "Back to Twenty Questions?"

I laugh. "I guess so."

She thinks for a second. "Paris."

"Really?"

"I know it's cliché. But I want to know if what people say about the Eiffel Tower is true or not.

"What do people say?"

"That it's nothing like what movies make it out to be. Practically not even worth seeing during the day. Still not much at night, but it's a little bit more romantic with the lights and stuff."

"You? Romantic?" My face scrunches.

She reaches over and playfully taps my arm. "Hey. I am actually very romantic." She takes a breath like she's about to say something else, but doesn't. Probably because that something else is something like '*when I want to date someone.*'

After just one question, the silence engulfs us both again. My eyes remain on her for the majority of the walk back. I don't like how she makes me feel. She has turned my confidence into submission because I'm smart enough to know the ball is in her court. Every time I think I've cracked the case, she shuts it right back up. She's in control and always has been. *But fuck. What else can I do? And how do I prove to her in the next seven days that this can't end with this trip?*

The weight of the unspoken words proves to be sitting on her shoulders too, because when we're back at the hotel, she says goodnight and goes to her room alone and remains there all night. Not exactly how I hoped we'd start our last week together.

We stay apart Sunday night too, but during our first day of work at this store, I've caught her staring at me more than once—watching as I move around the store like she can't get enough. Because she can't—no matter how hard she tries.

I climb up a ladder to hang a row of jerseys when I see her jerk the other way, pretending like she wasn't just caught. Once I'm finished, I make my way across the room and sneak up behind her.

"Excuse me, ma'am." My breath on her ear makes her jump. "If I remember correctly, lingering stares from across the room are against the rules."

She tightens her lips together, fighting a smile. "I don't know what you're talking about."

"Mhm," I respond sarcastically. "Maybe we should discuss it over dinner?"

She's quiet for a moment. "My place?" she whispers and darts her eyes around defensively, making sure no one is close enough to hear.

"It's a date," I say and walk away before she can tell me it's not.

Does she leave me spinning in a mess of whiplash? Yeah. But if it means spending time with her—pretending this won't end—then I'll chase the feeling, every damn time.

We finish out the week—benefits still intact—yet I still haven't brought myself to ask what happens after this. *Once we go back to Scottville, will we pass each other in the grocery store and pretend like we don't know each other?* It almost slipped out a few times while we were lying in one of our beds, but I decided to wait until the ride home. Tonight is the Lions' game, and I hope for a fun night together—no complications or awkwardness.

Ready to go, I knock on her door and she answers instantly. She's stunning as usual in a tight-fitted jersey donning the number 97 and a baseball cap that has her curls exploding out of the back of it. Her jeans are as tight as leather, and the rips in the denim expose slivers of her tan legs underneath. She's the perfect advertisement for our store.

"Ready?" I ask with a smile.

"Hell yeah, I am." She replies as she pushes past me, too full of excitement to wait for me to catch up.

At the stadium, we're led to our booth and introduced to all the people on the PR team. They tell us we'll pose for a handful of pictures, but that they can handle the on-camera interviews if we're not comfortable—which we both happily accept.

Once people start arriving, they just keep coming. The stadium is quickly filled with excited energy and a sea of Honolulu blue. It's been a good year for this team—the best one in years—and you can feel it in the fans.

Kory is in her element as she has soaked up all the fans' energy and is the one at our table that people are gravitating to.

I don't blame them in the slightest. The Kory I've seen over the years is back—her aura pulling people in before they even realize what's happening. It's no surprise she's *Home Team's* top sales associate.

I continue watching her spell fall over everyone she talks to until her body language immediately stiffens. My eyes jump to her face, and her eyes are wide with surprise, but not the good kind.

The aura that just reappeared vanishes just as fast.

CHAPTER TWENTY-NINE

Kory

"Nathan."

That was all I could say as I stared at my ex standing in front of me. The ex who left me to take a job in Phoenix. Except he's not in Phoenix—he's in Detroit with a blond on his arm.

"Kory." He responds, just as stunned as I am.

"Ooh, baby, I like this one. Can I get it?" the mousey-nosed barbie babbles.

He and I freeze, staring at each other while she continues. Eventually, my gaze moves to her, then back to him, and his stare softens. Almost saddens. It's the same look he gave me when he left.

I feel heavy—filled with betrayal and anger. He may have moved, but it wasn't to another state. It was just hours away, and instead of telling me the truth, he decided to pretend to do what everyone else had done to me. What he knew would hurt the worst.

The warmth of a hand against my back brings me back to the present.

"What's wrong?" Dom asks. His voice is low, and his eyes are locked hard on mine.

My eyes flick back towards Nathan, then back to Dom. "I need to go to the bathroom."

I watch his eyes mirror mine. I don't know if he knows who this is, but he registers that I am trying to get away. "Go. I can take it from here."

Without another word, I power walk away from our booth. I don't remember where the bathroom is, but my body moves in any direction that's not back towards the table. Eventually, a bathroom sign appears, and I push through the line to get inside, ignoring the dirty looks. I don't actually need to use a toilet; I just need to breathe.

Leaning my back against the cold brick wall, I inhale deeply four or five times. I just can't believe this. Can't believe him. I pull out my phone and text Autumn.

> Nathan didn't fucking move to Phoenix. He's here. In Detroit. With a new girl.

I copy and paste the same message to Olivia. Instantly, she is typing.

> WHAT? What a dick. Fuck him. Is she ugly at least??

Leave it to Liv to make me laugh in the midst of a breakdown. Then a message from Autumn.

> Maybe he's just there for the game? Ugh. Sorry Kay.

And leave it to Autumn to always try and see the best in people. I guess I didn't think of that. But the look on his face definitely screamed guilt. After a few more deep breaths, I tuck the phone back into my pocket and force myself to get back to work.

I am obviously followed during my escape because a voice calls my name as soon as I'm back in the hall. And it's not the voice I want to hear.

"What do you want?" I snap as I turn to face him.

I take in the face of the last person to stomp on my heart. Nathan's dark hair is shorter than it used to be—freshly buzzed. But his face is clean-shaven like it's always been. His deep blue eyes are clouded with ache, but they didn't have a hold on me anymore.

"I didn't cheat on you." He declares. "Kayla and I just started dating."

A laugh laced with sarcasm slips out of my mouth. "You still lied to me. You said it was over because you were moving to *Arizona*. Why would you do that?"

He lets out a deep breath and looks towards the ceiling. "I was going to. I really was. But the Detroit opportunity came up and I took that instead."

"Yeah, I'm sure that's what happened."

"It is. I swear. I texted you and I was going to tell you, but you never responded."

My foot taps out of frustration as I realize he's right about that part. He did text me once. The night I ran into Dom at the bar for the first time. And I did ignore him.

"I have missed you, though. You look great." He attempts to lean in for a hug, but I pull away.

"You have a girlfriend waiting somewhere for you." I clip then try to push past him, but he steps in front of me, blocking my path.

"Come on. Let's talk."

"I'd rather not. Bye, Nathan." I push hard this time, still trying to get past him, but he grabs my arm. I swing around just in time to see two tattooed arms grab Nathan and push him against the wall.

"She said no." Dom snarls—his voice grittier than I've ever heard it.

Nate puts both hands up for a brief second, then uses both of them to push Dom away. "Okay. Jesus. Bye Kory. Tell your boyfriend to chill the fuck out." He whines as he storms away.

Dom comes back over to me, gently placing both hands on my cheeks. "You okay?"

The combinations of his hands on my skin, the look in his eyes, the smell of his cologne, and the softness of his voice pull me in, and I lean into his chest, allowing him to envelop me in his arms. I nod, answering his question as we stand there in silence. I'm more than okay now.

"You shouldn't have left the table," I say once I peel myself away from him.

"Screw that table. I saw him follow you and had no idea what was happening. Your reaction told me it was something, though."

"It's actually nothing. Just my ex. He told me he was moving out of state, and that's why we split. I was just surprised, is all." I say, avoiding all the real emotions that came with that reunion.

"Brooks." He tilts my chin with his finger so I have to look back up into his eyes. That's another rule I forgot to add.

"I'm fine, Dominic. I promise." I nudge him with my shoulder—squirming back into the friend zone. "Let's get back to work."

The Lions win, which is incredible. The energy inside the stadium that was already palpable before the game is the craziest I have ever seen, once it's over. Crazier than any concert I've ever been to.

We grab dinner from the restaurant in the hotel and head straight to his room. I've spent the last six hours counting down the minutes until I could take these jeans off, so as soon as his door clicks shut, I shimmy them to the floor. I pull the hat off my head and shake my hair free as I toss it on the desk. The jersey comes off next, leaving me in a tank top and boy shorts undies before I park myself on the couch with my burger. With a quick familiar motion, I wrap my curls into a pile on my head so I can eat without them getting in the way.

He smiles slightly while also changing. A pair of basketball shorts replaces his jeans, and he reveals a tank top under his jersey, which he also wears.

It's in this moment that I realize just how comfortable we've become with each other. Not a single thought crossed my mind before taking my pants off and leaving them in the middle of his floor. Sex wasn't even on my mind until I watched him pull the jersey over his head with one hand. I just wanted to be comfortable. And with him I am.

He sits next to me and turns on the TV. After a channel has been settled on, we enjoy our dinner in silence.

When our food is gone, he throws our containers in the trash and then sits back down. As soon as he does, I throw my legs up across the couch, laying my feet on his lap.

"Comfortable?" he asks with a laugh.

"Very," I say truthfully.

We share a smile, then our attention goes back to the TV. Somewhere between bombs going off and people shooting at each other, he grabs my foot. The touch startles me at first, then the pressure of his fingertips causes my head to fall back. I cannot remember the last time someone massaged my feet. If ever.

I should really tell him to stop, but I can't. This feels too good. Almost as good as sex. *Almost.*

We stay quiet, my head relaxed back as he moves through each muscle of my foot—just the right pressure on each spot, even each toe. He switches from one foot to the other, and I hope he doesn't ask me to return the favor because I just may fall asleep.

"So earlier," he starts, rudely interrupting my relaxation.

"Yeah, sorry. I shouldn't have run out like a flake. It wasn't that serious."

"Kory," he protests. His use of my first name catches me off guard. "You can tell me the truth."

I stare at him, still rubbing my foot and looking right through me. There used to be two people I couldn't lie to. Now I think there are three. A breath puffs out of my lips in defeat.

"His breaking up with me didn't hurt all that much. But he said he took a job in Phoenix. That hurt because…" I pause, but look at him, and his eyes are soft, attentive, and he's still rubbing my foot. "That hurt because everyone I've ever loved has up and left me. My parents. My brother. Autumn. Him. Everyone."

"That's why you don't get close to anyone."

"Ding ding ding. Don't need a rocket scientist to figure that one out, huh?" I say making light of him, figuring out my issues so quickly. "So I thought he was gone, gone. Then, when I saw him tonight, I thought he lied just to hurt me more."

"You thought?" He adjusts himself to face me, and my body warms. Any body language expert would tell you that he's all in on this conversation.

"Yeah. When we were by the bathroom, he said that's not what happened. That his situation changed, and it's possible because he did reach out once, and I ignored him. Like I said, not a huge deal. Just took me by surprise."

"Well, I know you said you'd never love me, but I don't plan on going anywhere."

I swallow hard at the comment and look down at my feet, still in his lap. Anything but his face right now. He's right. I did say that I'd never love him. And I meant it. Then.

"So what about you?" I ask, changing the subject. "What's your trauma?"

"Oh no," he says, finally climbing out from under my feet and resting each of his arms on either side of me. "That's enough talking for one night." His eyes adjust to mine as he crawls up me, until our lips meet, ending all conversation completely until the morning.

CHAPTER THIRTY

Dom

I almost asked her what happened with us after this trip last night on the couch, but that conversation veered in a direction that I had no interest in continuing.

Maybe I should've shared my issues with her since she shared hers with me, but I couldn't bring myself to do it. I've already told her more than I've told anyone else.

She broke one of her own rules last night, falling asleep in my bed. She tried to sneak out early this morning so she could pretend she didn't, but she's not stealthy. Plus, she fell asleep long before I did. I went back to the couch to get my shorts and watched a whole movie before closing my eyes with her. I tried fighting my sleep—waiting for her to wake up and realize where she was—but she never did. Her head stayed nuzzled in my shoulder, her hair right where I could inhale the smell of her shampoo with every breath. The familiar scent of citrus, sugar, and… sweat. *My favorite.*

While I never asked the question, I feel like it's on both of our minds while we tiptoe around each other, loading our stuff into the truck. As we begin the drive, she opens her book and sits quietly, escaped into whatever world she's reading about. I should, but I don't bother her.

An hour into the drive, her phone rings. She gasps excitedly and holds the phone out in front of her face— obviously answering a FaceTime.

"There you are." A male voice says. "God, it's so good to see you."

I try to ignore the jealousy that causes my grip on the steering wheel to tighten. He says it with a smooth southern accent—"*Gawd, it's so good t' see ya.*" The way the vowels lingered made it sound like more than just a hello. Like he'd missed her. And that stung.

"Well, if you actually called every once in a while, you wouldn't feel like a stranger. I miss you, El." She tells him. My knuckles get a shade lighter.

"I miss you too, Kay. What are you doing? Are you in a moving truck?"

She laughs. "Yeah, I've been traveling for work. My partner insisted on this truck to haul his bike." She turns the phone towards me. "El, this is Dom, Dom, this is my brother Elliot."

While the jealousy subsides, two new things pain me. The use of the word partner, and the use of Dom—not Dominic. Ignoring those, a smirk crosses my lips. *Did she just break another one of her rules? Does this count as meeting the family?*

I wave while I drive, then they start talking back and forth. Their conversation is animated and excited, and I can see a new light in Kory's eyes. Her brother's phone call obviously means a lot to her. She squeals when he tells her that he's coming home for Thanksgiving. Apparently, Autumn will be here too, and she can't wait to have everyone at her apartment. Eventually, they hang up with promises to text more details.

"You sound happy," I say once she's quieted.

"I am. I really miss him."

"I get it. I miss my sister too." I stare out the window, regretting saying that out loud.

"What's her name again? I can't remember if you told me."

"Kami." I croak.

"That's a pretty name. What's she like?"

My knuckles have rewrapped themselves around the steering wheel—the bones screaming to break through the skin. I knew this would happen, and I know I have to say something. If I don't answer these simple questions, she'll ask harder ones, *like why haven't we spoken in ten years?*

"She was quiet in high school. You probably never knew her."

That's all I could bring myself to tell her, but there is so much more I should say. I should tell her how alike they are, how they both love to read, how they both love chocolate-covered pretzels, how they both love carnations, while no one else does. While there are some differences in their personalities, they also have so many little, more unique things in common. But I don't say any of that.

Thankfully, she's satisfied with that answer. "Elliot should have been born in a barn. He loves all the outdoorsy stuff—hunting, fishing, camping—I don't know where he got it from." She pauses before continuing. "He rides four-wheelers like you do your bike. You know, like ATVs?"

I laugh. "I know what a four-wheeler is, Brooks."

"Well, whatever. I don't know. Maybe we can all go riding together when he visits." She clamps her lips shut as soon as the words leave her lips. *Perfect segue.*

"I thought that was against the rules."

She thinks for a moment. "Well, those were friends with benefits rules. If we're not friends with benefits, then the rules don't apply."

I don't love that answer, but it's the perfect segue to question two. "So what does that mean for us once we get home? Will we not be friends with benefits anymore?"

She thinks for another minute. "Do you want to?"

Her response tosses the ball back into my court, temporarily. "I want more than that."

I know it's not the answer she expected, or probably wanted, but I had to say it. "Dominic," she starts, but I cut her off.

"But if that's what you're willing to give me, then yes, that's what I want."

"Then we can try to keep it going." She says with a smile, so I give her one back, even though I don't want to.

She may go out of her way to keep people at arm's length, but she can't ever say she doesn't know how I feel.

"My favorite manager!" John exclaims over the phone later that night. "How's it feel to be back at home?"

It sucks, John. I wish I were back in a hotel room with Kory on my lap.

"Good so far, but I'll go stir crazy in no time."

"I'm sure you'll find plenty to keep you busy." He laughs. "Anyways. Good news. We've been invited back to Detroit. Nominated for a small business award, actually. I want you and Kory to attend the ceremony banquet with me."

"A banquet?"

"Yes. We're nominated for being the fastest-growing new business. It's only right that you two come so you can accept this award if we win. When we win."

I did enjoy my time in Detroit. Of all the cities we visited during these trips, it's definitely at the top of my list to revisit.

"It's formal." He continues. "So you'll have to clean yourself up."

I hear the humor in his voice, friendly enough to entice a joke out of me in response. The thought is enticing—picturing Kory dressed up for a formal event—it makes me think of the ten-year high school reunion my ex made me go to. I should have never been there because by that time I knew I wasn't happy with her, but like many people do, I went to make her happy—to keep her image for the 'show off party'.

That night turned out to be a mess, and she couldn't help but be involved in all the Autumn, Jimmy, and Becca drama. We spent most of the evening apart because I couldn't stand to hear about it any longer than I had to. But then Jimmy showed up with Autumn, which sent everyone into a tizzy, including himself. Becca also had a date, and seeing her with someone else brought him out of the haze he had been living in with Autumn. He and Becca were back together shortly after. But amongst all that, Kory, looking like a runway model, had my attention. I couldn't pull my eyes away, which made me thankful Izzy would've rather been gossiping.

"I'm in. When is it?"

"December thirteenth, which is a Wednesday. We'll come in on Tuesday morning and leave on Thursday or Friday. We have a few weeks to prepare and find something to wear."

"Sounds good. I'll talk to Brooks."

"My man. Talk soon." He says, then ends the call.

I open up the internet app to look up a new place to go shopping for something to wear. It likely won't be in this town because I'm going for something nice. A regular off-the-rack suit won't do.

I'm not even one to enjoy dressing up—but to see Kory like that again—and to be by her side for the night—I'll do just about anything.

CHAPTER THIRTY-ONE

Kory - November

I look at each face sitting around my small dining room table with a smile full of contentment.

"This year I'm thankful for this. It may just be five of us, but this is the best Thanksgiving I've had in years." Autumn, Elliot, Olivia, and her date raise their glasses to my toast. "Now let's eat."

My whole year was made when Elliot got here. It felt like forever since I spent a significant amount of time with him. Three full days were a gift.

Unfortunately, he leaves tomorrow, but now Autumn is here until Sunday. Perfect timing to go shopping for a dress to whatever Dom agreed we'd go to.

I've spent more of tonight wishing he were here than not. It was the right choice not to invite him, though, because that would just make things harder. I know what he wants, and I can't give it to him. I look up at Autumn as she laughs at something my brother said. She nudges his shoulder with hers, and it makes me smile again.

We always used to joke that they looked more like siblings than him and me. He has the curls like I do, but a dark, dirty blond color more similar to hers. He lucked out with not only the blond hair, but mom's blue eyes, while I got hazel.

I thought about asking Dom to come more than once, but one, our benefits haven't been that consistent since being home, and two, I just can't bring myself to do that to Autumn. He and I still talk almost every day, but we've only seen each other a few times. It's too hard now that I'm back at the bar and my store, especially between football season and the holidays.

While disappointing to be missing out on my fix, I know the distance is necessary. Despite my juvenile list of rules, I'm failing at the no feelings thing. Coupled with his confession on the way home, I know I should have told him we should leave the benefits on the road and just be friends.

But I can't, and I don't really want to, which makes all of this so much harder.

Like the glutton for punishment I am, I pull out my phone to text him.

Happy Thanksgiving. How's it going?

I know he's at Jimmy's because his family isn't around. Even that conversation was a painful reminder of why we'll always be stuck where we are right now. He with Jimmy, and I with Autumn.

My phone vibrates.

Good. These kids are adorable. Keeping everyone laughing.

Kids. I totally forgot Jimmy and his brother had kids—two little girls. That has to be an interesting feeling for Dom—Thanksgiving as a fifth wheel to the two happy families, while I'm here drinking booze with my kid-less friends. I'm a jerk. I should've just invited him.

I hope they didn't stick you at the kids' table. Lol

Than another.

Ugh. Here we go again. This is why we needed distance. Every time we get into a comfortable swing, he reminds me that he wants more, and no matter the distance, it seems like the harder I try, the harder he does too.

"Can I just say, I love that I ended up being here for this," Autumn calls from outside the dressing room.

"Me too. I can't do this with Olivia." I slide the blue dress over my head. "She's worse than me when it comes down to what's a party dress and what's a formal dress."

The zipper glides up effortlessly, then I step out of the room. I turn around to face the mirrors, showing me the dress from three different angles. It's a long royal blue dress, satin and strapless. I don't hate it. I turn again to get Autumn's reaction and find her nodding her head with tight lips.

"Pretty." She says, which means she also doesn't hate it, but doesn't love it either.

"So uh, why didn't Tyler come with you?" I finally ask. I've been wanting to do it since yesterday, but we haven't been alone to ask. Neither of us says anything else about this dress, so I take that as my sign to move on to the next.

"He was going to, but changed his mind last minute." She shrugs. "I don't care."

"Trouble in paradise?" I call out from back inside the dressing room.

"Not really. He said he didn't understand why I wouldn't want to go to his family's. I mean, I get it, but we also see his family a lot. I never see mine, obviously. And I told him from the start of our relationship that I plan on visiting home as much as I can." I step into the next dress while she continues.

"Plus, I haven't spent a holiday here with my family where I wasn't acting like a depressed zombie, so coming here, whether alone or not, was more important."

Stepping out of the dressing room again, we both silently survey the new dress—a black halter with a corset back and sequins along the neckline.

"Oh yeah, how'd that go?" I ask referencing her family's Thanksgiving, which took place the day after due to her mom having to work on actual Thanksgiving.

"It was great. You'd never guess that my parents are divorced. It's still odd to me that they're such great friends."

I laugh and smooth my hands down the dress, looking to Autumn with the silent request of approval.

"Nah. Not that one."

I nod in agreement and go back in. Before long, I'm stepping out in another one to an immediate response from Autumn.

"That's it. That's the one."

I spin to see what she sees in the mirror and have the same reaction. It's a champagne color, with thin straps and a neckline that dips loosely. It's a thin, silky material that looks painted on me. The slit goes all the way up to the middle of my right thigh.

"Agreed," I say.

We finish up our trip, which includes jewelry, shoes, and a new bag—thanks to the extra money I set aside while traveling.

On the way home, we stop for food at our favorite diner, sit in our favorite spot, and order our favorite meals. It's the perfect day.

"You'd better send me pictures." She says as she shoves a bite of chili cheese fries in her mouth.

"You know I will."

"Dom is going to fall over dead when he sees you in that dress."

I know she's right, but I'm also kind of afraid of exactly that. "Do you think I should've toned it down?"

She scoffs. "Toned it down? Who are you and what has he done with my best friend?"

"He hasn't done anything." I lie and she knows it.

"Actually, I've *heard* what he's done to you, so I know that's a lie." She eyes my face and the lack of reaction to that comment. "What aren't you telling me? We said no more secrets, remember?"

She's right. But she's also the last person I want or should talk to about this. "He wants more," I admit.

"And?"

"And naturally it's made me pull away."

"Why?" Her question is short and pointed.

"Because I just can't."

"If you say this is about me, I am going to throw the rest of this plate right at you."

I take a deep breath. "But it is. Or maybe it's not. Maybe it's just me, but I can't see myself with him knowing I'll end up close with Jimmy."

"I think you hate him more than I do."

"As I should. I'm your best friend."

She takes a sip of her water. "Look, I love you. But you are being dumb. I can tell he makes you happy. Stop being so damn stubborn."

"I'm not being stubborn. I'm being realistic."

"Whatever you say, Kory. But don't use me as an excuse anymore. This isn't about me, and you know it."

I finish the last of my food in silence until we both hear my phone vibrate.

"That him?" She asks behind her straw.

I look at it. *Sure is.*

What are you doing later?

I just smile—at both the message and her.

"See? Tell me I'm wrong."

"You're wrong," I say as I put the phone down with no immediate response, but a sinking feeling that she might actually be right.

CHAPTER THIRTY-TWO

Dom - December

I haven't spoken to Kory much in the last couple of weeks.

I feared that might happen once we got home, but hoped it wouldn't. Part of me just hoped she'd actually realize how much she misses me, then naturally she'd realize she felt the same as I did.

After getting as close as we did while on the road, I can't be without her, and I've been miserable since being home. I miss the sound of her voice, the smell of her hair, the way she rolls her eyes at me. I miss her presence.

I know she has feelings for me. That too had been made more obvious as time passed. But it's almost like the stronger her feelings grow, the more reinforcement she adds to her walls. One of those new reinforcements is the fact that she drove herself here to Detroit instead of us riding together. I want to lie and say I wasn't disappointed about losing that extra four hours with her, but I was more than disappointed.

Bike rides used to help. She couldn't deny how much she enjoyed riding with me, but in Michigan, December means your riding time is up. Even if you bundle up enough to be comfortable, there's always a chance for wet spots or invisible black ice on the road.

There's not much else I can do right now. Knowing Kory and the walls she's erected, the more I try, the more bricks she'll continue to add. I've never had to exhibit patience like I have lately. But it's going to be worth it. It has to be.

I look over at the desk in my room to the bouquet of carnations sitting in a vase with a purple bow. During one of our first road trips, she told me they were her favorite flower. *'They're under appreciated because they're cheap. But I love them, and their smell is comforting,'* she said. That day, I made a point to look up carnations, and I'm glad I did because I'm pretty sure I thought those were roses before.

But now a dozen sit in a vase on the dresser—a mix of cream and shades of purple—I know purple is her favorite, and a little birdie told me that her dress was a cream-ish color. A little bag of chocolate-covered pretzels sits next to them—a snack for later. I may be a little presumptuous, but I'd rather consider it hopeful.

A text comes through.

> I'll be ready in 10.

While we drove to town separately, we agreed to show up to the event together since we were here as a team. *'Not as a couple'* is probably what she really wanted to say. I sit on the edge of the bed to put my shoes on and strain from the expensive fitted suit.

I ended up finding a suit shop that was relatively local—only an hour away. The two young people who worked there were more than eager to help once they heard I had no idea what I was looking for. I let them take the lead on the style. The girl, Alyssa, I think her name was, assured me that whatever girl I had my eye on wouldn't be able to resist me. I tried not to let the way she was looking at me make me uncomfortable—I just smiled and said thank you.

The suit is all black—the jacket, vest, shirt, pants, and shoes—all of it. It's a color I'm comfortable with, and they insisted it's a classic look. I don't have a tie, which felt weird for *'formal,'* but Alyssa insisted that's what all the celebrities are doing nowadays. Even further, keeping the top two buttons unbuttoned. The male stylist insisted the sheen on the lapels would draw the eyes right to my chest, and the open buttons would keep them there.

I stand up now, surveying the results in the mirror, and I have to say, I see the vision. These small store stylists may be heading somewhere someday. I grab the carnation made for my jacket and secure it in place. Then I grab the bouquet, pretzels, and head to her room.

Outside of her room, I feel like a nervous teenager—the one who shows up to pick up the girl for the first time, afraid to meet the parents. But that was never me. And this isn't a date.

After a couple of knocks, the door swings opens and I laugh as I step inside. She's pacing, hair and makeup done, but with a toothbrush in her mouth and wearing a robe. She looks adorable. "You said ten minutes."

"I know, I know." She says as she closes the door behind us. "I had a hair fiasco. Then I couldn't remember if I brushed my teeth. So now I have to fix my makeup too. Give me ten more."

"Your hair looks beautiful."

"Yeah, *now*. But thank you." Her eyes soften as she notices the flowers. I smile and hand them to her. "Carnations? You remembered?"

"I did," I say proudly.

She sticks her face into them and takes a long, deep sniff, then sets them down and sprints to the bathroom. I sit down on the edge of the bed, feeling satisfied, while she finishes whatever it is she needs to do in there.

"I'm almost done." She calls now, knowing she's almost past her *'ten more minutes.'*

I can't help but smile at her and at the flowers sitting on the desk. A smile filled her lips when she saw them, rather than an eye roll, and that was a good sign. The only sign I needed.

The area near the entrance brightens as she opens the door, and the bathroom light spills out. She steps into it as if it's a spotlight, and my breath is gone in an instant.

I knew she would look amazing, but I wasn't expecting an actual Goddess to be standing in front of me. The dress she's wearing leaves little to the imagination, but in a classy way. The fabric clings to every curve of her body as if it were poured onto her. The swells of her chest show just enough to make me ache for this night to be over already.

No one else should ever own this dress. It was made for her.

She looks at me shyly, which surprises me because we both know she's not actually shy, but still acts like it around me. But if she is feeling nervous like I am, then that's another good sign.

"Brooks," I say as she moves closer to me. "You look stunning."

Her smile grows a bit more confident, and she does a little spin. I want to grab her by her hair and strip the dress off in two seconds flat, but I won't. Not yet. I'm smart enough not to mess up a woman's hair after they have apparently already had a *'fiasco.'*

But I have to at least kiss her—it won't satisfy what my body is craving, but it will hold me over for now—and I need her to know that I don't see her as my friend tonight.

She doesn't shy away when my hand slides up her cheek; in fact, her eyes close, showing off the shimmer on her eyelids. I lean down and she welcomes the kiss, pulling me into her, before quickly pushing away.

"That's against the rules. Dominic."

"Fuck those rules," I say, pulling her hand so that she slams back into me. "Plus..." I add—my voice low, "It's not against the rules if we follow it up with sex." I wink, which causes her to laugh as she pushes off of me again and grabs her little bag.

"We both know there's no time for that right now."

"So, later?" My eyebrows waggle, and she laughs again.

"Let's go, Casanova. We wouldn't want you getting caught being anything other than the perfect gentleman you promised John you would be."

She passed by me again, pausing with her hand on the door. I step in front of her and slide her hand off the door so I can push it open instead. I hold my arm out into the open space, indicating for her to go.

"Ladies first. See? Gentleman."

She shakes her head but steps into the hallway. After pulling her door all the way shut, I join her, placing my hand on the exposed small of her back and leaning into her ear.

"And that promise was for our road trips. All bets are off now. I don't give a shit who knows what I do to you."

Her body shakes with the chill my breath on her neck caused. Neither of us says anything else as we make our way through the hotel to find the banquet hall.

We find our table according to the seating chart, then head outside to the riverfront cocktail hour. The scene is beautiful, despite the December chill. Kory's one of the only women out here without a coat on, and I can tell she's already cold.

"Here," I say as I pull mine off.

"No. Dominic, I'm fine. Don't be cold on my account."

"Gentleman, remember?" I whisper in her ear as I drape it over her shoulders. She grabs the lapels and pulls them in tighter, welcoming the warmth.

"Look at this! You guys are the epitome of a power couple! Well, partnership." A voice calls out. "Just look at you two."

John approaches us enthusiastically with a glass of brown liquor in his hand. He reaches out to shake my hand with the empty one, then leans in to hug Kory. I know it's just a friendly professional hug, but I can't help but feel a tinge of jealousy. Thankfully, I know he hasn't fully seen her yet—hidden under *my* jacket.

"Dom, can I see you for a second, actually? I want to talk to you about something."

"Yeah, sure, no problem. You okay?" I ask Kory.

"Believe it or not, I haven't grown co-dependent on you. You boys have fun," she responds.

John laughs, then throws his arm over my shoulder, pulling me away.

"She's a spunky girl. I like her a lot," he says.

"Yeah. Me too." I respond as I look back to find her smiling back at me from behind her glass.

CHAPTER THIRTY-THREE

Kory

Keeping myself away from him tonight might actually kill me.

He slides his jacket back on once we're inside, preparing for the main event to start. I can't help but watch as he does. I don't understand how one person can hold all the traits he does. He looks dangerous—maybe not typically dangerous—but definitely dangerous for me. Even the way he walks and the way he talks to people sends tingles from my head to my toes.

More and more people slowly fill the room—all dressed to the nines like us. I'm thankful I didn't end up overdressed, but it's still a slightly uncomfortable feeling. I've never been to something quite like this. Everyone looks so… regal. It's so much more than I had pictured for just a small business award ceremony.

"Need a drink?" Dom asks against my ear.

Yes, I do. I need a million every time he does that. Which has been a lot tonight, and I can't help but wonder if he's doing it on purpose. His smooth voice slides right into my ears and straight to my stomach—and other places. But I don't tell him all that.

"Yes, please." Is all I say.

As he walks away, Lacey, a young blond at our table, introduces herself. We chat for a few about why we're here—

she being the co-owner of an all-natural smoothie/nutrition cafe, one that focuses on vegan and gluten-free options. They just opened a second store and are nominated for the same award as us.

A tan hand sets a glass in front of me as I feel another on my shoulder. "I'll be right back," Dom says. "John wants me to meet someone."

I look up, meeting his eyes, and in this moment, it feels like we should kiss. Or he should kiss my head. Just a quick reassuring one like couples would do before separating. But we're not a couple, so we don't, even though his eyes linger for an extra couple of seconds. Instead, I nod, and he walks away.

"So how long have you two been together?" Lacey asks.

I take a sip—Crown and Coke—my favorite. I smile appreciating the fact that he still remembers, and that the last time he brought me this drink, I ended up puking all over him.

"Oh no," I say with a laugh. "We're not together. Just partners. Work partners."

Both her eyes and nose scrunch together before she laughs, too. "You're kidding, right? I don't believe you for a second."

My heart beat speeds up a little, and I'm not sure why. I also don't know why I'm suddenly annoyed by her line of questioning.

"Not joking. We've become close friends. That's it."

"Girl, you might need your eyes checked because I've never seen anyone look at a *friend* the way he looks at you."

My annoyance grows at the false familiarity in her comments. She doesn't know me or him. That's a rude thing to say to someone you don't know. I take another drink, unsure of how to respond, but I don't think I like her anymore.

"So, he's available then?"

My eyes jump up to her. I definitely don't like her anymore.

I didn't mean for my eyes to react as strongly as they did. I wish they hadn't because I can tell by the way she raises her eyebrows and shakes her head before taking a drink, that she took my reaction as a hard no. Thankfully, before the conversation can go any further, he and John return to the table together and take their seats.

Dinner gets served shortly after, and the conversation returns to easy and light. It's mostly business talk since that's what we're here for. There's Lacey and her partner Renee, and three other people—older men who started a travel agency focused on all the things to do in Michigan that are beautiful. It's a great idea. There are so many hidden gems that most people don't know about. That leads John to gush about how many people thought he was crazy to start a business in a small town, but *'look at us now'* he says with open arms.

Music plays in the background as an overlap for people who are still eating and those who are done. A few people gather on the dance floor, then more follow. Lacey tries to convince her friend to get up, but she refuses to budge. Giving up on her, she looks directly at Dom.

"What about you? Join me for a dance?"

While my cheeks heat, he laughs and shakes his head. "No thanks. I don't dance."

I'm embarrassed to admit the relief I feel when he says no, or the satisfied smile on my face that follows.

"You're missing out." She says with a shrug.

That song ends, and a slower one starts playing. No one says anything—the air at the table is now a little awkward. Before the first verse has finished, Dom holds his hand out to me.

"Come on."

"Where?"

"To the dance floor," he answers with the smirk that disables me from saying no. I place my hand in his and stand up.

"I thought you didn't dance?" Lacey protests.

"Changed my mind," he says, then whisks me away.

On the dance floor, I put my arms around his neck and he rests his on my hips. We both begin to sway for a few minutes before I look up and find his eyes waiting for mine.

"What are you doing, Dominic?"

His shoulders rise and fall under my arms. "This wasn't one of your rules, so why not?"

"That girl asked if you were available." I spit out bluntly.

He laughs. "Oh, I know. I clocked her looks as soon as we sat down." I look at him incredulously, and he smirks. "Are you jealous, Brooks?"

My cheeks grow pink. "No."

He chuckles, not believing my answer for a second. "Well, what did you tell her?"

"I didn't answer."

He leans down to my ear. "You should've told her I've been unavailable for months."

Goosebumps are back, and I can't respond, but I do rest my head on his chest and enjoy the rest of the song and this—the feeling of us together. Something about this moment—our bodies held together intimately, but not sexually—has my hardened insides melting. I breathe in his cologne while my cheek rests on his heart. I feel the faint patter beneath the fabric, and it makes me smile as I pull myself tighter into him, which he welcomes without question.

When the song ends, I find myself hoping for another slow one to start, but instead, the beat picks up, and I know that neither of us plans to dance to it. But I wish we could just stay right here, just like this, without ever having to stop.

We don't completely disconnect, though. As we walk back to the table, we're hand in hand. My fingers intertwined with his for the first time—and I don't pull mine away. Once we sit down, Lacey smiles and winks at me. *Maybe she wasn't actually interested after all.*

Only a few more songs play before the actual ceremony starts. To be honest, it's long and boring as hell. But Dom's hand is resting on my thigh underneath the table, and I don't stop him then either.

With the push from my best friend—and apparently the stranger at our table—I think I've finally stopped fighting it. I don't know what exactly that means, but I know now that we can figure it out tomorrow—that I *want* to figure it out tomorrow.. I thought staying the distance would prove that I would be fine, but each day that passed, I missed him more. Being here with him now, I can no longer deny that I want him around me. All the time. Just like this.

I'm not at all paying attention—only able to focus on his thumb swiping gently on my thigh—when I hear *Home Team* announced and John shoots from his chair. People are clapping, and he ushers me and Dom out of our chairs to join him on stage. I can see *the Growth Excellence Award* displayed on the screen. Dom helps me up the steps, then I turn to see the hundreds of people looking up at us with smiles on their faces as they clap.

It suddenly makes me anxious, and I wonder if Dom can tell because he subtly pulls me in closer to him.

John grabs the plaque from the announcer and steps to the podium. "Thank you for this. It means the world to me. To us. The growth we experienced and the success of not only the new stores, but the original two, wouldn't have been possible without these two." He opens his arm to us, and I smile and nod while Dom waves.

"I hoped this would happen for obvious reasons," he pauses to laugh at his own joke. "But I also hoped to end up on this stage to share a special announcement." he stops again, looking back at the two of us. I have no idea what this announcement is, but Dom's widened eyes make it obvious he does.

John turns back to the podium. "*Home Team* is growing even more! We are officially expanding outside of Michigan."

The crowd cheers louder, and Dom's pull on my waist tightens.

"I'm so excited to spend the next year—hopefully even more—opening more locations across the country. My right-hand man here, Dom, has already agreed to take on these projects and make these stores as successful as the ones here in Michigan."

My stomach falls to my feet, and if I could see myself, I'm sure all the color has drained from my face with my stomach. People are now standing and cheering, and it takes every ounce of power in me to keep my composure in front of all of these smiling, clapping people. The crowd now appears ominous. The spotlights feel like flames, and there are beads of sweat racing down my back.

As soon as I hear John say what sounds like his final *'thank you,'* I push Dom's hand away and head straight for the table.

"It was nice to meet you." I spit out to our table guests as I grab my clutch and rush out of the banquet room.

The hallway already feels cooler than it did in there, and when the cool air slaps my cheeks, I can feel that they're wet.

I hear Dom call my name as I step into the elevator, but I'm already pushing the close door button—repeatedly. I watch him running to catch them as they finally slide together.

On my floor, I try to sprint, knowing he will probably catch me, but it's impossible in heels.

I just can't believe this. But I guess I should. It's what happens to me. Every time.

As soon as I change my mind and think this could work—that maybe I could let myself be happy with him—he's leaving, just like everyone else.

CHAPTER THIRTY-FOUR

Dom

Damn it, John.

I hit the button on the elevator over and over again, hoping it will open faster.

We talked about this plan briefly, but I had no idea it was official enough to be shared. It probably isn't. He shared no details. The scotch he'd been drinking all night probably convinced him it was a good idea.

Her door is shut, as I expected it to be, so I knock loudly. No answer. I knock again.

"Go away!" she yells.

"Not a chance. Not until you talk to me."

"Then you'll be standing out there a while. I don't want to talk to you, Dominic. Leave me alone!"

I stop pounding. "That's not happening. I'll happily stand out here all night if I have to."

It's quiet for a minute until she finally answers the door. She's already in sweats and a T-shirt with her dress, a champagne puddle on the floor.

"What do you want? I'm going home, so make it fast."

"Don't be crazy. You've been drinking, and it's already eleven. You are not driving four hours home."

"Why do you care? I'm fine on my own. Always have been. Always will be, apparently," she says in a fit while she throws things in her bag.

I step closer to her. "Let me explain, please."

Her head jerks up to look at me. "Did you or did you not agree to leave for this new little adventure?" The last couple of words are dripping in sarcasm.

"Yes, but..."

"Exactly," she cuts me off. "That's all I need to know."

"I didn't know he was going to announce it like that." I plead. "I didn't even know it was like, a solid plan. He *just* asked me tonight."

"But you said yes! And then what? Just tell me, *'Hey, I'm gonna be gone for a year, sorry.'*" She laughs and shakes her head. "Just like Nathan did." She continues pacing through the room, looking for more things to aggressively slam into her bag. "And you know what's worse? You've been begging me for more. Convincing me that you'll do anything and that you're different. But then when it comes down to it..." she pauses and sniffles. "Something else is more important than me. It always is."

I grab for her arm to stop her. To have her look in my eyes so I can convince her she couldn't be more wrong.

"That's not true at all. Yes, I agreed to it. But I told him that only if I got to pick my own team. I want you to come too. I want to do it together."

She pulls her arm back and wipes her cheek. "Yeah, of course you'd say that now. God forbid you lose your fuck buddy, right?" she laughs and shakes her head. "Just when I'd convinced myself we could actually be more."

"That's bullshit and you know it," I respond angrily. But I'm not angry at her. I'm angry that she refers to herself like that. And mad at John for fucking this whole thing up. I knew we were close. *I felt it.*

"That I convinced myself we could be more? Yeah. I know."

Already exasperated, I stop trying to explain myself. It will only make her angrier and everything worse. "Will you please just stay here tonight? I'll leave you alone. Just don't drive tonight. Please."

She stops the frantic pacing, replacing it with foot tapping instead. "Just go. I'll take care of myself."

"Fine. But I'm telling you the truth. I never planned on leaving you. I wouldn't do that to you."

"That's what they all say. Until they do."

I nod and back out towards the door. She's sat down on her bed with her phone out, pretending I'm not still in the room. I just hope that means she's staying put for the night.

Back in the hall and wandering to my room, John finds me in the hallway. "Hey, what happened? She okay?"

"No, John, she's not. Why didn't you warn me that you were going to do that?"

I run my hand through my hair. *Why would she care?* That's what he's going to ask. *How do I even explain why she's not okay without telling him everything?*

"The announcement? I didn't know it would be an issue. That's what upset her? Let me talk to her. I didn't mean to make her feel left out."

He starts to walk towards her room, and I stick my arm out to stop him from going into her room. "No," I say a little more firm than I meant to. "Just leave her alone. It's not that."

"Then what is it? We were having a good time, but I don't understand."

Well, here goes nothing. "It's me, John. We're... something. And she's mad at me, not you."

He rolls his eyes. "Seriously, Dom? This was exactly what wasn't supposed to happen."

"I know, but it's not what you think. Remember when we were talking at the restaurant? Before she got there? And I said I was already interested in someone? It was her. It's been her all along."

He takes a deep breath, followed by a shake of his head. "Why didn't you say anything?"

"Why would I, John? Come on. We enjoyed spending time together, and everything was great. Until tonight."

"But I still don't understand what exactly the problem is."

"She doesn't want me to leave. And she heard it for the first time in front of all those people, not from me."

I don't tell him why this is so important to her because that's not my business to tell. But maybe now that he knows we care about each other, that answer will be enough.

"She'll be okay. I'll talk to her tomorrow." I insist.

"Fine. We'll talk more tomorrow, too." He turns to get back on the elevator, and I go to my room.

As soon as I'm inside, I take my jacket off and throw it onto the chair. I fall backwards, and almost as soon as my back hits the bed, I'm asleep.

I wake up at 9:30 a.m.shocked that I actually slept that late. I get in the shower, hoping to wash the previous day away —the second half of it, anyways. With emotions calmed and no alcohol in our systems, we should be able to talk today. I pack up my things so I'll be ready to go once we're done.

I navigate the hallways between other guests leaving and housekeeping carts. I find what I think is her room, but double-check the numbers. This is it, but the door is opened— propped that way with one of the cleaning carts.

She's gone.

CHAPTER THIRTY-FIVE

Kory - January

Was he telling me the truth? I don't know, but I knew all along that it was going to be better this way.

My reaction to the idea of him leaving was exactly what I had been trying to avoid. It's why we shouldn't have even attempted being friends with benefits—I had a sinking feeling from the start that I would fail. I didn't even react that strongly to Nathan leaving, and I was with him for almost two years. I knew this is exactly how shit would end if I got attached to anyone.

After that disaster in Detroit, I returned to life on my own —back to my store and to the bar. The bar was slow in the winter, but it kept me out of the house and busy, which is how I liked to be, how I was used to being.

I did get to visit Autumn for Christmas, which was nice. I called her the day after the ceremony, but didn't tell her what happened. I know we said no more secrets, and she's my best friend—but my aversion to getting close to people because they always leave is not exactly a subject we talk about much, considering she's one of them who has done it more than once. It was a nice trip and all—and I was thankful not to spend the holiday alone—but being the third wheel was not super fun.

It was comforting to see them in their element, though. I hadn't seen them together much except for the weekend she moved into his place, and seeing them move around their kitchen together—comfortable and easy—had my stomach tightening a little. Happy for her, admittedly sad for me. I missed that feeling.

Autumn and I spent Christmas afternoon alone while he went to visit his parents. I thought it was strange that she didn't go with him—*again*—but I didn't complain. There was no telling when the next time I'd be able to see her would be.

"So what's new?" she asked while curled up on the couch with a blanket and a mug of tea. "What's happened since Thanksgiving that you haven't told me?" Her blue eyes glared at me while she blew the steam away from her cup.

"What do you mean?"

"I mean, you haven't brought him up once. So what happened?"

I naively hoped we wouldn't talk about him at all while I was there, but I should've known better. "Just wasn't going to work. Like I told you." I shrug my shoulders.

"But for what reason? It's not actually because of a job."

I scrunch my face in confusion. *How does she know that?* A mischievous grin grew, partially hidden behind her mug.

"He messaged me." She confessed. My head rolled back heavy with annoyance. "He's worried about you, Kay. That's all. I am too honestly. I've never known you to be one to self-sabotage. That's my job."

"I'm not self-sabotaging. Exactly the opposite. It's just better this way." I said, repeating the line I'd been telling myself over and over again.

"Is it though? I've never seen you light up the way you did when you talked about him. Even now—look at you—your cheeks are all red." Instinctively, my hand goes up to my face. "I'm sorry for leaving you." She says quietly. It takes me by surprise, but now I know for sure that Dom talked to her and made her feel guilty, which made me want to stop talking about him even more.

"It's fine, Autumn, we're good. Look at us?" I scooted closer to her with my own blanket draped across my legs. I lean my head on her shoulder and get a whiff of the cinnamon in her tea. "I always want you to do what makes you happy. Even if it isn't my first choice."

"Same with you," she responds, leaning her head onto mine.

I knew she was talking about him—and I knew she meant it—but it wasn't what was important at the moment.

"None of that matters. You're here, I'm here, so let's put on some cheesy, predictable Christmas love story and laugh at it together, forgetting about everything else. Okay?"

She laughed, nodded, and then we did exactly as I suggested. We remained in that spot, even falling asleep until Tyler got home and woke us up.

I rang in the new year at work since I had nowhere else to be or anyone else to be with. Olivia—once again single—and Morgan came out to celebrate *'with'* me. Part of me hoped Dom would show up, but part of me was glad he didn't. But I was missing him, and I kept finding myself there, despite knowing I was better off. The ache for him almost convinced me to reach out—just to say hi—but the fact that he hadn't reached out since Detroit stopped me. He obviously didn't care about me as much as he said he did.

After surviving the holidays the best I could, life got real quiet again.

Working both jobs wasn't enough. I was bored all the time and craving company. A company that Olivia and Morgan can't fulfill. *One thing that's always made me feel better, though?* Rearranging my furniture. That's exactly how I ended up here right now—sweating and my living room in shambles on a Wednesday afternoon. I've always done this—even when I was a teen and only had a bedroom. With my parents being gone as much as they were, it turned into a game. Elliot and I would move things around the house—subtly at first—to see if they noticed. They never did with the small things, like lamps switched, or pictured moved from one room to the other, so it grew from there. Eventually, it became almost normal to be sitting there bored, and one of us would say, *'Let's move the couch over there.'* I pause, taking a sip of my wine and smiling at the memory. To a normal person, it might sound crazy that rearranging my furniture reminds me of my brother, but not me.

After setting the glass down on the counter and returning to work, a knock on the door startles me from trying to rotate the heavy couch. I'm not expecting anyone, and I hope whoever it is doesn't mind me in an oversized T-shirt that's not mine, bike shorts, and my hair thrown up on the top of my head with a bandana headband to keep the curls out of my eyes.

I leave the couch and swing the front door open to find the absolute last person I would've expected.

"Nathan. What are you doing here?"

"I've been home for a couple of days and couldn't help wanting to visit. Can I come in?"

I shouldn't, but I motion for him to come in anyway. Maybe wine in the afternoon wasn't a great idea.

He looks around and chuckles. "Rearranging again?" He smiles—familiarly—as this is something he has shown up to before. Something he told me was cute before.

I shrug. "Yeah. You know me."

"I do." He says, piercing me with a smile that grows more than familiar. One I forgot he had. "You look adorable, by the way."

"Thanks," I say and scurry away from him—to the kitchen to offer him a water—and to drink some myself, avoiding the wine, and the way he's looking at me and how incredibly lonely I've forced myself to feel over the last few weeks.

"So I hate to sound like a jerk—but really—what are you doing here?" I ask as I hand him a bottle.

"I told you. I just wanted to see how you're doing. I go back tomorrow, so I just wanted to visit. Thought maybe we could get dinner tonight or something."

The reminder of his new life in Detroit—and how mine fell apart there—takes away any warm fuzzy feelings that may have tried to creep back in thanks to the wine and recent isolation.

"Well, thanks, I guess. I'm fine. Just staying busy like usual. But I'm going to pass on dinner. I have to finish this before I get any sleep tonight."

I go back to the couch that I was trying to move. I hear him laugh, and when I look over at him, he's unbuttoning his shirt.

"What are you doing?"

"Relax. Clearly, you need some help. Go over to that side."

His bare arms grab the end of the couch that needs to be moved the most. I motion with my head in which direction I am trying to go. My eyes watch him as my feet maneuver the space, thankfully without tripping. My eyes scan the room to look at anything but the way his muscles define under the strain of lifting. But it's not just to avoid staring at Nathan's *'okay'* arms—even though, yes, I have to admit there is a certain part of me that feels desperate enough to make a really dumb decision—but it's really to avoid thinking about how much better they'd look covered in tattoos.

"I don't think I've seen you do this much work, ever," I say as I swipe at my forehead with the back of my hand after we set the couch down in its new spot.

"I don't think so either," he agrees.

That makes us both laugh, and for a second, I'm glad he showed up, until I hear a cough at the door.

CHAPTER THIRTY-SIX

Dom

The door wasn't shut, so I let myself in. Actually, I didn't even go all the way in; I just stood in the doorway.

I gave her time. I gave her space. Autumn assured me that would work—not that I'd find her laughing with her half-naked ex. When I make my presence known, Kory jumps back, her smile sinking. He doesn't flinch at all, and his smile remains unwavering.

"Dominic," she says, surprised and out of breath. "What are you doing here?"

"What is *he* doing here?" My words come out full of fire, and I can't help but walk towards him.

"This was my apartment. Who are you?" he spits back.

Kory steps in between us with a hand on each of our chests. "Yes, *was* your apartment. It's not anymore, and you were just leaving."

He looks between the two of us—his darkening eyes leading me to believe he didn't think he was on his way out. He didn't look like he was on his way out. He scoffs, stepping back to grab his shirt, and she turns her attention to me.

"What are you doing here, Dominic?"

"I'd say I came to get my shirt, but I guess you're still enjoying it," I smirk and wink—both on purpose—and he takes the bait.

"Real cute, Kory." He angrily puts his shirt on and works the buttons together. "And roses? Really? Come on, bro, we're not fifteen."

I look down at the flowers I forgot I was holding—the stems probably broken from my grip. "They're carnations, dumb ass." I snap.

This time, he approaches me, but once again, she intercepts. "For one, I don't know why either of you is acting like this. And two…" she looks at Nathan. "They're my favorite flower, and the fact that you don't know that is a perfect reminder as to why you were just leaving." She walks to the door and stands there with folded arms. "It was good to see you. Drive safe."

He contemplates what to do, looking between us before huffing out the door with a "whatever" on the way out.

Once he's gone, I let a smile paint my lips until she slams the door shut and swirls around. "What the hell was that?"

"I thought you didn't like that guy?" I try to hand her the flowers, but she pushes them away as she brushes past me.

"I don't, but who do you think you are? I don't hear from you for a month, and you show up unannounced, acting like some possessive boyfriend?"

"Well, I didn't know he'd be here. I'm sorry. I just wanted to talk."

"Yeah, apparently everyone did today," she laughs sarcastically, then falls back onto the couch, so I set the flowers on the coffee table and join her.

"So what do you want?" she asks.

"You know what I want."

She takes a deep breath and exhales even bigger. "Why won't you give up?"

I put my hand on hers. "Because I told you I wouldn't. I can't. I was trying to give you space, but I can't do that anymore either. I miss you."

Her head turns in the opposite direction from me, staring at the wall. She inhales deeply but doesn't say anything, so I keep going.

"I know you feel something for me, too, and I'm not going to let you keep pushing me away. I'll keep trying forever if that's what it takes." She hasn't pulled her hand from mine, but she hasn't looked up at me either. "You could never push me away far enough, Brooks. You could shove me straight into the depths of hell, and I'd walk right back through the flames with a smile on my face to find you. Every single time."

The sniffle she makes has me pulling her chin back and up to finally look at me. Her eyes are red and wet. "I can't," she whispers.

"Stop saying that. You can do whatever the fuck you want to. This is about you and me. Not a single other person. No one on this planet will ever mean more to me than you do. I could never even see another person for the rest of my life, but you and I'd be fine."

She pulls her face away, then stands up to pace the room. I give her a few minutes of silence before standing in front of her and pulling her into me. She leans into my chest, so I wrap my arms completely around her. The sweet scent of her hair goes straight to my veins.

"I love you, Kory. I've never loved anyone before. It's all been saved for you, and it will never be for anyone but you."

This confession wasn't planned, but it's my last-ditch effort. A Hail Mary.

I don't know that I expect her to say it back, but my body tenses with hope. *Just maybe.* Instead, she pushes away from me and returns to pacing.

"Hey, I'm sorry," I tell her. "You don't have to say it back. I just needed to say it out loud. I've known it for too long."

She sniffles again and shakes her head. "No. You can't."

"Can't?"

"You can't love me." Her wet eyes turn into streams running down her cheeks. I try to hold her again, but she pushes me harder. "You can't love me, Dominic." She yells. "You can't do any of this." I stand there waiting for her to take it back, but she doesn't. "I'm serious. I'm better on my own. Just forget about me already. I'm begging you."

"No, I won't. Kory, I can't." I reach for her again, but she jumps back.

"I don't know how many times I have to tell you that I can't be what you want me to be. I don't want to be. Just go. And take the flowers with you."

"You're serious?"

"I'm sorry," she whispers.

I haven't felt the feelings taking over my chest since the moment I realized my family was never coming back. I've tried to tell her I understand how it feels to be left alone. I've shared this with her. But now the pain is back, and she won't even look at me, and despite months of *really* trying, I can't play it cool anymore. I storm to the table and swipe the flowers, accidentally knocking over the wine glass. The maroon liquid runs along the smooth surface, dripping some onto her feet and puddling on the floor.

"I'll get it." She says, still avoiding my eyes and quickly jumping up to leave the room. When she returns, she stands there still silent with her back to me.

"Kory…" I try to bring her back into conversation, but she throws her head up angrily.

"I don't want to be with you, Dom. What don't you get?"

I still don't believe her, but those words out of her mouth cut my heart straight in half. The hurt I've been pretending not to feel finally manifests into anger.

"You know what? Fine then. Do whatever the fuck you want. I don't care anymore." I head to the door, but stop before leaving. "Just know, I meant every word I said." I choke out before slamming the door shut.

I drive straight home, and I'm not sure if my brain is empty or if it is too full of thoughts to distinguish any.

I know I am finally in with her. She said it herself. But then she locked me out again. I don't get it, and I officially don't know what else to do.

There's only one thing that helps in a time like this, so once I'm home, I toss the crumpled flowers onto my counter with the box that was sitting on my front seat. A gift I hoped I'd give to her tonight. I storm straight for the garage, and it takes two seconds for me to jump on and take off like a rocket down the street.

I don't care that it's January. The freezing cold air stinging my face like needles is exactly what I need. You can't feel this with a helmet on. Everything blurs past me, and nothing else registers except the feeling of my face slowly turning to ice.

It's the last sensation I feel.

A screech and a crunch are the last things I hear.

The warmth of her skin is the last thing I imagine.

Then darkness is all I see.

CHAPTER THIRTY-SEVEN

Kory

He meant every word he said, yet I didn't mean a single one.

I don't think I stopped crying for hours after he left. I didn't want to.

Because not a single part of me actually wanted to do what I just did, but he was right. He would've never given up. I had to hurt him, even though I wish I hadn't.

I stop crying long enough to realize just how long it's been and to try and force myself to sleep. I heard my phone buzz a handful of times during my fit, but I ignored it. I couldn't hear his voice because it would break my heart more knowing that even after I hurt him—he would still be trying—and I'd have to hurt him again.

The only other realistic possibility would be Autumn or Olivia calling. I know he messaged Autumn before, so I wouldn't put it past him to message either one of them again, but I can't bring myself to talk to any of them. This isn't a break-up, but the whole thing hits differently than any actual break-up I've ever been through. Nothing either of them could say would help this time. This is everything I had been trying to avoid.

There is no sleep anywhere in my future, so I sit and grovel instead. Discretely wishing I could go back in time, back to when we were on the road and expectations were clear.

Boundaries were intact. It was so easy then. Back before, I really believed that our connection was real, not just a hormone-induced convenience.

But that's because I also almost forgot why I'm better off on my own. Why I always have been. I can't risk allowing him to continue burrowing himself deeper into my soul, because the gaping hole he would leave behind when he left would be too much for me to handle. It might already be.

My phone rings again, and I look at it this time. It's a number I don't recognize, but with a local area code. At this time of night, it can only be pre-teens up past their bedtime making prank calls. Life was better back when we were that age, when you couldn't trace the number back to you. Maybe you can still hide it, but I don't think this generation has figured that out yet. It starts ringing again as soon as the last call ends. *Good God.* I think about answering just to tell them to shut up, but I also don't want to argue with twelve-year-olds. I hit the ignore button, then look at the recent call log. There are eleven missed calls—from two numbers—both local and neither of them saved in my phone.

The thought crosses my mind to Google them, but before I do, a small circle with a message attached pops up on the screen. I see Jimmy's face in the message bubble, which causes my eyebrow to crease through my crying-induced headache.

> Kory, call me. It's about Dom.
> 7182630784

That's one of the numbers that's been calling—nine of the eleven times. I'm instantly cold as the blood in my veins turns to ice. *It's about Dom.* Something is wrong.

I immediately click the number so that it calls him. he answers right away.

"Kory?" his voice is breathless.

"What's wrong, Jimmy?"

"He was in an accident. He wasn't wearing his helmet. You should get here."

Now it feels as if my stomach has frozen, too. It's hard and heavy. I feel like I can't breath. My body feels too heavy for my lungs to expand. *He wasn't wearing his helmet?*

"His helmet? Why was he on his bike? It's freezing outside?"

"I don't know, but you should just get here."

I say some words, then he says some words. Some must have been what hospital they're at, because the next thing I know, I'm speeding down the road.

My veins are still frozen solid, but my face is hot, and the longer this drive takes, all that ice melts into beads of sweat and streams of tears.

This is my fault. He was on the bike because of me. It hits me as I practically blow through a stop sign. He rode his bike when he had a bad day. He had a bad day because of me. I hurt him emotionally *and* physically.

My lungs all but stop working, leaving me struggling to take a breath in. Then a switch flips and I can't keep up with the amount of breaths my lungs want to take. With my whole body heaving, I have no other choice but to pull over. I close my eyes and lean my head back against the seat. Both hands still grip the steering wheel as I talk myself through breathing. *In 2, 3, 4... Out 2, 3, 4. In through the nose. Out through the mouth.*

After a few moments of steady breathing and logical thinking for the first time since I saw Jimmy's message, I know I won't be any help when I get there if I'm a mess. I need to at least try to keep my shit together. I lean forward until my head rests on the steering wheel instead and say a little prayer —a real, genuine one for maybe the first time in my life—both for him to be okay and for me to be able to hold it together.

It works enough for me to resume driving and make it there safely, but once I'm in the hospital parking lot, I find myself once again out of breath and frantic as I search the hallways for the right waiting room—forgetting the details I'm sure Jimmy already explained.

A very sweet nurse sees the state I'm in and directs me to a desk with another nice lady who asks for his name. I spit it out, and she explains he's in the OR but tells me where I can go to wait. The first nice nurse offers to walk with me, but I tell her no, thank you. I need another minute.

The OR? Surgery?

I wish they'd told me what kind. But maybe they didn't for a reason. At least surgery meant he's alive, I guess.

I barrel through a glass door to find Jimmy sitting there alone. He jumps up, and I run into him, throwing my arms around him, surprising us both. I don't know why, but he returns my embrace and holds it there until I pull away.

"What's going on? What happened?"

He sits back down, pulling me down into the chair next to him. "He was on the bike, and it appears he lost control—sending him and the bike… into a guardrail. They're not sure if another car was involved yet or not."

"So what's wrong with him? Why is he in surgery?"

"He had bleeding in his brain, a broken wrist, and one of his legs was also broken. Their biggest concern is obviously his brain, but while he wasn't awake, his body was still responding, so it didn't appear that the bleed needed surgery. The surgery he is in is to put his leg back together." he pauses. "They are a little concerned about him waking up, though. Just from a pretty intense surgery combined with a brain injury—even if the brain injury seems mild."

Tears begin falling again before I even register them. I can't sit still, so I jump out of the seat and start pacing, much like I was doing hours ago in my apartment, when I caused all of this.

"So we just sit here? What about his parents? His sister?" Jimmy's eyebrows crease. "Did you call them? Are they on their way to Michigan?"

"What are you talking about?"

"His *family,* Jimmy. I know they don't talk, but surely they would want to know this. Did you call them?" I demand again.

Jimmy stands up and approaches me. Instinctively, I want to back away, but I don't, allowing him to place both his hands on my shoulders. His brown eyes look softly into mine.

"I can't call them."

"Then I'll do it. Give me their numbers."

"There are no numbers to call."

"What does that even mean, Jimmy? Of course, there's a number somewhere."

"No, there's not. They're dead, Kory."

CHAPTER THIRTY-EIGHT

Dom

I know I'm dreaming because I've seen this all before. I try to force myself awake because I don't like where I know this memory is heading, but I can't.

My parents' entryway is in front of me with a bunch of suitcases surrounding it, packed full of excitement and hope.

Kami got into college in New York. It was her dream school. Mom and Dad were going with her to help look for an apartment in the city, so that they could come home and pack all her things, then move her there for real.

I chose to stay home to work and house sit. I would be lying if I said I wasn't a little bit upset about the new school of hers. My sister was my best friend, and the thought of her being in another state indefinitely irritated me to my core, disappointing me most. *If only I'd known it would end up so much worse than just a few states away.*

Further confirming that I am dreaming—or something—I watch myself walk past me and grab the suitcases. My mom and dad follow, then Kami. Dad holds the door open, and I help them carry all the bags to the car.

I blink and we're suddenly at the airport, parked in the drop-off lane with other eager early morning commuters. Standing invisibly in the middle of the road, I watch as I hug each one of my family members for the last time. I remember telling them that I loved them, even though deep down I was not happy about the whole thing.

I remember hugging my sister for an extra minute, telling her that she's not going to love it that much and that she'll change her mind and decide she doesn't want to live there and wants to come home. She laughed but said nothing as we held each other tight with tears gathered in our eyes. *Twins—never have been separated before—seconds away from being separated forever.*

They grab their suitcases and begin wheeling them away. All three of them stop at the door and wave one last time before disappearing into the sea of people inside.

Another blink puts me in my bedroom, sitting on the edge of my bed, my phone on the floor. I know what just happened. I just got the call. The call saying there was a catastrophic engine failure on the Manhattan tour boat. It caused an explosion. No one survived. My only three family members were on that boat.

My family had been gone for over twenty-four hours before they were able to identify who they were and figure out who to contact.

Fucking Kami. I knew that was her idea. She just had to get all the touristy things out of the way because she refused to be a transplant who still acted like a tourist. She insisted on doing all of those things during this trip.

And because of that, I would never see her again.

With the next blink, things go back to being all dark.

CHAPTER THIRTY-NINE

Kory

"What do you mean they're dead?" I ask, suddenly feeling faint.

Jimmy looks back at me with wide, confused eyes. I glare back at him, but then the faintness I felt turns into heaviness that makes me sit back down. I lower slowly into the stiff waiting room chair, both trying to process what he just said and waiting for some type of response.

Kami. His twin. His best friend. *We've talked about her? How has he never mentioned the fact that she's not alive?*

Jimmy sits down next to me. The chair squeaks while he adjusts himself before finally responding. "They died right after we graduated high school. A boat accident."

My forehead rests in my sweaty hands, still in shock. I just don't understand. "All of them? In the same accident?"

"Yes. Dom was the only one who didn't go on that trip."

I turn my head to look at him, hoping the horror in my eyes will be met with joking in his. It isn't. He keeps talking.

"He took it hard. He didn't have any other family, so when that happened, he was left on his own, to take care of it all."

Inside my head, there is a tornado right now, swirling all of our conversations around, trying to pinpoint where I may have missed this information. His family was a touchy subject, but there was never a time that he alluded to them being dead.

I thought they just left him—that we had that in common—this is so much worse.

"But he told me they went to New York?"

Jimmy nods. "They did. That's where it happened."

I stare ahead of me at the textured wall and chew on my lip. "I can't believe he never told me."

"I can. I'm honestly surprised you knew they existed at all. I haven't heard him say anything about them in years, since the funerals, actually."

"But why talk about them like they're still alive?"

Jimmy shrugs. "I don't think he's ever really grieved them. He just kept going, almost pretending like it never happened. He's obviously comfortable with you, though. He listed you and me as his emergency contacts in his phone. That's why the hospital called us."

I lean forward, putting my head back in my hands. All this time, I've been fighting what I feel for him. Acting like a stupid spoiled brat who doesn't want to get attached for selfish reasons. Pushing someone away who's just trying to love me. Venting to him about how awful my life is because I can only talk to my family on the phone, when his is gone completely. I've probably sounded like such a crybaby. I wonder how many times he wanted to say 'At *least your family is alive.'*

And then there's him. I've done nothing but try and push him away, and he's done nothing but try harder. I'm his fucking emergency contact for God's sake. Because he has no one else. And because he loves me.

My cheeks are hot and wet, and a tear drips onto my arm. I feel Jimmy's hand pat my back, and I appreciate his silent support as I sort through all this.

"He told me he loved me tonight."

"About time." He says with what might be a chuckle.

"I told him I didn't want to be with him." A deep jagged breath hits my lungs, causing my body to stutter, as if it's trying to stop the sobs that are imminent with that confession.

"It will be okay," he says.

"Jimmy," I whisper, pausing then forcing the next words out of my mouth. "What if he doesn't wake up?"

Just as I finish the sentence, sobs rake violently through my body, and my tears are no longer quiet. He pulls me in, and I let myself fall into his chest and break.

How do I live with myself after this? I love him too. I can't deny it. I won't. The thought of living without him existing causes another shaky sob to bubble out. *What if he's gone after our last conversation?* This can't be how it ends for us. I have so much to say to him. So much that I should have said. He was right and I was wrong. I love him. And I need him to hear me say it.

For the second time in my life, I pray. Curled up practically in the lap of my best friend's ex—my one enemy—sobbing loudly in this hospital room, I beg God to bring him out of this.

To bring him back to me so I can fix this. So I can say it back.

CHAPTER FORTY

Dom

My eyes want to open, but I struggle under the bright light. After a few strained blinks, they finally open and stare straight up at the sun.

The sound of waves reaches my ears, and all of my senses turn back on. I feel under my bare feet that I'm standing in sand.

Why am I here? I take in my surroundings, pretty sure this is Lake Michigan, but it's hard to tell. There's no one here. Or so I thought.

"Hey, shithead."

My skin prickles at the sound of the unmistakable voice. A voice I haven't heard in years.

I turn around and, despite it being impossible, see her walking towards me. She is glowing—maybe literally—wearing a flowing white dress. My chest pounds as the figure comes closer into view—light skin and onyx hair—genetics that almost identically mirror mine.

"Kami?" My voice cracks with confusion.

"The one and only," she replies as she opens up her arms.

It takes me only a second to close the gap and wrap my sister up tightly, lifting her off the ground. We squeeze each other until I realize the only way that this is possible.

"Wait. Am I?..."

She smiles and shakes her head. "Almost, but no, you're still alive. People dressed like that never stay for long." She reaches for my hand, and against mine I can see that she does, in fact, have a faint glow to her while I'm just in a regular black T-shirt and jeans—what I last remember wearing—*I think.*

We sit down on a log, and she stares out at the water, but I can't pull my eyes off of her. They swell as I stare at my—dead—sister beside me, trying to figure out how this is even possible. Her long, straight hair blows in the wind and tickles my arm. I can physically feel her. This cannot be real, but it sure feels like it. She looks over at me and giggles, then lays her head on my shoulder. I lay my head onto hers.

"What happened?" I ask. "Why am I here?"

"Accident on dad's stupid bike. You'll be okay, though. You did just enough damage to come visit me." She smiles mischievously, and I feel a tear slide down my cheek.

I missed that look on her face so much. I'm still struggling to accept that any of this is real and the fact that, apparently, I'm pretty messed up. But if I had to almost die to see my sister again, it was worth it.

"Was I by myself?"

"Yes. Just you. No other drivers. You lost control."

I let out a sigh of relief, knowing it could've been worse. We sit together quietly watching the water. I feel like we should take advantage of this weird limbo state and talk, but I don't know what to say. I'm just happy to be here.

"Are you going to tell me about her?" She breaks the silence.

"Who?"

"The girl you were worried about being on the back of your bike." She looks up at me and smiles again.

"Her name is Kory. With a K- like you." I start to cry again—or more—I don't even know. *Does she know how much I've wanted to have this conversation with her? How much I've needed to have this conversation with her?*

"She's a pain in the ass. But she's funny—witty, smart, strong, independent. She makes me laugh without even trying. She's insanely stubborn."

"She sounds like you," she says.

The waves crash closer to us each time they come in. I watch them and continue talking. "Sometimes, her eyes remind me of the caramel candies grandma always used to have. But then other times they remind me of the green of Dad's. Her voice sounds like mom's, especially when she sings or hums like mom did while she's working, cleaning, and reading. Oh yeah, she loves to read, she's always reading—looks just like how you did with your face in a book all the time. Her favorite place is this lake. Guess what her favorite snacks are?"

"Chocolate-covered pretzels." We both say in unison.

"It's like she was put here to complete me—to fill in all the pieces of me—she has pieces of all of you." I stop and sniffle.

"You love her." She says. She doesn't ask. She doesn't sound unsure at all. She's telling me.

"I do, and I told her, but she didn't say it back."

"She loves you, too, Dom."

"Can you tell *her* that?" I make a joke and bump my shoulder into hers and sniffle.

"Oh, she knows now." We are quiet for a few minutes as the water comes in even closer, touching my toes now.

"I don't know what to do, Kam. I've tried everything."

"Waking up would be a good start." She laughs, then stands up, so I follow. She links her arm in mine as we start to walk, feeling the sand shift beneath my feet and watching the cattails sway with the wind.

"I don't want to wake up yet," I admit.

She tightens her hold on my arm and rests her head back on my shoulder. "You can't fix anything from here."

"I'm so sorry, Kami. I should've been there." I tell her, fighting back tears again.

She smacks my arm. "Stop it, Dom. You couldn't have done anything differently. If you had been there, then you'd be dead too. At least we have someone to watch from up here."

"But you should be there too."

She scoffs. "Look at this place? The weather is perfect all the time. I never get sick. I don't have bills to pay. This was my favorite place and literally what I hoped Heaven would be. And now I'm here forever with no more concerns, ever. I promise you, I'm fine here." She stops and faces me. "But you. You have things to do. A life to live—to build with the perfect girl for you. I know, I picked her out myself."

The last comment chokes me up, and she smiles up at me as she takes a step forward and tucks her arms under mine. She rests her cheek on my chest, and I hold on tight with a sudden feeling that I won't be here much longer.

"All I want for you is for you to go and live life." She says, "Do all the things you don't believe you should because we're not there to see them. Be happy. Get married. Have kids. Name one Kami."

We both laugh at her comment, and I lightly kiss the top of her head. It's still crazy to me that this isn't real. I rest my cheek back on her head and breath in the calming scent of her shampoo—the one she and my mom always used.

"You've got a deal," I tell her.

"Also, quit being a weirdo and tell her about us. She'll listen."

For the first time since they left, the thought of telling Kory the truth about my family doesn't completely scare the shit out of me. I might just be able to do it.

"I love you, Dominic."

"I love you too, Kami," I say, before everything is dark again.

CHAPTER FORTY-ONE

Kory

I stare at him, waiting for something—*anything*—to indicate he is about to wake up.

They said he's breathing on his own and is *'just sleeping,'* so it should be any minute. But that was ten hours ago. I watch as his eyelids flutter, just hoping that one of these times means they'll pop open and the emeralds hidden underneath will be looking back at me.

The staring has also been necessary to adjust to him looking the way he does. His face is bruised, somehow not cut, but he's definitely bruised and swollen. His head is wrapped in white bandages, and I know he'll be mad as hell when he wakes up to find out they had to shave his head. It was done as a hasty precaution, before they realized they—thankfully—weren't going to need to operate on his skull. His leg—fully casted—hangs elevated for the majority of the day. But he's alive, and every time I see a finger twitch, or his eyeball roll under one of the lids, I know we're getting closer.

Jimmy's passed out with his head leaning back on the extra chair. I've seen a different side of him since we've been here—one I forgot existed. Jimmy was never the bad of a guy, and watching him pace this room alongside me and share my concern for his friend reminded me of that. I don't know that I'll ever totally forgive him for what he did to Autumn—and Becca, for that matter—but maybe I'll try.

The stiff plastic chair creaks as I sit in it, causing Jimmy to wake up. "How long was I out?" He asks, rubbing his eyes.

"I don't know. An hour, maybe?"

He runs his hands through his hair, then checks his phone. He looks over at Dom, then back at me. "Anything?"

I shake my head. Still nothing. *Lots of nothing.*

"I need to go get Em," he says as he stands. "It's my week, so I need to get her and take her to my mom's. Then I can be back."

My eyes grow wide as I realize what he just said. "Your week?"

He nods. "We're separated."

"Wow," I respond, both surprised and a little annoyed. *He put Autumn through all of that for what? To still end up divorced five years later?*

"She left me." He adds, as if he can read my mind. "It's new. She said she just couldn't do it anymore. That when she realized she was only staying with me because of Emery; she couldn't be 'one of those' people."

"Ouch. She said that to you?"

His lips tighten in a straight line while he nods his head. That does sound like something Becca would say, though. Honestly, I was surprised she even took him back in the first place. "I'm sorry," I say, able to fill my voice with more compassion than I would have a few days ago.

"Don't be. I'm okay. We tried to recover—played the part as best we could—we just couldn't ever get there." We stare at each other for a moment, neither of us entirely sure what to say. I never expected him to want to tell me this much of his personal life, and I don't think he did either, but he continues, already at the point of no return. "It wasn't directly related to what I did; I really feel this would've ended up happening regardless."

We both know he's talking about him and Autumn's affair without coming out and saying it. I nod. I can hear in his voice that he believes what he is saying. There isn't an ounce of mourning for his marriage in it. Just *it is what it is.* Maybe he's right, but it's not my problem. *Well, as long as Autumn stays her ass in New Jersey, it won't be my problem.*

"Still sorry. Not a fun thing to go through, even if you are a total dick."

The laugh he responds with lets me know he knows I'm joking. *Mostly.*

"There's the Kory I know." He pats his pockets for his keys. "I'll be gone just an hour or two at the most. Call me if anything changes, please?"

"Will do," I say as he leaves.

I lean my head back in the uncomfortable chair and go back to staring at Dom in the bed. He looks peaceful. And I hope he is, because I'm silently cursing at him for pulling me in after all, causing me to still be stuck having to hear about Jimmy and his relationship problems.

CHAPTER FORTY-TWO

Dom

A steady cadence of beeping alerts me that something has changed again. *What am I dreaming now?* I still can't see anything, but I can hear the short, high-pitched noises.

I listen closer and then also hear footsteps, then someone clearing their throat.

"I brought you some food."

It's Jimmy's voice. Kory's voice follows, and I smile—at least I think I do—it feels like I do.

"You didn't have to do that," she tells him, then I hear the crinkling of paper bags.

As my senses continue to wake up, the strong salty smell of greasy fast food fills my nose, but is immediately followed by her familiar citrusy scent. The sweet, delicious aroma has me wanting to taste it, and suddenly, I think I do. My tongue tingles just imagining the taste of her, and it wakes up my sense of touch. Now I can feel the course blanket underneath my hands.

Jimmy's voice registers again. "You haven't left this room in almost two days. You need to eat."

I think I feel a smile again. *Can I talk? I have to try.*

"And… you don't… even like… me." I scratch out slowly.

I hear her gasp, then she's at the side of my bed, with one hand on my shoulder and the other gripping my hand. *I'm so glad I can feel again.*

"Dominic. Oh my God." She takes her hand off my shoulder and touches the side of my face. I lean into the feeling as I attempt to open my eyes.

It's so much brighter in here than either of my dreams. It takes so much effort and so much blinking before I can finally pull my eyes all the way open. Finally, Kory is the first thing that comes into focus, just as I hoped, staring at me with wide, honey-dripping eyes.

"Jimmy! Go get somebody!" she demands, without breaking eye contact. As Jimmy follows her orders and heads out of the room, she leans down and squishes our lips together.

"Are we about to hook up in this hospital bed, or are you breaking your own rules?" I croak, my voice still barely audible.

"Fuck those stupid rules." She says through a tearful laugh. "I thought you were gone," she continues, still tearful, but no longer laughing.

"I think I was," I say and wince. With all my senses finally waking up, so has the pain.

"Shhh, don't move." She says and rubs my head before reaching and pushing the red button on the wall as incessantly as I was pushing the elevator button in Detroit, trying to get to her.

"What hurts?"

As I try to focus on it, I realize I can't really pinpoint it. Everything kind of hurts. My head, my back, my arm, my legs. Shifting—which just makes all the pain worse—I realize my right arm and leg are in casts. My leg is restrained all the way up to my hip.

She must notice my reaction. "You broke your femur, and they had to replace it with metal. You also broke your wrist, bruised your lung, and had a small bleed in your brain."

I reach up and rub my hand along my head, now realizing it's bandaged. Before I can respond or even continue processing everything she just told me, people pour into the room.

"Dominic, how great to see you awake. I'm Dr. Hayes. Nice to finally meet you." The woman in the white coat says with a bright smile. A few others in navy blue scrubs start working around machines and taking my vitals. "Quite the spill you took, young man. How do you feel right now?"

"I think everything hurts."

Dr. Hayes chuckles. "I bet it does. We'll get that taken care of for you here in a second."

"What happened?" I ask.

In the background, I can see Kory and Jimmy glance at each other before the doctor answers me.

"You were in a motorcycle accident. Lost control and hit the guardrail. You are very lucky to be alive, especially after not wearing a helmet. Do you remember any of it?" I shake my head no. "Do you remember anything from that day?" She adds.

I squint my eyes as if that will help me focus. I remember my sister—the dream version of her—explaining this already, but I can't pull an actual memory of the accident. I don't even remember getting on the bike. The last thing I have a vivid memory of was speeding home from Kory's apartment. Broken by the fact that she told me she didn't want to be with me. I look up at her and see the guilt strewn across her face. She quickly avoids eye contact and looks at the floor.

"No, not really." I lie.

"Well, you were pretty banged up and again, very lucky to be alive. Your memory will come back in time."

I look over at Jimmy, who thankfully isn't scowling at me just yet. He always gave me shit when I'd jump on for a quick ride without my helmet. An *I told you so'* is definitely in my future. The doctor keeps talking. "We had to repair your lung and reconstruct your leg. Thankfully, your wrist just needed casting, but the leg is going to have your longest recovery time. You need a lot of healing and therapy before you can hold your weight." Kory comes back to the side of the bed, grabbing my hand again. "But all your vitals look great. I'm sure you will have no issues recovering with these two. They haven't left your side, so it's good to know you'll have good support through this process."

I look up at Kory, her eyes still wet, then over at Jimmy, who is approaching the other side of me.

"Thanks, Doc," I say as she starts to back away.

"They'll be in with your meds any time now."

"Good to see you, bro," Jimmy says once she's gone, lightly tapping on my shoulder.

"Yeah, you too." I struggle to cough. My rib lights on fire. "Can I have some water, please?"

Kory grabs a cup with a straw already hanging out of it and holds it to my mouth. The cooling sensation that takes over my mouth and body as I rehydrate myself is one of the best feelings I've ever felt. My eyes look up at hers, and they become locked together—suddenly I'm remembering the *top* best feeling I've ever felt and wish Jimmy wasn't in this room. I can't fight the smirk that forms around the straw as I continue to welcome the hydration into my body, or eyes never leaving each other.

"Well," Jimmy slices through the tension. "I'm going to go call and check on Em. I'll be back in a few." He disappears from the room as soon as he finishes his sentence.

Once he's gone, Kory sets the cup back down on the table, then returns to the side of my face.

With just a little more effort than normal, I am able to slide a grin across my dry lips. "So, do you sleep at hospitals for two days for all the guys you don't want to be with?"

CHAPTER FORTY-THREE

Kory

I don't get a chance to respond to his smart ass remark before a nurse comes into the room with some pain relief.

She asks him his pain level, which he responds with an eight point five. He gets a couple of pills and a tiny cup of water. As he is swallowing those, she also puts something in his IV.

"We'll start you off with these for now. Let us know if it helps you or not."

He nods, and she smiles back. A few seconds later, we're alone again.

"I'll have you know, sir, I only stay at hospitals for guys I really, *really* don't want to be with."

His smirk instantly mirrors mine, and suddenly I'm fighting tears again. None have escaped, but he sees the change and reaches his good arm up towards me.

"Come here."

The way he notices these things about me is exactly why I'm holding these tears back, and as I climb into this tiny space next to him in the bed, they start to flow freely.

"When did you get so soft?" he asks as he strokes my hair.

"I'm so sorry."

He laughs, followed by a wince. "For what?"

"For everything." I sniffle. "For being a stubborn brat. For pretending I didn't like you when all you've done is care about me and be nice to me. For going out of my way to be a bitch to you, just to prove a point." I stop and look up slightly —into his eyes. "For telling you that I didn't want to be with you." I place my hand against his cheek. "That was the biggest lie I've ever told."

He leans down to kiss me, and his lips feel slightly warmer than they've ever felt before. Maybe it's because we both know now that we want *this*. We want us. It's not a warm-up to sex. It's not something I'm going to brush off and pretend means nothing. My whole body can feel this kiss. Every nerve ending from my toes to my scalp is lit up. *Something has changed.*

My body instinctively pulls closer to his to intensify the kiss when he jerks quickly back. "Ow, ow. Damn it."

"Oh my God, your rib. I'm so sorry." I push up on the headrest to get out of the bed, but he grabs my arm.

"No. Please, stay." He says, "Just…" He adjusts us both as much as he can so that he is up against the other side, giving me the tiniest bit more space on this side. He folds his arm around me and tucks my head near his armpit and peck muscle. "Much better."

I feel his chin nuzzle in my hair, and neither of us says anything. I lie here inhaling his scent with every breath. Two days in the hospital and yet he still smells like—him. While enjoying being putty in his arms, it occurs to me that he never responded to my apology, nor did I actually tell him I loved him.

"So do you forgive me?"

He doesn't answer, so I bend my neck back to see his face and have to stifle a laugh.

The meds must have kicked in, and he is knocked out— mouth open and all. I tuck my head right back into its place, content to stay here until he's conscious again. Maybe I might actually get some sleep, too. But just a few minutes later, Jimmy comes back into the room and I pretend not to notice the smile on his face when he sees me in the bed. I don't care. After sitting back in his chair, he must have realized that the food he got me still sits there untouched.

"You know, you still need to eat something. He's not getting out of that bed and disappearing anytime soon."

"Ha ha," I say sarcastically—feeling my hot breath rush back into my face with how tight I have myself cuddled into his chest.

But he's right. Now that the adrenaline of him waking up, seeing him be his normal self, and getting part of what I needed off my chest, I realize I am *starving*. I slide out of the bed, careful not to push on him, and go straight for the food. I shovel McDonald's fries and chicken nuggets into my mouth so fast, I'm not convinced that they aren't sitting in my stomach as intact pieces. I stuff the empty containers back into the garbage can.

"Feel better, don't you?"

"Much. Thank you. Made it even better, that was my favorite."

"I know. That's why I got it."

My face creases so hard, causing my eyes to squint. "How would you know that?"

He nods his head towards Dom. "He has a list in his wallet. I found it when they gave me his stuff, and I was trying to find his insurance card."

My mouth falls open, but no words come out. He chuckles, then reaches for the bag that has what I now assume are Dom's things. Taking the creased piece of paper in my hands, I open it to find a handwritten list. One that looks similar to the list of rules I gave him, but this one is titled "Kory's favorite things." There are words scribbled in different colors of ink; obviously, he added things as I mentioned them. No wonder he always knew what I wanted; he carried this list with him everywhere.

A tear hits the page, and I quickly shake it before it messes anything up. Jimmy reaches his hand out and as he returns it back into Dom's wallet, he looks back at me. "Don't tell him I showed you that."

I nod, agreeing with him, but my mind is spinning with the amount of effort this man put into winning me over. All the while, I put the same amount of effort into keeping him away.

"Hey," Jimmy says, pulling me back to the present. "You guys are gonna be okay."

CHAPTER FORTY-FOUR

Kory

With Jimmy gone again, once again dealing with dad duties, I take advantage of his absence to ask one of the questions I've been dying to.

"So Jimmy's separated, huh?"

I also want to ask Dom about his family, but I won't. I want him to want to tell me more than I want to ask.

"He's telling people? He said he wanted to keep it quiet for a while."

"He told me at least."

Dom adjusts himself in the bed so that he's sitting up a little bit more. I help him fix the pillow behind his head. "Well, good. I think he was a little embarrassed. Like, they went through all that for what? I get it, but I'm glad he's coming around to just accepting it."

"He didn't want it to end?" I hand him his cup, which he can now grab from me and drink himself.

"No, but I think he realized he made the wrong choice." He pauses, and I know he's talking about choosing to stay with Becca instead of Autumn. "Did he mention that it wasn't because of the affair?" I nod my head, and he laughs. "Yeah, he keeps saying that like he's trying to convince himself. And he didn't seem upset by her leaving him at all, which is weird, right? He just said he wasn't telling anyone right away, which then turned into not talking about it at all."

I respond with nothing but a quiet *hmph,* wondering if he hears the irony in his words. His entire family has passed away, yet he talks about them as if they just moved to another state. I watch him lie his head back on the pillow—eyes shut —wondering if he's thinking about it too. I really want him to tell me on his own time, but I also don't know how long I can pretend Jimmy didn't drop a whole bomb. Well, two of them, if you count his own.

That makes me think of Autumn and ignites the internal debate of whether I should tell her about his separation or not. I probably shouldn't, but as her best friend, this is the exact kind of gossip from our small town that she relies on me to call her about. I look back at Dom, who has dozed off again— taken under by his latest dose of medication—and grab my phone. In the hall, I hope for service, and thankfully, it connects right away.

"Kory! God, I've been waiting forever for you to call. How is he? How are you?" She rambles the second her face fills the screen.

"I know. I'm so sorry. It's been crazy."

"No, no, you're fine. I'm just happy to see your tired face." She flashes a sympathetic smile, and it makes me smile back.

"That bad, huh?"

"You're beautiful as ever. I can just tell you've been sleeping in a hospital chair." She pauses. "So, how's your man?"

For the first time, my instinct i*sn't* to say he's not. I smile instead and let the butterflies in my stomach flutter freely, finally let out of their cage. Autumn catches my response and smiles widely.

"Look at you! I don't know that I've ever seen that look on your face, Kay! Feels good to stop being so stubborn, huh?"

"Fine, okay! I give up! My best friend was right. He was right. Everyone was right except me. Happy now?"

She leans back, and I can tell by the bob of her head that she's kicking her feet like a teenager.

"Ahh, yes! I love it. And I love you. And I love this *for* you. I just wish it hadn't taken this to happen. Now tell me, how is he?"

For the next few minutes, I explain what I can remember. Every few hours is another visit from a doctor, a new specialist, a new therapist, and they all have new information, new things they are watching for.

"It could be up to six months for his leg to completely heal enough to walk. He didn't take that well."

"My God..." she says.

"I know." I'm so engrossed in the conversation that I don't hear anyone approaching until he's already talking.

"How's he doing?" Jimmy asks as he pauses next to me before opening the door.

Autumn's eyes widen at the sound of his voice, though she tries to recover and pretend they don't. Then, to make it worse, I see him glance over my shoulder, and they both notice each other before he quickly turns away and goes back into the room.

I debate following that brief but awkward interaction with the news of his impending divorce, but I can't bring myself to do it. *Not now.* Instead, I fill her in on the other bomb he dropped.

"Hey, do you remember Dom having a sister in high school? A twin?"

"Maybe, but I've been trying real hard to forget most memories from back then."

We both laugh, knowing that was an ode to who just walked by. "Well, he did apparently. A twin who was his best friend, and a mom and dad who all died." I whisper close to the phone. "And he never told me."

"Well, I mean, you were keeping him at an arm's length, weren't you? I don't know if I'd open up completely to someone like that either."

"Okay, but that's not the point. We talked about them—a few times—he never mentioned them being dead." I whisper the last word again. "I told him about my family, and he talked about his as if he knew how I felt. But that's crazy because my parents just don't care."

"Maybe he just doesn't want to deal with it. I don't have a sibling, Kory, but I'd probably rather die if I knew I could never talk to you again. I'd pretend you were alive too, for my own sanity."

I purse a puff of air through my lips. "I know. I just wish he'd talk to me about it. Especially now."

She laughs lightly. "Kay, the guy just had brain surgery and woke up to find out he almost died. Give him time, I'm sure he will."

"It wasn't brain surgery, but ugh, you're right."

"Again," she shows her teeth through her obnoxious smile.

"Yeah, yeah, whatever. I'm going to get a snack. I'll call you later."

"Or try and sleep. Call me tomorrow."

"Okay. Love you."

"Love you too."

I slide my phone in my pocket while walking to the vending machine. Her point is valid. All of them. That's exactly why you need a best friend to remind you of a different perspective other than the one you're consumed in.

I know I love him. I know I've been feeling that way for some time, but now that Autumn has me thinking about it, I still haven't said it back.

I wouldn't open up that vulnerably to someone who kept pushing me away, either.

I kept saying that this wasn't serious, that it was only temporary. *Why would he share his darkest secret with someone who planned on leaving him?*

And just like that, the irony of what *I* was saying hit me like a ton of bricks.

Exactly what I am most afraid of happening to me, I was doing to him all along. In order to keep myself from getting hurt, I became what I hated the most.

I lean my forehead against the vending machine glass as I listen to the bag of pretzels fall. Inhaling deeply, I fight the emotions trying to resurface from that revelation. I stand back up straight to see a nurse watching me with concern in her eyes.

"I'm okay, thank you. Just tired."

She nods before retreating, and I grab my snack out of the bottom. The package crinkles in my hands as I fidget with it, still wrestling with too many thoughts. Pushing back the conversations and questions that don't need to be asked right now and trying to figure out how to finally say the one thing that *does* need to be said.

CHAPTER FORTY-FIVE

Dom

It's amazing how they expect anyone to sleep in here when every thirty minutes someone comes in to check on me —scanning barcodes, shifting my stiff body parts, shining lights in my eyes, handing me cups of pills to swallow.

I had finally just dozed off when I woke to my nurse switching out an IV bag and clicking away on her rolling computer. Jimmy is standing near the window, but Kory is missing.

"Where is she?" I try to shift myself to sit up.

His head turns towards me with a laugh. "Hello to you too. She's in the hallway talking to Autumn."

My head tilts. "Autumn's here?"

"No," he says, rather quickly, and I don't miss the disappointment in his voice. "They're on the phone."

"How are you doing? Kory said you told her about Becca." I know that he knows I'm not really asking about Becca, but I also know he doesn't want to actually talk about Autumn.

"I'm fine. Just getting used to all the going back and forth. Em's with my mom for the day." He lifts a plastic shopping bag from the table. "I grabbed some stuff from your place. Shower stuff. Clean clothes when and if you can ever wear them again." His lips pick up in an amused grin.

"That's awesome. Thank you, man." I cannot wait to be able to shower myself with my own stuff.

"So, speaking of what I told Kory," he starts, rubbing his fingers into the back of his neck. "She knows about your parents. And Kami."

It takes me a second to register what he's just said. As it's settling in my brain, I ignore the pain to sit up straight. He comes around the side of the bed to help.

"I'm sorry. I didn't know she didn't know. She got here and started demanding someone call them."

That actually makes me smile. I can picture it. The fire she has inside of her was probably bursting out—invisible smoke blowing from her nose and ears. *For me.*

"It's okay. I should have just told her already. I just hate saying it."

"I know." He nods. "I know you do. Just wanted to give you the heads up so you're not blindsided if she brings it up."

"I appreciate it. All of this, too." I motion around the room with my uncast arm. "Thank you. Seriously."

"Don't worry about it, man. You'd do the same for me."

I nod in agreement because he's right. "When she comes back? Can you give us a few minutes?"

As if on cue, Kory walks in the door carrying a bag of chocolate-covered pretzels in her hands. I watch her toss one in her mouth and think of my sister's recent words—*tell her about us, you weirdo.*

Answering my question with a single nod of his head, Jimmy walks towards the door. "My turn for a snack," he says before he vanishes into the bright hallway. Kory chews and waves with the other hand, and he passes by her. Once he's gone, she sits in the chair up by my head.

I take a minute to look at her before talking. He hair is thrown up, haphazardly, tendrils falling throughout and around her face. Her loose T-shirt—my T-shirt— exposes a bit of her shoulder and collarbone. As my eyes take it all in, an ache that medicine can't fix takes over.

Proving that she can, in fact, read my mind, a smirk spreads across her lips. "See something you like?" she pops another pretzel in her mouth suggestively.

"A few things. Come back here." She knows I'm asking for a kiss, so she leans right in. Her soft, chocolate-flavored lips push into mine, making the ache so much worse. "Does my door lock?"

She laughs as she pulls away. "You have quite some time, sir. Simmer down."

I lean my head back into my pillow petulantly. "I'll never make it."

Her laugh continues as she sits back down. My eyes remain fixed on her again, but for a different reason. For the moment that just happened. An action as simple as her getting up and kissing me. For no reason other than I wanted one. We haven't really talked about *'us'* yet, but now I know we have time. She's here. I'm alive. That's all that matters.

We do need to talk, though, but not about us. It's time to have the conversation I've never had with anyone—never planned to have with anyone—except for Jimmy. But in this moment, watching her sit there enjoying her and my sister's favorite snack with a smile on her face, I *want* to have this conversation with her.

"Hey." I start and clear my throat. "About my family."

Her eyes bulge, and her hand immediately goes up. "It's fine, Dominic, you don't have to talk about it." Her curls shake with the motion of her head. It seems as if she may keep talking, but I interject.

"No. I want to. I want you to know everything about me. That's a huge part of who I am, why I am the way I am."

She puts the package of pretzels down and replaces the head shake with a nod, giving me her full attention.

"My family was always close. We had the perfect one. Two happy parents and two kids—one boy and one girl—twins who were truly best friends. Even as a young kid, I knew we were lucky. Kami was quieter than me, though, in public anyway. On the surface, she was the introvert, and I was the extrovert." I pause to smile at the memory. At the fact that I always knew a different Kami at home than everyone else did. "But that didn't matter. I did my thing at school, she did hers, then when we got home, we were probably doing something together. Once we got to high school and started getting more into our own things, she became obsessed with drawing. That drawing turned into sketching clothes, which then became her passion. She knew by sixteen that she wanted to design clothes. She was good at it, too. And our parents would've done anything—paid anything—for either one of us if we told them it was our dream."

I close my eyes and take a deep breath, preparing for the part of the story I've worked hard to avoid.

"Like most aspiring fashion designers, she knew she had to get to New York. I hated the idea of her being that far away, but I couldn't convince her to change her mind. She applied for and got into her dream school out there. My parents decided to take her on a trip to scope out the city and to find a potential place. They hated the idea of her hotel hopping for an unknown amount of time. They tried to convince me to go with them—to make a family trip out of it—but I was feeling resentful about the whole thing and refused to go, offering to watch the house instead." I pause again, swallowing the lump that's gathered in my throat. "It's my biggest regret. Not going with them."

We both stay quiet for a minute, both obviously waiting for the worst part of the story to come. After another deep breath, I continue.

"Since they turned it into a trip, they wanted to explore some *'fun'* stuff too, obviously. They went on a boat tour, one that took them to the Statue of Liberty. 'Catastrophic engine failure,' 'explosion,' 'freak accident,' 'no one on board survived.'"

The terms roll off my tongue in an automated tone. Terms I kept hearing repeated on social media videos, news reports, and read in articles. I can't fight another pause, and the silence in the room grows heavier. Ruminating on the weight of the room, the touch of her hand on mine makes me jump. She doesn't say anything. She hasn't said anything this whole time, but she doesn't need to. Her eyes are wide with attention, but they aren't filled with pity; they're full of something else.

"It took a few days for them to figure out how to identify everyone, then find their families from all over the world, but I knew something was wrong. I didn't hear from any of them for the rest of that night, then into the morning. I stayed up all night waiting for one of them to call. But they never did. I went from having the perfect family to having none at all."

"I know that was scary to deal with." Her thumb strokes my hand as she says it.

The comment surprises me because I expected an *'I'm sorry.'* But that's not what she says. Her first reaction is about how I must have felt, and somehow I think she's gotten me to admit something I never have before.

"It was, even though I tried to pretend I was fine. Well, fine enough. And I'm the first to admit we were spoiled, or privileged kids. I never needed to worry about anything because I knew my parents would be there. Then they weren't, and I was lost and mad at myself for how clueless I felt. I had to do so many things I had no clue how to do—planning funerals, dealing with probate court, and selling the house because I wasn't prepared to take on a mortgage at the time. I wasn't even twenty years old. It was so overwhelming that I blocked most of it out. Then I decided to just block it out completely."

I point to the cup of water on the table, and she hands it to me with her other hand, never taking her other one off mine. "Pretending they just lived in New York was easier than saying they died there." I hand the cup back to her so she can return it to the tray. "Then you started talking about your family, and I thought about telling you a few times, but I always chickened out. You've been on your own, too, and would understand. I should've told you. I'm sorry."

"No. Dominic. I could never understand. You lost the three people who meant the most to you and who loved you. I've been on my own because my parents just don't care. Never did. They're the reason I don't have my brother because they pushed him away, too. If I had the family you had, I don't think I could've recovered." She gets out of the chair and climbs into my bed like she did the first night I woke up. "You're stronger than I could ever be." She whispers into my chest as her fingers trail along the few exposed tattoos. *God, I love when she does that.*

"Don't sell yourself short, baby. You've dealt with your shitty hand pretty impressively, too."

"I've never been one to fold," she tilts her head up to look at me. "Until I met you."

I respond with my lips instead of words. I still can't believe it. I knew from the first time I saw her that she was the one, but I'll never get over that finally coming to fruition. Everything about her is perfect—including the way she just handled this conversation. She hasn't drug it on, she hasn't asked a million questions I don't want to answer, and just let me tell it at my pace and *listened.*   Nor did she correct me when I called her baby,

After a few minutes of quiet cuddling, I decide I'm ready to tell her more. "Her favorite snacks are—were—chocolate-covered pretzels."

She lifts her head again to bring our eyes together. "So that's *really* why you remembered," she jokes, her hand playfully colliding with my chest.

"I remember everything about you, Kory May Brooks."

"Ew, please pretend I never told you that."

She pushes up off my chest, then reaches behind her to grab the bag of pretzels. She hands me one and holds one herself.

"To Kami then." She tips her pretzel towards me, and it only takes me a second to realize what she's doing. *We're toasting with chocolate-covered pretzels.*

I tap mine to hers. "To Kami," I repeat, then toss it in my mouth. She fights to keep her lips closed through a smile while she chews hers.

I have the same fight with my mouth as realization sets in that if I wasn't completely in love with her before these last thirty minutes, I definitely am now.

CHAPTER FORTY-SIX

Kory - February

His emerald eyes stare up at me begrudgingly, moving from my face to the wheelchair in front of me, to my face again.

"Your chariot awaits," I say with all the enthusiasm I can, trying to lighten his mood.

"I'd rather not."

"Well, they're all out of horse-drawn carriages, and you can't bear any weight for at least five more weeks, so this is the best I can offer. It's either you sit your ass in this chair and leave with me or you stay in that bed and stay here with them." I flash him the biggest—most annoying—smile I can.

He groans, and I lean down so he can throw his arm over my shoulder to get into said chair. Although his wrist is still cast, he is able to use his arms far more than he can use his leg. I know he is going to be bored out of his mind, but we're about to leave this hospital, so underneath his grumpiness about being stuck in a chair, I know he's actually happy.

I rest on one knee so I can put the footrests down and lift his immobile leg onto it. As I brace myself to stand, I look up to see him smiling down at me. "While you're down there…"

I smack his leg and jump up quickly. "Knock it off, Dominic. We're not even home yet." I pause, then quickly correct myself. "Your house, I mean."

It's an honest mistake. I'm never home anymore. I can't remember the last time I slept in my bed, but referring to home as something the two of us share sends a tightening to both my chest and stomach that I wasn't prepared for.

His smile never wavers. "My hat, please." I hand it to him, and he immediately hides his buzzed head with the damn thing on backwards.

"Problem?" He asks with a smirk. What I was thinking must have been written on my face.

"Just the same one as you." I throw him a wink and laugh as he shifts in his chair, adjusting his pants in between his legs with a different groan.

He rolls his chair towards the door, and I watch him look at himself in the mirror. He pulls the hat off and readjusts the strap to make it tighter, now that he is missing a layer of hair. He hates that they shaved it—especially for no reason—almost as much as he hates the wheelchair. Personally, I think the buzz cut is kind of hot on him. I also don't mind if he never takes the hat off, either. Maybe it's time to admit it doesn't matter what he is wearing or how his hair is styled. It's just him.

He's in the home stretch, though. Still a long road ahead, but the worst is over. He is expected to rest at home for another two weeks on bed rest with a physical and occupational therapist visiting him five days a week. After those first two weeks, he should be cleared to spend more time in the chair than in bed. His doctor said the physical therapist will have him gradually start adding weight to the leg until eventually he can walk again.

I thought he might cry real tears when they told him not to expect full mobility or the ability to walk freely until this summer—at the earliest. But he can go home, and I'll be right there with him for the foreseeable future. He needs almost constant help and tried to insist that it wouldn't be me, *but who else would it be?*

Turns out, Dom has money. More than I would have ever guessed. Between his family's life insurance, selling the house, and a settlement from the tour boat company, he has a pretty penny in the bank. Working at *Home Team* is just something he does because he enjoys it. So, he tried to say he would hire a nurse, but I told him absolutely not. He teased me for being jealous, and I insisted that was not the case, even though maybe I was a little.

At this point, after weeks together in the hospital, I can't imagine not being anywhere but with him. I don't want to be. I can't see myself going anywhere else after this but his house.

I think we're a couple, though we still haven't officially labeled it. Honestly, I'm not sure we need to. It seems we've been on the same page since he was almost taken from us completely.

I also feel funny asking at this point. *Hey, we've been together for weeks, kiss all the time, I help you with your meds, food, and sponge baths, but I was wondering, am I your girlfriend?* Again, after what we've been through, it feels almost ridiculous to ask. Plus, it's obvious how we both feel. That won't change with a relationship label.

I look around, doing one last sweep of the room, making sure we don't forget anything, and right on time, the nurse brings his discharge paperwork.

"You two take care of yourselves. You're an incredibly lucky man," he says and shakes Dom's hand.

I'm almost positive he was referring to the fact that he's still alive and being discharged from the hospital so soon, but Dom looks up at me and rests his hand on mine that sits on his shoulder before saying, "I sure am. Thank you."

My stomach tightens, and an ache surges through me as I push him through the hallways; thankfully, he can't read my face. *God, how I can't wait for him to get the all clear.*

His right leg and arm are both free, so he is able to push up and stand enough to swing into another seat. My jeep is only stock, so it's just tall enough for someone of Dom's height to do it with ease. I fold up the chair, stick it in the back, and climb into the driver's seat.

"Ready?"

"You have no idea." He rests his hand on my thigh as I pull out of the parking lot, and that ache becomes so intense my thighs clench together.

His townhouse has a first-floor entrance, thank God.

I love where he lives. It's not a huge multi-level apartment complex, but a single stretch of two-story townhouses. Each home front looks like its own little house with a small stretch of yard, some have personalized. The inside is beautifully updated and modern. It's the perfect type of modern to showcase his minimalist style, well, what looks like a minimalist style, because he doesn't have much. He had just what he needed. It looks like a cottage on the outside and a New York City apartment on the inside—which I would never tell him.

After successfully getting him inside, he swings himself a little too effortlessly onto the couch, then pats the cushion next to him. "Come here," he says, then holds his arm up and open for me to join.

"You've gotten quite comfortable saying that to me," I say, but oblige, leaning into him, letting out a soft moan as I feel his arm wrap around my back and pull me tight. I close my eyes and appreciate the moment—*him home*—*us here together*—no awkwardness. I inhale the scent of ocean air and driftwood while he runs his fingertips up and down my arm.

"Do you hear that?" he asks.

"What?"

"Not a single fucking beep."

Both of us erupt into laughter, and I push off his chest to sit up.

"You know what else?" I add. "Real food!"

"Yes, oh my God," he groans.

"Please tell me you have groceries."

"Honestly? I wouldn't remember if I did."

Shooting myself upwards, I run into the kitchen to raid the fridge and cabinets. I've only been here a few times, and none of those times did I pay attention to where anything in the kitchen is. As I approach the table, his helmet is sitting there in a box. It stings a little, seeing it sitting there when it should've been on his head. It might have been a different couple of weeks if he had worn it. But then again, *would we even be here in his apartment if this hadn't happened and kicked me in my ass?* I don't know.

"What do you want me to do with this?" I rest my hand on top of the box and turn my body back to face him.

"Oh," he pauses. "Well, I guess whatever you want. It's yours."

"Mine?" I stare at it for a moment before sliding it out of the box. It's then that I notice the purple pin stripe that runs along the side. *He bought me a helmet with my favorite color on it.*

"I was going to give it to you that night at your apartment." He goes quiet, and I know why. He's talking about the night I told him I didn't want to be with him. The night he almost died because of me.

He's still saying something when I go back into the living room and straddle him on the couch, one leg out a little bit farther to avoid the cast that stops halfway up his thigh. I grab his face and kiss him with every ounce of strength I've been holding back while at the hospital.

"I love you."

The words finally fall out of my mouth for the first time, without control, while our lips are still against each other. He stops and looks at me, and keeping my hands on his cheeks, I pull back and look directly in his eyes.

"You're the sweetest, most thoughtful, yet sexiest person I've ever met. And damn it, Dominic Rissi, I'm in love with you."

His hands rest on my thighs. "Even if I weren't also in love with you, I'd still do anything for my girl."

"Your girl?" My voice squeaks.

"You've never *not* been my girl. You just weren't ready to accept it yet."

I can all but feel the glisten that covers my eyes. Now that I've said it, I don't want to stop. "I love you," I tell him again.

"I love you too." He responds before our lips crash together, more chaotically than ever before.

And just like that, the doctor's words faded away, lost beneath the sounds of our quick breathing. But to my dismay, they come right back in bold, all capital letters in front of my face as Dom's whole body tenses and he sucks in a huge breath of air that he can't seem to release. I jump off his lap, immediately mad at myself for forgetting that he's nowhere near ready for anything like that.

"What do you need? Tell me what to do?" I ask, waiting for him to let himself out of the trance he's locked his body into to avoid the pain.

When his eyes finally meet mine, I see it—the fear, the fight, and the flicker of trust he's still trying to believe in. And right then, I know this isn't going to be easy. But I also know —now more than ever—that it doesn't matter. I'm here, and I'm going to love him through whatever happens.

CHAPTER FORTY-SEVEN

Dom

I've been staring at the same corner of the ceiling that hasn't changed in two hours. But I keep my eyes locked on that one spot like it might. Like maybe if I look long enough, it'll give me something—answers, patience, a fast-forward button. But all it gives me is the same damn crack in the plaster and the same reminder that I can't move. Not really. Not the way I want to. My leg itches under the cast, my back aches from lying in bed, and the wheelchair parked beside me feels more like a prison than a helpful tool. I hate this. I hate being still. I hate needing help.

Kory's sitting in the chair across the room, her legs tucked under her, glasses adorably on her nose, and a book open in her lap. She's trying to read, but I know she's not really reading. Her eyes keep drifting to me. She's waiting. For me to need something. Again.

"Stop watching me," I mutter.

She doesn't look up. "I'm not."

"You are."

She closes the book and sets it on the nightstand. "You're grumpy."

"I'm useless."

"You're healing."

I scoff and look away. "You shouldn't have to do all this."

She stands and walks over, sitting gently on the edge of the bed. Her hand finds my head, rubbing the back of it and onto my neck like it's the most natural thing in the world. I miss when she used to run her hands through my hair. I can't wait until it grows back enough for her to do it again.

"You'd do it for me," she says sweetly.

"That's different."

"Why?"

"Because you would never be a burden to me."

Her hand stills. "And you think you're a burden to me?"

I don't answer. I don't have to.

She leans down, pressing her forehead to mine. "You're not. I could've let you hire that nurse, but I didn't. Because I'm right where I want to be." She kisses me gently, then a smirk crawls across her lips. "Thank God I didn't, then you'd be lying there being mean to someone who doesn't love you enough to tell you to stop being a baby."

I smile at that but close my eyes as a pang of fire hits my leg. I still can't believe she loves me. I wish she would just say it over and over again.

She knows the routine, and that pang must mean it's time for another dose of meds. She hands me the familiar pills and my water, which I take with no discourse. She sits back in the chair she was in, attempting to go back to the book.

"Have you written anything in a while?" I ask, changing the subject from me.

"No. Not since the day of the book fest."

"Oh yeah? On that board?"

"No," she grins, "I wrote something in my hotel room that night."

"And you didn't share it?"

"Why would I do that?"

"Because you love me?" I flash her a smile.

"Did I then, though?"

"Pretty sure you did, but I'll let you keep believing that you didn't."

She smiles, causing one to grow on my face. I love that she's near me, but I hate that she's just wasting all her time in my bedroom—not the way we should be. I don't remember what it was like to breath without pain. I would rather be sleeping, which makes me feel guilty leaving her just sitting here by herself, while I sleep my pain away. I can't shake the feeling that she is just suffocating, stuck by a sense of obligation. I can't let her forget who she was before my caretaker. The word makes me wince. She loves me, and I finally have her, and that's exactly why I can't let her grow resentful and change her mind.

"How's Olivia?" I ask her. "You haven't brought her up in a while."

"She's fine. Dating some new guy, so she's been pretty preoccupied with that."

"What about Autumn? You going to visit her soon?"

She closes her book and looks at me with her head cocked to the side. "Dominic, are you trying to get rid of me?"

"No. But I'm sure your friends miss you."

She leans back, her eyes soft. "I can see them when you're better."

I shake my head. "Don't wait on me. You're allowed to do things for yourself, Kory. You don't have to put your life on hold because I fucked mine up."

"You didn't fuck your life up. You got hurt. That's not the same." She gets out of her chair, coming towards the bed.

"It feels the same."

She sighs and lies down beside me, like in the hospital, careful not to jostle my leg. Her head rests on my shoulder, her hand on my chest. "You're not a burden. You're my person now. And I'm not going anywhere." I nod and close my eyes, letting her words take me over. *I'm her person.* "Plus," she adds, "I'm supposed to be the stubborn one here, just let me love you already."

I laugh, and it hurts, but it's worth it.

I swallow hard. "You're too good to me."

She lifts her head just enough to meet my eyes. "You're good to me, too. Even now. Even when you're the ornery and stubborn one."

I laugh again. Still painful. Still worth it.

She settles back down, and I let my hand drift to her curls, tangling my fingers in them gently. "You've been good to me. You did so many things for me, you didn't have to, Dominic. Just hush and let me return the favor. Especially since this is my fault."

"That's what this is?" I ask, straining my neck to look down at her. "You think this is your fault, so you feel like you're stuck here?"

I hear a faint sniffle and feel her head shake. "Had I not been so awful to you, you wouldn't have jumped on that bike and…"

"Hey," I say firmly, cutting her off. "This is not your fault. I could've been in an accident in my car, or walking down the street, or…" I pause, "On a boat. It's an accident. They happen. Stop blaming yourself."

"Only if you promise me that you've stopped blaming yourself."

I inhale deeply, then kiss her head, engulfing the scent that calms me. It works. "I promise, thanks to you. But I want you to promise me something too." I say into her hair.

"What's that?"

"If this starts to feel like too much, please tell me. I won't be offended if you need to leave and take a break."

"I won't, but I promise."

And for the first time in days, I don't feel stuck. With her head on my chest, I feel still. And when I look at it from this angle, still isn't so bad.

CHAPTER FORTY-EIGHT

Kory - March

The weather outside is just as gloomy as it is in this apartment. An early spring storm is rolling in—the ugly kind —grey skies slowing darkening as the atmosphere stills. The calm before the storm.

He's struggling today. I was warned it may get worse before it gets better. Some days have been better than others. But just as we seem to get him out of a dark spot, his clouds return.

I can tell the exact minute he's ready for a dose of meds without checking a clock; I see it in the way his jaw tightens and the way the light in his eyes shifts from patient to proud to don't touch me in the span of a breath. But none of it bothers me because I know that's how I had been treating him for months—without serious injury as an excuse.

"I'm fine," he says when I walk in with a mug of tea.

"Who said this was for you?" I quip.

He rolls his eyes with the faintest tightening of his lips. *Almost* a smile. It's the smallest victory—that eye roll and almost smile—but a victory nonetheless. Today has been rough.

"You need to rest," I say, the way I always do when he starts to get agitated.

"I need my life back." He says it like he's daring me to disagree.

I sit on the edge of the bed, ignoring the pinch in my chest. "You'll get it back. One step at a time."

His mouth flattens. "I hate that phrase."

"I know." I offer him a crooked smile. "Hate it enough to do your ankle pumps?" He tries not to laugh. He loses. Barely, but another small win for me.

"You're impossible."

"You already knew this." I tuck my feet under me and pull the blanket straight again so that I have an excuse to touch him. He watches my hands, and I ignore that too.

This sucks for me too, but not the way he thinks. Being with him like this, 24/7, and not able to touch him the way I want to, would have me just as crabby if I didn't have to be the positive one in the room.

For a little while, we do our usual dance—the small stretches we learned from PT. I count with him out loud, and his words through gritted teeth, and when the wince turns to a curse, I whisper my worst joke so he groans for the right reason. Well, almost the right reason.

Once we're done and he settles with a dose of meds, I prop my chin on my fist and study him. Admiring the strength he doesn't see. But I see it. In the way he apologizes for nothing and insists that I need to be doing anything other than taking care of him. The way he tries to pretend he doesn't need me, just to make *my* life easier.

"You're staring," he says.

"You're pretty," I say back.

He snorts out an actual laugh—a small one, but a real one—then winces as he leans forward, trying to itch beneath the cast. He won't ask me to, so I reach over and do it for him, letting my fingers linger on his skin.

Thunder rolls like a faraway train as the storm finally hits. The smell of rain and laundry detergent turns the room into something that almost feels holy.

"Want to pick out something to watch?" I offer, reaching for the remote.

"I want you."

There it is. *No bravado. No coy.* Just the truth, bare and a little shaky. My pulse misfires. This is not a new thing for him to say—with a hundred tiny moments like this stitched into the last seven months. But this is different because he can't move, because pain has made him careful and pride has made him quiet, and because every decision now has to be weighed against a leg and ribs that won't allow mistakes. We're both reminded of that as he takes a sharp inhale, clamping his teeth and eyes shut tightly.

I slide onto the bed on his uninjured side, facing him, my knee bumping the mattress near his hip. "Show me where it hurts," I say.

He takes my hand and places it high on his thigh, inches from the cast. Heat radiates through the thin basketball shorts. The muscle is trembling beneath my palm as I apply just a small amount of pressure with my fingertips and knead.

"I hate needing you for this," he says, eyes closing as if the admission stings.

"I love being needed by you."

"You deserve easy."

"Why would you think that? I've never been easy." I lean in and kiss that little furrow between his brows like I could smooth it completely with my mouth.

A lightning bolt flashes through the window, and as thunder cracks loudly right above the roof, a shift happens—as if the storm planted itself above this house to remind us what we are together.

I stop and look at his face, his eyes darkened in the way that catches my breath. His eyes flicker to where the neckline of my shirt hangs down before coming back up to meet mine. I bring our lips together again, feeling him soften under my lips. His good arm finds the small of my back, pulling me closer, silently begging for what I know he *doesn't* hate needing from me. I pull back, keeping my forehead against his. "Tell me what you can handle."

"Slow," he says, reading both mine and the storm's energy. "And close."

"Okay."

We begin taking inventory like we're making a grocery list. Pillow here, another there. His one hand can curve around my waist, but not pull that hard. My knee can cross his hip, but not press. His one leg can be bent, pushed into the mattress to keep him from sliding. We laugh through it—soft, private laughter—the kind that makes my ribs expand until everything feels loose and bright again.

"Sit up a little straighter," I whisper, sliding my arm behind his shoulders.

He grips the temporary side rail with one hand, my wrist with the other, and we move on the count of three. He winces, but I kiss the corner of his mouth and whisper, "Now stay right there," to distract him until his wince turns into a sigh.

"Bossy nurse," he murmurs.

"Would you rather have a nurse after all?" I lean my chest over his head to adjust the pillows until his chest angles more towards me.

"No. Keep going." He breathes.

I kiss him again, soft at first, then deeper when I feel the tension in his shoulders loosen. We slide into an even deeper kiss like we are inching into hot water, like we have all the time in the world—because we do. His palm finds the curve of my waist beneath my—*his*—shirt; his thumb strokes idle, missed circles there that make my breath hitch.

"Is this okay?" I ask against his mouth.

He nods. "More than okay."

My hand cups his jaw, rough with his unkempt stubble, and I trace the line of his throat with my thumb, feeling the drum of his pulse. It makes me braver. I kiss his cheek, his temple, the shell of his ear. I breathe him in—soap and rain, and the smell of him that's familiar, even though he's been stuck in this bed—and let the ache of missing the ease of us transform into something warm.

"Tell me if anything hurts," I murmur, shifting my knee the smallest bit.

"I am only saying something if you stop," he says, and the smile in his voice makes me laugh into his skin.

We navigate the boundaries like explorers. A little closer. Not there. Here. Yes, that. The bed complains, though he never does. The ache in my chest—that steady attendant since the hospital—loosens its grip as he presses his forehead to mine and breathes me in like I was air he's been rationing.

"God, I love you," he says suddenly.

"I know," I whisper, because I'm allowed to be as cocky now as he has been. "I love you too."

He kisses me again, slower, and for a few long heartbeats, everything, including the storm, disappears. No rattles of medicine bottles. No stretching. No rotating angles and checking for range of motion. *Just us.*

When we stop to breathe, I tuck myself along his side, my leg draping lightly over his hip, the way the PT said not to do, yet, except we've been making it work since in the hospital. He closes his eyes, and the line between his brows is finally relaxed.

"Stay," he says, like we hadn't already established I'm going anywhere.

"Always." I kiss his shoulder. "But I'm still making you do ankle pumps after this." He groans partly in protest, partly in pleasure at my mouth on his skin.

"Way to ruin everything."

"Uh, I'm pretty sure I just fixed everything," I correct, smug.

"You act like I did nothing." He argues.

"Keep it up, and you might actually be back to doing nothing." I lie through my teeth.

I feel the bounce of a little laugh on his chest, and his hand tightens the grip on my ass cheek just slightly. My body attempts to laugh back, but it is caught in a bubble in my throat, one I struggle to swallow down. Because this—this stupid back-and-forth is the exact shape of our happiness, and losing it even temporarily has felt like misplacing a whole part of me.

"Tell me something you haven't yet," I ask after a while, voice low, our bodies unmoved, eyes on the window where lightning stitched itself briefly across the sky.

He's quiet long enough that the rain fills the spaces his words should have. Eventually, he speaks. "I keep waking up convinced you're going to realize this is too much and leave," he said, so softly I might have imagined it if not for the way his fingers slide up and tighten on my waist.

My chest goes hot and protective. I draw back enough to look at him. "I didn't come here, or just agree to stay out of pity," I say, even though this is a conversation we've already had. "I am here because I know you need help and because I *want* you to have mine. I love you, Dominic. How many times do I have to say it until you believe me?"

He doesn't even flinch. "As many times as I had to try and convince you that you did."

My mouth falls open just briefly in shock, but then closes into an amused grin. I push up—on a safe spot on his chest— to look at him. His grin mirrors mine, amused by his comment. For once, I'm left without a comeback, so I decided we've breathed enough for now.

The kiss that follows is a bit more hurried than a little bit ago, a frenzied, we can't keep our hands off each other kiss we haven't shared in months. My hand slides beneath the edge of his shirt, finding warm skin, and his breath stuttered in that way that turned my bones to honey.

"Okay?" I check again, because love is sometimes just a thousand tiny permissions.

"Please." He breathes.

It wasn't long until his hand was curled back at the base of my neck, holding me in place. I welcome the tight grip as it's not to brace himself from the pain anymore, but finally to welcome the relief.

CHAPTER FORTY-NINE

Dom - April

I hate every stupid rule she made last year, but my favorite one to be abolished? Sleeping in one bed.

The first month at home was hard, but she was the most patient, perfect person to have by my side. I don't even think about the fact that my physical mobility is still a bit limited anymore—rather, I fully embrace the good parts about this situation. There is nothing better than waking up to a face full of her sweet, citrusy-scented hair. Most days I'm up before her, but I lie there just enjoying her in my bed—in my arms. Whether her head is on my chest or her back flush against me, it's all heaven.

I asked her to stay, but not live here. It wasn't until days after that conversation that I realized I don't know if she knows I meant forever. When I reflected on the conversation, *'stay'* suddenly didn't feel like a strong enough word. *Does she think I meant just for now? Until I'm better?* I don't want her to ever leave, and I don't think she does either. *Why would she?* She loves me. And I love her. She's reminded me so many different times and so many different ways since we left the hospital. Shit, since way before that. But now her words meet her actions, and I can't get enough.

A few days a week, I have to suffer without her as she leaves for a couple of hours to check in on her place, but she always comes back. We haven't spent a night apart since my accident. I do appreciate her convincing me not to hire a nurse to help. I have a feeling she would still be here every day, and three would just be a crowd.

I am starting to get a little bit of my mobility back, thanking my attitude adjustment for being part of the change. My doctor said I can also credit my great physical shape before the accident as part of why my healing is going exceptionally well. *'Taking it easy'* initially felt like a punishment, but now it's as easy as it sounds.

The taking it easy part would probably suck, though, if it weren't Kory I was spending time with. If it were a nurse, or even Jimmy, they'd never compare, especially if you consider what her definition of me taking it easy has turned into. I could do that forever and never, ever get bored.

So that's what we do. Take it easy. Together. Rarely leaving my place, *but why would we need to?* Everything I could ever want is here. And it's not this place. *It's her.*

I can now stand for short periods of time, not that it's easy with a cast that still covers my entire leg. I'm limited to five minutes still or one hundred steps, but it's better than nothing. It's just enough to get up and hobble like an unoiled tin man to where she's making us lunch.

Coming up behind her, I thread my arms underneath hers and wrap them around her stomach. She stops and leans her head back into me, humming in response. We stand like that for a peaceful moment before I abruptly swing her around and lift her onto the counter. Her hands scramble behind her, trying to move the sandwich ingredients out of the way.

My hand pulls her face to me, and her arms slide under mine this time, pulling me in closer and wrapping her legs around my waist. Our tongues dance for not nearly long enough before she stops, resting her forehead against mine. "You are definitely not supposed to be lifting me like that," she says, her voice breathy.

"Yeah, well, you definitely shouldn't be in my kitchen, making me lunch, wearing nothing but one of my shirts, if you don't want me to attack you like that."

She looks into my eyes, and I stare back at the green and golden swirls until she places a quick kiss on my lips and jumps off the counter. After handing me a sandwich wrapped in a paper towel, she turns back around and goes into a cabinet.

"Go eat. Jimmy's coming by. I'm going to go talk to John about going back to work." She spins and effortlessly tosses me a bag of chips, which I catch with my good hand.

"You didn't have to call him," I tell her, allowing myself to fall back onto the couch. "I don't need a babysitter."

Watching her distaste for my best friend fade has been refreshing. I would have never expected her to be friends with him, but it *has* been nice since she lost the daggers that used to shoot from her eyes at the mention of his name.

"He wanted to come anyway—asked if we were busy. I think he wants to get you out of the house for his birthday."

"Damn, it's spring already?"

"Babe, it's been spring. We just haven't left this room." She says, now standing in front of me.

The way *'babe'* rolls off her lips wakes up every nerve in my body. The way my shirt rides up her legs as she slowly lowers herself onto my lap sets them on fire.

"I haven't eaten my sandwich," I whisper as her face inches closer to mine. She pushes her lips into mine while grabbing the sandwich and setting it aside.

"Well, I thought about it," Her whispered breath feels hot on my wet lips. "I can't go on with my day without finishing what you started."

Kory's in the shower when Jimmy walks in the door. I hear the fridge open and shut, then the pop and subsequent fizzing of two beers being opened. He hands me one as he sits down next to me.

"How's it going?"

"Amazing," I tell him as I hear Kory move from the bathroom to the bedroom. He looks at me, eyebrow raised, searching for sarcasm. I raise mine back at him along with a nod towards the hallway. He laughs and takes a sip, getting the hint with not many words at all. I change the subject, though, because while sharing details of my love life with him has never been off limits, with her, I need those details all to myself.

"What about you? How's Em doing?"

"She's great. Perfect as ever. I think her still being so young has helped with the whole divorce thing. I'm glad we didn't draw it out any longer."

"Oh yeah, that's official, right?"

He nods and takes another drink. "Yup. Divorced as of yesterday."

"Well, shit. Cheers, I guess," he laughs and taps his bottle to mine. "How's Becca?" I ask. "I mean, like how are you guys getting along?"

"Surprisingly, fine. We talk about Em and that's it. I guess I'm really not all that surprised, though."

"What do you mean?"

"The divorce was her idea. She's not going to make it difficult because it's what *she* wants."

His point is valid. I never disliked Becca, but I didn't love her for him. They never really fit, and he became a watered-down version of the friend I knew. I obviously hoped he would be okay, but was also relieved for him when he said they were splitting—*again*. And now that I think about it, if he wants to get me out for his birthday, that's what we'll do. It's time for him to have some fun back in his life.

"I think she's seeing someone already," he says, surprising me.

Kory comes out of the bedroom just as he drops that bomb, distracting me from answering. She looks effortlessly stunning as always. Casual in leggings and a T-shirt hanging off her shoulder—purposely this time. Her hair is pulled half back, hanging down long, but still exposing her face.

"I'll be back in a bit." She says with a quick kiss before heading out the door.

"So you two are finally official now, huh?" he asks with a laugh after a brief silence.

"Nah, let's go back to what you just said first. She's seeing someone?"

He shrugs. "She was late picking Em up this morning. She's never late. *Ever*. And she didn't look like herself. She wasn't put together, which leads me to believe wherever she slept, it wasn't at her own place."

"Does that bother you?" I ask, watching his face to gauge his true reaction.

"No? Yes? I'm not sure. I mean, we were just divorced yesterday morning. I guess that's the one part that does surprise me. It's not like her."

"Everyone changes. It's part of life. Look at me."

"Yeah, so now back to that," he says with a chuckle. "She living here now?"

I return a chuckle of my own through the swallow of my beer. "Yeah, that's the thing. I don't know what is official for us and what isn't. We haven't talked about anything, just been in a haze, going with the flow. I asked her to stay, and she said always, but not sure if she meant while I'm stuck here, or forever."

"So wait, you're not even dating?" amusement laces his face.

"Yes? I mean, I would say yes, but we've never said those words out loud." I stop for a minute, bracing for the next part. "We tell each other we love each other, though."

He chokes back the beer in his mouth, as I expected him to. "So you can tell her you love her, but not ask her to be your girlfriend?" I simply shrug with a smile hidden behind the mouth of my beer bottle. He shakes his head. "So what are you waiting for then?"

"The right time, I guess? Speaking of which, I'm glad she's gone. I need your help with something, and I really need you not to be mad at me for what I'm about to ask you to do."

CHAPTER FIFTY

Kory

I didn't lie, but I couldn't tell the whole truth either.

I had been talking to John about going back to work, but he insisted that neither I nor Dom was ready for me to go back. He was taking care of everything while we focused on his healing. He needed his Dream Team back and was willing to wait as long as it took.

What I really needed to do was check in with the body shop that was fixing up his bike. They were almost done, but wanted to run a few things past me. Dom not being able to leave the house very easily has made this secret so much easier to keep, considering there are only three auto shops around here, and only one of them knew what to do with a crotch rocket.

Once he told me about what happened with his family, I knew the bike meant something completely different. It wasn't just something his dad left behind and didn't want anymore—it was one of the last pieces of him that Dom had left. There was no way I was going to let him lose that.

I told Jimmy we needed to get it back, and he immediately jumped on finding it. Thankfully, just like the body shops, there aren't many junk yards around, so it didn't take him long. He got it delivered to the right shop, then handed the reins over to me. I provided the shop with some pictures I found in his place and some I took on our road trip. I didn't know anything about bikes, especially motorcycles, just that I wanted it to look exactly the way it did before the accident. They assured me they could do it.

Before I go to the shop, though, I stop at my apartment to grab the stash of cash I have stowed away for emergencies. He'd be mad at me for using it on him, but I don't care.

As I climb up the stairs and round the corner, I'm taken aback by a tall figure standing in front of my door. Once I register the broad shoulders and sandy blond bun, his name flies out of my mouth.

"Elliot!?"

My brother turns around, greeting me with a wide smile, flashing every single one of his perfect teeth.

"Surprise!" he says with his arms wide open.

I drop my purse and jump into them, squeezing his neck, and he spins us around.

"What are you doing here?" I ask excitedly as he puts me back on my feet.

"I got bored. And I've been thinking about it since Thanksgiving, so I'm back home. For good."

I think the tears are already pooling in my eyes before my brain fully registers what he's just said. My brother is back. A piece of my heart is back home. One of the only ones that matter. I fling myself into his chest again, unable to speak. He hugs back again, and after a few seconds, I feel his chest bounce with a laugh.

"I didn't expect you to be such a crybaby. Who are you and what have you done with my tough little sister?" he shuffles his hand in my hair, and I laugh. "Think we should go inside and do this? I've been standing out here for like twenty minutes."

"Yeah, yeah," I say as I shuffle back to my purse and fish out my keys. "Why didn't you call?" I ask as I stick the key into the knob.

"I was trying to surprise you, but apparently that was harder than I expected. I've been home for a couple of days now, and this is the third time I've come here hoping for this exact surprise."

As we step inside, I look around, realizing this no longer feels like home. *Because I don't live here anymore.*

"Yeah, about that," I say as I set my bag down, and he makes himself at home, going into my fridge.

"Kory, there's nothing in here."

"Yeah, I was about to say, I'm not really here much anymore. Well, like at all."

He fills up a cup of tap water and then sits down at the table. "Work or a boy?"

The childishness of the word boy makes me roll my eyes, but warms my soul at the same time. This is what life should've been like all this time. My big brother. Questioning me about boys.

"A boy," I say happily while joining him at the table.

We spent the next hour sitting there talking. I tell him all about Dom—how we met—sparing him the gritty details, but how our relationship started—how it almost ended, his accident, then how we've been for the last few months, and finally how I'm trying to get his bike fixed for him.

"Shit. I was coming home to go to the shop. I totally forgot." I say as I stand out of the chair.

"I'll go with you. Maybe they need some extra hands."

"Since when are you a mechanic?" I call as I run to my room and grab the money.

"I can do anything." He says with a laugh as we exit my apartment.

On the ride to the shop, it's his turn to talk—explaining a little bit of what he's been doing all these years. Working with kids who are aging out of foster care. Helping them learn the skills they need in adulthood. I almost cry again listening to him talk about it with so much passion. After being left behind by our parents, left to fend for ourselves, he took that and turned it into something so beautiful.

"In college, I realized there were so many kids who were like us; many actually had it worse. I put a twist on my social work degree and focused on teaching these kids—boys *and* girls—the skills I had to learn on my own. Home improvement, paying bills, lawn care, car work, shit, even laundry. That's made me pretty much a jack of all trades now."

I pull the car into a parking spot. "El, that's seriously amazing. No wonder you were too busy to talk to me. You must have like a hundred little brothers and sisters at this point."

"Yeah, I actually started thinking about that a lot—how I focused on them more than my own sister. That was a jerk move."

I send him a smile, "It's okay. I'm sure those kids needed you more."

He pulls me in for a half-hug as we cross the parking lot. "You've always been such a tough cookie. I am proud of you, Kay."

"Stop it before you make me cry again." I fling his arm off my shoulders, and he laughs.

"Fine. Let's go check out this bike for your lover boy then."

The laugh that bubbles out of me is light, as light as the rest of my body. I walk into that noisy, stinky shop feeling closer to while than I have in years—pieces of me snapping back together with each step.

CHAPTER FIFTY-ONE

Dom

Fresh air drifts through the open window, carrying the smell of dew and just-cut grass. The kind of scent that makes you want to breathe deeper. The TV hums low in the background, but I'm not watching it.

I'm watching her.

Kory's curled up on the other end of the couch, legs tucked under her—the spot that's become her favorite—her hair spilling over one shoulder. She's holding something—a folded piece of paper, edges jagged like it's been ripped from a notebook. Her fingers keep smoothing it out, then folding it again.

She's been quiet all night. *Too quiet.* And Kory Brooks doesn't do quiet unless something's eating at her.

"You've been staring at me for five minutes," I say. "Either say what you're plotting, Brooks, or take a picture."

That earns me a laugh, but it's shaky. Her knuckles whiten around the paper.

"I'm not plotting," she says softly. "I just... have something to show you."

I mute the TV and shift, ignoring the dull ache in my leg as I sit up straighter. "Okay," I say slowly. "You've officially got my attention."

She hesitates, then blurts it out like ripping off a Band-Aid. "Remember the book fest? The poetry wall?"

I grin. "How could I forget? You made me smell a book like a psycho."

That gets another laugh, but it fades fast. She unfolds the paper, and I realize it's not just any scrap—it looks like the list of rules she gave me months ago. Same jagged edges. Same stubborn handwriting. My chest tightens.

"What I wrote that night," she says. "I want to show you."

My throat goes dry. "Read it to me."

Her eyes flick up to mine, then back down. And then she starts reading, voice low and uneven:

"People always leave, forever leaving scars, silent wishes of return lost to life on Mars.

She pauses, looking at me again before reading the next line.

"Some people never left. They were just waiting to be seen.

The one I wrote. After another quick pause, she continues.

Sometimes, if you'd look beyond where you've always been,

You'd find far more than just silent nights and distant stars."

She pauses as I put together what I just heard. She took my words, and her words, and put them together to make something beautiful. And I recognize the last line too.

"Was that part of the poem you wrote in high school?"

She smiles, happy I remembered again. "No, but you said those two words and I remembered part of it—I like this version best."

"Me too."

"There's more. That's what I wrote the night of the Bookfest. Before I came to your room." She stops, and we both smile at that memory. "But I wrote the last time you asked me about it. While you were sleeping."

"Okay," I say, nodding for her to continue.

"Some stars don't burn out, they just hide in the night, waiting for someone to see their light. And maybe I was blind, maybe I was scared, but now I can see that you were always there."

The words hit me like a punch to the chest. I can't move. Can't breathe.

When she finally looks up, her eyes are wide, uncertain. "Say something," she whispers.

I swallow hard because my voice feels like gravel. "You have no idea what that means to me."

She tries to laugh it off. "It's just a poem."

"No," I say, shaking my head. "It's not *'just'* anything. It's you. It's everything I've been hoping you'd let me see all these years. Can I?" I reach my hand towards her, asking to see it. My fingers brush the edge, looking at the different color ink, and I can't help but smirk.

"You know what this reminds me of?" I go to the table where my wallet is sitting, then bring it back to the couch, sliding out two folded sheets that've been through hell—creased, worn, but still intact. I hold one up between us.

Her eyes widen. "You kept that?"

"Of course I did." I unfold the infamous Rules List, the one she wrote in bold, bossy letters like she was drafting a legal contract. "No kissing unless sex is involved. No romantic walks. No nicknames." I grin and pause for dramatic effect. "You know we broke every single one."

Her cheeks flush, and I swear I've never seen anything cuter. "I can't believe you still have that."

"Oh, that's not all I have." I reach into my wallet and pull out another piece of paper, smaller, lined, scribbled in different handwriting. I hand it to her.

She takes it slowly, eyes scanning the title: *Kory's Favorite Things*.

Her lips part as she reads down the list—*Vanilla Coke. Chocolate-covered pretzels. Carnations. Crown and Coke. Favorite color: purple. Favorite season: summer.*

"You…" Her voice cracks, and she presses the paper to her chest. "You made a list?"

"Had to keep up somehow," I say with a shrug, trying to play it cool even though my heart's pounding. "You think I just magically remembered all that? I wrote it down the first week we were on the road. THEN I remembered."

Her laugh is soft, almost shy. "Jimmy showed me this in the hospital," she admits, cheeks pink.

I groan. "That traitor."

She laughs harder, and the sound is everything. Then her eyes soften, and she looks at me like I'm something worth keeping. "I still can't believe you kept all of these."

"Every word from you meant something," I say. "Because from the second you finally walked directly into my life—or me—I knew I couldn't lose you."

Her breath jumps, and before I can say anything else, she's in my arms, kissing me like we still have time to make up for.

When we pull apart, her forehead rests against mine, and she whispers, "Happy early birthday."

"Best one I've ever gotten." I smile, because damn, this feels like the only gift I've ever wanted.

She laughs through tears, and the eye roll, I love almost as much as I love her. I tuck her against me, breathing her in like oxygen. For the first time in years, not only do I not feel stuck, but I feel whole.

CHAPTER FIFTY-TWO

Kory

I'm bringing a load of clean clothes from the laundry room back to my apartment when a voice floats out from the living room—his phone on speaker, loud enough for me to catch every word.

"August! My man!" a guy crows. "How's it going? Everything good?"

August? I freeze, both intrigued and confused. I've never heard anyone call him by his middle name—ever. He spent our whole childhood trying to make sure no one knew that was even on his birth certificate. Our parents must have used up any creative juices they may have had on our first names, *because our middle names?* The months we were born in. They honestly could've just let those lines blank, but here we are. Kory May and Elliot August.

Hugging the laundry basket against my hip, I stand by the door wanting to listen to whatever this is.

"Yeah, yeah, I'm good. Actually feels good to be home." Elliot says, which tugs my lips into a smile.

"I wouldn't call that home, but whatever." I hear the friend laugh, but I squint my eyes. This is his home. I don't care what anyone from Tennessee says.

Before Elliot says anything back, the friend says, "So anyway, you gonna tell me about that mystery girl who ran out on you in the morning?" The friend laughs. "We never got to finish that conversation."

"Not much to tell, other than what you already know," Elliot starts, but I march into the room, hoping that he stops because I don't know that I want to hear where this is headed. Thankfully, that's exactly what happens. "Yeah, let's talk about that later." He says, then after a few more short sentences, they hang up.

I start moving my clean clothes into a bag and can't help but ask, "So… Who's August?"

He laughs, but it's slightly rigid. "Right." He winces. "Guess you heard that."

"I'd have to be deaf not to. You had your phone on speaker like you are an old man." I fold my arms. "Now, care to explain why my brother has an alter ego I don't know about?"

He hesitates—like he's choosing between a joke and the truth. "It started as an escape. When I left, I wanted to be someone new—start fresh, ya know? Pretend I wasn't Elliot, whose parents were pieces of shit. I could be August—someone knew who could make up his own story."

He pauses, as he typically does when we talked about our parents and/or his absence—a silently apology for what that absence meant for me.

"But then it turned out to be a good thing for work. Social work isn't all sunshine and rainbows with happy endings—especially when what I was helping with were children who were not going back to their parents. Some teens got angry and blamed us for things. Sometimes parents get angry. All of them can get violent and have at some point. Having a different name made it harder for them to find me. I don't think anyone did, but it felt like a safe move anyway, just in case."

I stare at him for a minute, taking in the somberness that has overcome him. It feels heavy in here now, and I don't want it to feel heavy; I've had enough recently. I nudge him with my hip.

"Hey, well, thank God Mom and Dad ran out of baby-name inspiration and defaulted to birthday months. They did you a favor there. What a conversation starter."

That earns an annoyed look from him and a huff of a laugh out of me. "May and August," I say with dramatic flair.

"Just think, we could've been November and—oh no—February. Imagine being called 'Feb.'"

"You could have been July and called Julie or Jules."

"And you could've been April and been the boy named April."

He finally smiles, a full one with a laugh behind it. "August isn't so bad, then."

I'm never going to call him that, but if he likes it, then that's cool for him. I fall onto the couch, trying to force myself to picture him as an August. I stare at him and repeat it in my head, but it just makes me laugh.

"Okay, so anyways. Tell me the truth," Elliot changes the subject as he leans against my kitchen counter like he owns the place. Although I guess that's kind of the case since he's been staying here by himself. Each time I come back to this apartment, it feels less and less like my home. I did some laundry today, just as an excuse to hang out with him for a bit. "How are things? Any better?"

I nod and smile. "Better. Like… much better. No storms. No lightning. Just… calm."

He raises an eyebrow, skeptical. "Calm? You?"

"Shut up," I shoot back, grinning. "I'm serious. We've got a routine now. Slow mornings, therapy in the afternoons, dinner together at night. No drama." I pause. "No running away."

Elliot smirks. "Sounds suspiciously like happiness."

"It is," I admit, and the word feels good on my tongue. "I'm really happy."

He tilts his head, studying me like he's trying to read between the lines. "I was a little worried about you a couple of weeks ago. You sounded tense on the phone. It's one of the reasons I gave in to my thoughts about moving home."

I shrug, remembering that day—Dom in one of his worst moods—the air in the apartment so tense I could've cut it with the knife I was using to spread peanut butter. Tense enough that he picked it up through the phone. "I was. It's just been hard. I think I was still waiting for something to go wrong. That's what I do, right? Brace for impact."

"And now?"

"Now…" I pause, smiling at the thought of last night—Dom laughing in the kitchen, singing off-key to some old country song while stirring pasta. "Now I'm not bracing. I'm just… there. With him. And it feels good."

Elliot grins. "About damn time." He glances at the phone, which has been lighting up with notifications from Brody at the shop. "So, what's the final plan?"

"No final plan yet," I say, reading his reply that it's ready. "I want it at the restaurant before he gets there. I didn't think about how I would pick it up or get it there, though."

Elliot smirks. "Lucky for you, part of *'I can do anything'* includes that I can ride. I'll pick it up and get it there early. You just make sure he doesn't suspect a thing."

"He definitely doesn't. We haven't even spoken about the bike. Honestly, with how things were going at first, I almost squashed this whole idea, but with how they are now, I think he can handle it. So, deal." I grin, feeling that familiar rush of excitement—the kind that used to come from spontaneous bike rides or sneaking glances from across the store—knowing what was coming later. Except this is better. This is all for him.

I leave my apartment with yet another bag, slowly adding more and more of my things to Dom's instead. Another bag of clothes, another couple of books after I've finished the ones I have there already, and random things from my bedroom to make it more comfortable for Elliot.

By the time I get home—*yes, home*—the apartment smells like garlic and butter. Music drifts from the kitchen. It's something quirky, yet melodic—something unmistakably Taylor Swift. I freeze in the doorway, biting back a laugh.

He's at the stove, spatula in hand, head bobbing to the beat like he's in his own little concert. The muscles in his toned, bare back flex as he sways ever so slightly to the beat. The man who swore he'd never admit to being a Swiftie is currently singing about how he's the problem under his breath.

"Busted," I announce, leaning against the doorframe, arms folded smugly across my chest.

His head snaps up, eyes wide, cheeks flushed. "I—uh—this is just what was on the playlist."

"Sure," I tease, walking over and plucking the spatula from his hand. "Next, you'll tell me you don't know all the words to *All Too Well, The 10 Minutes Version*."

He smirks, pulling me in by the waist. "Maybe I do. Maybe I don't." His lips brush my ear as he whispers, "Guess you'll have to stick around to find out."

"That's the plan," I say before landing a quick peck on his lips. Just as I pull away, he slaps my ass before I can jump away from it—because that's become part of our routine too.

"Almost ready to eat?"

"Yeah, let me put this stuff away."

He doesn't ask me what stuff I'm talking about, or where I'm going to put it. He just shares a knowing smile as I silently move myself all the way in. Once I'm done with what I can make a place for at this moment, I reenter the kitchen to find him with plates set out on the table. He stands there waiting for me, clearly proud of his setup. Two plates of a sauced chicken dish with rice on the side, a generous serving of zucchini and squash on the side, and a single teeny tiny candle in the middle.

"It was the only candle I had." He says sheepishly.

"It's perfect," I say as I sit down in the chair, and he pushes me into the table. "Aren't you working yourself a little too hard?"

He shakes his head as he sits across from me. "I just cooked some food. No different than what I've already been doing. I'll be fine."

My head subtly nods in agreement as I prepare to take the first bite of whatever this is that smells amazing.

"Plus," he adds. "I've been waiting a while to share this dining room table with someone, and cooking is the only hobby I'm left with at the moment, so I'll do it every day even if it makes me sore."

Our eyes meet across this little table, and just like that, I know—storms or no storms—I'm really never, ever leaving.

CHAPTER FIFTY-THREE

Dom - June

For the last two months, I've watched the Kory I knew and loved back in high school return.

Her brother being back in town relit the spark that seemed to have dwindled a little—a spark I'm not even sure that she knew was missing.

She brought him to my place a few days after she learned he was here, reluctantly. I had to reassure her a hundred times that I wanted to meet him—that I'd love to meet him. I knew it was my feelings she was worried about, but with her, it has never been easier to talk through those. "Just because you can't meet my sister doesn't mean I don't want to meet your brother," I told her before smacking her on the ass and telling her to stop treating me like a fragile piece of glass. I know I acted like one before, but again, thanks to her, I'm not one anymore. It's like she's put me back together-cracks and scars forever visible—but both my healing and my family are topics I can think about with a smile now.

Seeing her and Elliot together is even nicer than just hearing her excitement about him. He comes over a couple of times a week and watches her with him—seeing the happiness radiate from her—is worth any pang of sadness I may have felt from not being able to do this with my own sibling.

They're sitting at the table now, and her eyes catch mine from across the room. She purses her lips together, blowing me a kiss, and I catch it, slapping it against my cheek. She laughs, then returns to whatever they were laughing about, and my heart swells. I love being part of her happiness.

Elliot gets up, heading for the door. "Seven thirty, right?" he asks, confirming the time for dinner.

It's my birthday, and even though I insisted that I prefer a homemade meal, she insisted we go out and celebrate the birthday I almost didn't make it to.

"Yup," she chirps.

"See ya'll in a bit then." He says and moves two fingers from his head towards us in a goodbye salute.

"That southern accent is never *not* going to be weird," Kory says to me after the door shuts. "I'm going to get in the shower. You okay?" she asks—concerned for me as always. I nod, then she scampers down the hallway.

As I watch her retreat—just the slightest hint of her round cheeks peeking out of the bottom of her shorts—I'm glad I was just recently granted more freedom and lost the cast. I'm still in an annoyingly large brace, but scans and PT have gone well, so I keep getting better and better each week. The brace is so much better than the cast, though, giving my knee some mobility back. The cast on my wrist was also removed last week, which made me feel almost new by itself. I follow her, knowing there's something we haven't done yet since my accident, and I've decided that there is no better day than my birthday to change that.

She's standing in the bedroom in her bra and underwear, like she's undecided if she's actually going to get in the shower or not. Spoiler alert. *She's not. Not yet.*

She sees me come into the room and must recognize the look in my eyes because she sits down on the edge of the bed, welcoming me into her space by spreading her legs just enough for me to stand in between them. I gather her hair in both of my hands and pull her head back so she's looking up at me.

I lower my lips to hers, softly at first, but it doesn't take much for the intensity to grow. As it does, she leans back until we're lying flat, me completely on top of her.

"I've missed this," I whisper in her ear, then pepper kisses down the side of her neck.

"We kiss all the time," she whispers back.

"No. This. You beneath me." My tongue trails back up the path I just made with kisses. "You aching for me. Not the one in control."

"Do something about it then," she breathes.

Thankfully, due to this brace, I've been living in loose-fitting basketball shorts, so it takes about half a second before they're on the floor, and I do exactly what she asks me to.

My leg is a little sore at the restaurant, but it was worth it. Anytime with her is magic, but you're a liar if you say changing things up every once in a while doesn't make a difference. It felt like forever since we had any other kind of sex but careful, step-by-step, basically rehearsed and memorized sex, just to cater to my sorry ass. We stayed in bed for so long, I wasn't sure either of us would actually accomplish anything else today, including this dinner.

But we made it—only fifteen minutes late—and my hand rests on her thigh underneath the table. Elliot, John, Jimmy, and Emery are here too. It's a combination of people I would have scoffed at had you told me a year ago this is who I'd be spending my birthday with. But it works. I smile. These are my people now.

As dinner winds down, I notice Kory has gotten fidgety. She's looked around for the waitress almost constantly since asking for the bill.

"You okay?"

"Yeah, I'm good." She kisses me quickly, then goes back to scanning the room again.

Once it's finally paid, we all stand up in unison. I catch looks shared between Kory, Elliot, and Jimmy, which leads to more suspicion.

"Okay. What's going on?"

"Come on." Kory orders as she grabs my hand and pulls me along.

Outside the restaurant, she continues to pull me until we round the corner. I look at Jimmy behind us, carrying Em and smiling. Once we stop, she says. "Happy birthday."

I turn back to face in front of me, and my bike is here. The bike that was practically in two pieces last time I saw it, well, pictures of it. I walk up to it, circling it and running my hands along the perfectly smooth gas tank.

"Once I put it together that it was your dad's, I knew you needed to have it back," Kory says.

I hear her words, but it takes a moment of strength to control the knot in my throat before I can respond. She didn't have to do this. I didn't ever plan on seeing this thing again. It was one last piece of my dad that had disappeared, yet thanks to her, I have it back.

"Jimmy helped," she adds.

"This was all her man," he humbly responds.

Still not being able to form words, I move pointedly back around the bike and b-line for Kory, grabbing her with a force a little too strong. We stumble, but I settle us both with her face in my hands and my lips on hers.

"I love you," I tell her. "So fucking much." I kiss her again.

"I love you too," she responds, thumbing a tear off my cheek.

Once I can pull myself away from her, I turn to Jimmy and throw my arm around him. I feel Emery's tiny hand on my back, too. "Thanks, man." I choke out.

"No problem. Being a part of two secrets that are not about me has been the highlight of my summer," he says quietly with a wink.

I smile back at him—ready now more than ever to follow through on what *we've* been planning.

CHAPTER FIFTY-FOUR

Kory - August

"You literally got the all clear yesterday. We do not need to go to the beach today."

Dom is moving around the room like a worker bee, insisting we go to the beach tonight. "Yes, we do. You've spent the whole summer taking care of me and haven't gone to the beach one time. And it's going to rain tomorrow. You need this. So grab a book and get your pretty little self in the car."

My lips tighten, trying to stop the smile. I don't think he's stopped moving since we got home from Ortho yesterday. The thought of him maneuvering the shifty sand on a barely healed leg has me nervous, but I can't say no when he says stuff like that.

"Fine," I say, then head to the bedroom to grab my current read off my nightstand.

It only takes us about twenty minutes to reach our destination, a stretch of beach more familiar with locals than tourists. It's slightly more secluded with difficult parking, so it's not often busy.

As we make our way through the tall lake grass, the water finally comes into view, and I try to hide from him the fact that it takes my breath away. There is a sense of peace that Lake Michigan has always brought me. A sensation that immediately returns as soon as I hear the first lap of water on the shore. I notice him staring at me and realize I didn't succeed in hiding how I felt at all. I haven't been able to since he came into my life.

"Told you," he reaches his hand out, and I take it, rolling my eyes at the same time.

After just a few more feet along the sand, my breath escapes me again.

"Dominic." I gasp.

There's a blanket in the sand in front of us, with two short beach chairs and a make-shift table adorned with carnations in various shades of purple. There's also a candle, a bottle of champagne, and two flutes. As we inch closer in silence, I can see there is a platter of chocolate-covered pretzels in all shapes and colors.

"What sunset on the beach is complete without snacks and drinks?" He motions for me to sit while flashing a downright devilish smile.

"This is amazing." I lean back in one of the chairs as he pops open the champagne and then fills our glasses.

"Cheers," he says, holding the glass out to me. "For finally making it to the beach before summer is over."

I laugh, then tap mine to his. "Cheers."

We sit in a peaceful silence for a few minutes, watching the water and alternating sips of bubbles and bites of salty sweetness. I don't know why he told me to bring a book. I can't take my eyes off either of the views in front of me.

Not many sights can rival a Lake Michigan sunset. The sun is huge and deep orange, halfway to the water's surface at this point. It sends streamers of color through the sky—first orange, which fades to pink, which turns to purple right at the horizon's edge.

Even the water is painted with color. From where the sky meets the water, it alternates strokes of blue, pink, then more blue, and purple again. It's an artist's dream to be able to accurately pull off painting how beautiful this looks in person, on a two-dimensional canvas. Not many can quite do it justice.

"There's seriously not much better than this," I tell him, breaking the silence. "Thank you."

"That so?" he asks with a smirk.

"I said not much."

After a light chuckle, we fall back into a relaxing silence with his hand resting on mine. I am tempted to throw these chairs out so we can lie together when a bug tickles my arm. I brush it away, but then feel another. As I look down at the sensation, I realize it's wet. It happens again, then again, and I see that it's not bugs, and it's coming from above me. I turn my neck to look up and around, and don't quite understand what I'm seeing. The intensity picks up, and while it still doesn't make sense, it's now clear what is falling.

"Is it… Snowing?" My words come out sounding as confused as I feel.

I know it sounds crazy, but there is no other explanation. We are being snowed on right now. Sitting on a beach. In August. I look over at Dom, who isn't confused at all—rather amused—smiling and taking it all in as well.

"Snowstorm on the beach?" his smile turns smug. "You don't remember?"

As those words leave his mouth, it all comes back in an overwhelming rush. My hand flies to my mouth as he stands.

"I'm pretty sure I said you'd love me so much you wouldn't be able to stand it." He reaches down and grabs my hands to lift me to stand with him. "Then you said, *'maybe when there's a snowstorm on the beach in August'* or something like that? Right?"

I don't respond as I listen to him paraphrase my smart ass remark from a year ago while snowflakes fall all around him. The intensity of the snow picks up. It's *really* snowing. And he's right. Absolutely right.

He continues. "Then you said I was crazy, to which I replied, maybe, but I'm right." He winks, which makes me laugh through budding tears or melting snowflakes on my lashes. I can't tell the difference.

"How did you? How did you remember?"

"I've told you before, I remember everything about you. If it has anything to do with you, it's locked in here forever," he taps the side of his head.

He pulls me into his arms and holds me tight while it's somehow still snowing.

"So, what do you think? Do you love me so much you can't stand it?"

I laugh as I wipe what's definitely a tear from my cheek. "Yes, stupid."

"Good, cuz they worked really hard to help prove me right." He motions behind us, and it's only then that I take in the fact that we're not alone.

The *'snow'* is blowing out of four black machines held by Jimmy, my brother, Olivia, and Autumn. The sight of Autumn here in Michigan causes the tears to spurt out and a bubble in my lungs. I can see her eyes are glossy too. She's here for me, next to Jimmy, which was one of the things I was most afraid of for her. But she's here anyway, crying for me.

I suck in a breath and turn back around to Dom, who is now down on one knee with a box in his hand.

"Kory Brooks, from the moment I saw you, I knew you were the one for me. You may not know that was when we were fifteen, but I do. I knew that day that timing would eventually work out and we'd be here. Well, I didn't know it would be on the beach during a summer snowstorm, but I couldn't picture it any different. This may sound crazy because I never even asked you officially to be my girlfriend, or to move in, but I never want to be without you. Marry me. Please."

"Yes." I spit out with no hesitation. I spent enough time hesitating with him. That's all over now. "A million times yes!"

He grabs my hand and slides on the solitary diamond before standing and scooping me into his arms in one easy motion. We kiss, and he spins us around, and I can't believe this is happening. Once I'm on my feet, the snow is gone, and Autumn is next to me. I throw myself at her next. We're both a mess, sniffling and wiping our wet faces in between giggles. Next is my brother, who squeezes me tightly. Olivia takes a turn to squeeze me, then I even hug Jimmy before flying back into my fiancés arms with no plans on ever leaving them again.

He picks up the champagne flutes, handing me mine. "To having you by my side—forever."

I tap my glass to his and kiss him. "To having you *forever.*"

EPILOGUE

Kory - Three Months Later

"So, is Lake Michigan still your favorite place?" Dom asks as he kisses my cheek and hands me a margarita.

He relaxes into the long beach chair next to me, every inch of his exposed skin glistening in the Florida sun. My eyes linger—as long as I want them to—on every ridge of muscle carved just for me. He notices and simply blows a kiss my way, causing a laugh to bubble out of me. I turn my attention back to the ocean.

The view is similar to what I'm used to, but still different. The waves break harder on the shore than they do back home, and the air has a different, distinct smell. The salt air, while different, is no better or worse than the fresh lake air, but it is glorious in its own right.

"Yes, that will always be my favorite place. It's home. But this is paradise."

"Well, cheers to paradise."

I laugh as he lifts his glass to mine. This is something he's never going to stop doing, apparently. There's always a reason to toast to something.

"Plus, Lake Michigan got me this." I lift my hand, flashing my ring at him.

"It definitely wasn't the lake that got you that." He winks, then downs his drink. I watch the liquid move down his throat and suddenly can't wait to get back to the room.

Life has been completely different these last three months —in the best way. I don't know how I ever claimed to be happy living inside the walls I had built. Ever since Dom broke them down, I realized just how much I was missing. And to no fault of anyone but myself.

We haven't done any wedding planning yet. Neither of us feels the need to rush. Surprise surprise. We're happy just like this, and considering I didn't have much time with him as my boyfriend, I'm fine with having him as my fiancé for a while. Plus, we're deep into the cross-country project with *Home Team*, which is why we're planted on a Florida beach right now. John was overjoyed when Dom was cleared to fully return to work.

We started with closer states—Ohio, Illinois, Indiana— states we could drive to. After those few trips, we became frequent flyers, visiting a handful of states on the East Coast. Our first trip was to New York. John had no idea why that might have been an issue, and while it was hard to wrap his mind around it at first, Dom decided he was really done hiding from what happened to his family. We went, enjoyed our trip, and even looked at the Statue of Liberty—from land. We talked about them a lot while we were there—I think he could feel them—and it was really good for him.

John's still working on getting us out to the West Coast, and I have no doubt he will succeed.

It's amazing to imagine life without Dom ever existing. If you had asked me to describe my dream man two years ago, he checks every box. He's a pro at making me laugh—among other things—but he's also not afraid to challenge me or call me on my occasional BS, which I need more often than I'd like to admit.

And thankfully, despite our long, drawn-out declaration of love for each other, banter is still our love language, and I wouldn't have it any other way.

I lean my hand back against the chair and close my eyes, soaking in the sun like a lizard on a rock, and listening to the water, the screech of seagulls, and the giggles of children wading in the waves. I could, in fact, stay here forever, but I know I'd miss home. Traveling has been awesome, and I've enjoyed every second, but I don't think I could put down roots anywhere but Michigan.

Even though my eyes are still closed, there's a sudden darkening, like the sun has just slipped behind a cloud, except I haven't seen a single one all day. My eyelids lift to find abs in my face where the sun should be.

"Excuse me, sir," I say, looking up at him. "This seat is already taken."

His knees lower so that he is straddling me, straining this beach chair beneath us. "Oh, I'm aware," he says before planting a kiss. "I'm going to go into the room and figure out what to make for dinner. Join me when you're done roasting." He kisses my forehead before lifting and disappearing behind me.

I lean my head back with a small content sigh, but no sooner has Dom left than my phone rings—FaceTime from Elliot. I answer, raising a hand to my forehead to shield my eyes from the sun.

"Sup," he says when we connect.

"Rotting away and miserable," I say sarcastically as I move my phone to show him the view.

"Yeah, seems like it." He shakes his head.

"What are you up to? How's the new house?"

It's strange sometimes that my brother is home in Scottville while I'm usually the one in another state, but knowing he's there—and seeing him almost every day when I'm home—gives me a comfort I didn't realize I'd been missing. He, Dom, and even Jimmy have all hit it off and become friends, which makes everything feel lighter—yes, even with Jimmy. The night Dom proposed made me see things differently. Watching Jimmy and Autumn interact, laughing like they were *actually* just old friends, I realized that maybe the hurt *had* already faded. Maybe I'd been holding onto problems that didn't exist. Maybe, for the first time in a long time, we could all truly be friends.

And as we all sat there on the beach, I let that hope finally burrow itself inside me. I looked at Dom, his best friend, my best friend, and even my brother—thinking about each of the things that all of us have healed from this year, and the life he and I were about to start together—peace swelled in my chest. That alone was almost sweeter and more grounding than even the moment he proposed. I don't know that he'll ever fully understand the magnitude of what he's done for each of us, just by being in love with me.

Elliot stayed at my place for a while after I *officially* moved into Dom's. He didn't like the apartment life, though, so not long after he moved back he found a house he liked and, lucky bastard, got his first offer accepted. *Who would've thought the one to put official roots down first would be him?*

"It's good. Finally think I'm completely unpacked and settled. It was nice to be able to take my time. Thanks for helping with the apartment."

"Of course."

I had to be the one to give notice since I never let them know that another person had moved in—technically illegal, but something a sister does for a brother when they live in the same town—so I was more than happy to be able to.

"I actually want to talk to you about something. When do you come home?"

"Talk about what?" Nerves tighten in my stomach. That's almost always bad.

"It's nothing bad," he laughs, reading my mind.

"I don't come home for two more days. Tell me now or I'll go crazy."

"Fine," he pauses, looking around to see if anyone is near him. *Where is he?* "I met someone."

My eyes grow. "Really? Already?"

"Already? What does that mean?"

"Nothing really, you're just talking about it like it's serious already."

He runs his hands through his curls. "Not serious yet, but I do think I really like her."

It could be my eyes straining from the sun, but I think his cheeks turn pink. "Awe, El, look at you!" He rolls his eyes, and I add, "Is she like from town?"

"Yeah. She's actually my new neighbor."

"Oh! This is good!" I say excitedly. "Okay. I can handle that for two days, but when I get home, you have to tell me everything!"

He laughs. "Sounds good. Bring some of that sun home for us."

Such a Michigander thing to say. He fit right back in. "I'll try. Love you!"

"Love you too." He says before the screen goes black.

I return my head to resting back on the chair with my eyes closed. A smile rests on my face, happy for my brother.

We didn't talk much while he was in Tennessee, so I don't know much about his dating life there, if there was one at all. I'm excited to finally be able to share these things with each other—to have the sibling relationship I've always wished we had. I also can't wait to gush and tease him about a girl he likes.

But the more I think about it, the more curious I get. She's his neighbor. We know everyone in town. *Who could he possibly be dating?*

STORY INSPIRATION SOUNDTRACK

You're on Your Own Kid — Taylor Swift
Bejeweled — Taylor Swift
Mastermind — Taylor Swift
Question — Taylor Swift
Glitch — Taylor Swift
Labyrinth — Taylor Swift
Maroon — Taylor Swift
Midnight Rain — Taylor Swift
Bigger Than the Whole Sky — Taylor Swift
The Great War — Taylor Swift
Lavender Haze — Taylor Swift
Snow on The Beach — Taylor Swift

Honorable Mentions
Vigilante Shit — Taylor Swift
Paris — Taylor Swift
Anti-Hero — Taylor Swift

BOOK CLUB/DISCUSSION QUESTIONS

1. In the early chapters, both characters seem detached from their current or recent relationships. How might this detachment foreshadow their eventual connection?
2. People always leave. Kory's mantra becomes a lens for understanding her choices. How does her history of abandonment shape her approach to love and friendship? Do you think her fear is justified or self-sabotaging?
3. Autumn is the one person Kory considers "home," even when they live states apart. In what ways does Autumn serve as Kory's emotional anchor, and in what ways does their distance force Kory to learn to self-soothe?
4. Motorcycles often symbolize risk and freedom. How does the first bike ride use that symbolism to reflect the emotional stakes of their relationship?
5. How does the kiss in the pool blur the lines between physical attraction and emotional vulnerability? Why is Dom's decision afterward important?
6. Kory's list of "Friends-with-Benefits" rules is both humorous and heartbreaking. Which rule feels most revealing about her fears? How do these boundaries reflect her struggle between craving closeness and fearing loss?
7. Dom's gestures—remembering her drink, detouring to the book festival—are sometimes subtle but just as powerful as their physical connection. Which acts do you think were more pivotal to the growth of their relationships? The small moments or the big physical ones?
8. John's announcement about Dom's new role shatters Kory's fragile sense of security. Why does this moment feel like betrayal to her?

9. Kory once said she doesn't beg people to stay. How does this scene after the announcement force her to confront whether she truly believes that, or whether she's just learned to leave first emotionally?

10. Before the accident, Kory's fear was being left. After the accident, the fear becomes losing him. How does that shift deepen—or complicate—her ability to love?

11. Dom didn't just pretend his family was alive—he maintained the life he wished he still had. What does this suggest about how grief can make us hold onto the version of ourselves that existed before the loss?

12. Jimmy becomes unexpectedly gentle and supportive during Dom's recovery. What does this reveal about who Jimmy is, beyond the way Kory viewed him?

13. How do the hospital/recovery scenes reveal the transformative power of tenderness and patience? Which moment feels most symbolic of Kory stepping into the role Dom once held—positive, unwavering, and full of hope?

14. Dom believed from the start that Kory would love him "By Next August." How does this confidence shape your understanding of his character? Was it faith, persistence, or something deeper? How does this certainty contrast with Kory's fear of attachment?

15. What moment from the story do you think changed each of them the most? What moment or event felt most healing?

Bonus Question:

Compare the first line and the last line of the book.

"People always leave," and "To having you forever."

How does the shift from the opening line to the closing line encapsulate Kory's emotional journey? What does this transformation reveal about her growth in trust, vulnerability, and love?

ACKNOWLEDGEMENTS

To the readers—thank you so much for loving my work and giving me the chance to continue doing this. I'll never be able to explain how appreciative I am.

To my husband—I'll probably say this in every acknowledgment page I ever have, but thank you so much for your support. This used to be a hobby—and I suppose it still is —but it has also turned into something life-consuming. I just can't thank you enough for being by my side through all of it. I love you.

To my very best friend—the Kory to my Autumn—thank you for just being you, and getting a new job which was the last puzzle piece I needed to use for Kory's story. LOL! But seriously, though, to then watch you find your happiness while writing about Kory finding hers was incredible timing. You both deserve it for being the best friends there ever were.

To my friends and family who have watched me carry around my notebook or my laptop and tune out of family events while engulfed in the fictional world I created—thank you for embracing that part of me and also not asking me what I'm working on because you know I'll tell you it's a secret. LOL!

To my street team—I love you guys and the fun we have in our group chat. It's so nice to have a hype squad to not only share secrets with, but to just connect with and become fellow bookish friends. Random people connected from all over the place, yet you'd never guess it when we get to yapping.

To my beta readers—I am deeply grateful that you took the time to read a draft and offer your feedback. It was all invaluable and just what I needed to take it to that next level. I cannot wait for you all to read the final edition!

To my talented team of supports—K. Jaspersen's cover designs and formatting, Elaine's editing, Delilah's artwork, and Elisabeth & Jay's awesome voices—I'm so lucky to have connected with you all. You each take my visions and turn them into something so perfect. I couldn't be where I am today without the addition of all of your incredible talents!

As always—closing with an additional thank you to the readers. I hope you love book 2 in The August Series as much as you did book 1, and will continue this journey with me from here. :)

ABOUT THE AUTHOR

Ashley Pierce lives in Southeast Michigan, where she was born and raised. A lifelong fan of psychological thrillers and romances, she brings real-life Michigan moments into her fiction, blending hometown charm with emotional depth and suspense.

She writes a wide range of stories—some gripping and intense, others heartfelt and romantic—giving readers something fresh and unexpected with every book. She prefers handwriting her stories— with a pen dripped in experience, emotion, and hometown pride.

Ashley spends her non-writing time reading and spending time with her husband, kids, and dogs, usually outdoors or at the lake.

THANK YOU FOR READING!

Please visit my social media to keep up with all new announcements and events!